D1324726

FALL
OUT

FALL OUT

C. G. MOORE

uclanpublishing

Fall Out is a uclanpublishing book

First published in Great Britain in 2020 by
uclanpublishing
University of Central Lancashire
Preston, PR1 2HE, UK

Text copyright © C. G. Moore, 2020
Cover illustrations copyright © Shutterstock.com

978-1-912979-18-9

1 3 5 7 9 10 8 6 4 2

Set in 10/16pt Kingfisher by Becky Chilcott

A CIP catalogue record for this book is available from the British Library.

Printed and bound in Great Britain by Clays Ltd, Elcograf S.p.A.

'Hope will never be silent.'
Harvey Milk

For my grandad, who taught me young
that there is hope even in the darkest places and times.

Chapter 1

EXPLOSIVE TEMPER

Chop. Chop. Chop.

'Mum, can I speak to you for a minute?' Mum was chopping carrots.

Chop. Chop. Chop.

'Is it important?' she responded.

'Yeah, kinda.'

Chop. Chop. Chop.

'Well, if it can't wait . . .'

'I don't know the easiest way to say this.'

Chop. Chop. Chop.

'I guess what I'm trying to tell you is . . . is . . .'

Chop. Chop. Chop.

'I'm trying to tell you that I'm gay.'

Chop. Chop. Ear-splitting scream.

'Mum?'

'Shit. Shit. Shit.'

'Mum? Are you OK?'

'Get me a tea towel. Get me a bloody tea towel!'

I grabbed one. Mum can barely drive with eight fingers and two thumbs. Looking at the severed finger next to the carrots, I called an ambulance. Mum went ballistic, cursing and shouting. I could taste my salty tears and I was seriously freaked out. I didn't know what to do. I had a plan and that was most certainly *not* part of the plan.

By the time the ambulance arrived, the tea towel was more red than white. I climbed in. Mum wouldn't meet my eyes. I attributed this to the dismemberment.

We arrived at St. Andrew's A&E department. Mum was ranting and raving like she just lost a leg. I walked alongside her, mortified, thinking, *Jesus*, it was just a finger. I'm pretty sure they can grow them in petri dishes.

The doctor asked a hysterical mum how it happened. I'll never forget her answer. Ever. 'How do you think it happened, you specky twat?'

I whispered to the doctor, 'She cut her finger off with a knife.' When she caught me talking, she pointed and said in an indifferent voice, 'my son is gay'. So, it could have gone a lot worse.

I always imagined "coming out" would be my moment. A sacred ritual like Communion or marriage. I'd ask mum if I could speak with her. We'd sit on our black pleather sofa and I'd tell her 'I'm gay'. She'd cry but they'd be tears of happiness. She'd be so proud to see me come to terms with who I really was and whip up a chocolate "coming out" gateaux for me – because she knows chocolate is my favourite everything.

Dad would come home from a long day's work on the site. He'd take off his high-vis vest and ask if I was OK. Mum would give me a little push and I'd stand up like I was going to deliver the Queen's Speech. I'd tell him and he'd hug me so tight that I'd have to say he was hurting me. We'd laugh and after collecting Kayleigh from her playdate, we'd sit as a family and watch a movie.

I'd tell Em at Lizzie's house party. We'd laugh and cry, and we'd talk about all the silly things we'd done. We'd do shots and some hot guy would ask me to dance. We'd go out to the porch and stand next to the heater, watching the stars and the full moon – kissing and holding hands.

That's how I pictured it.

Now, that picture was fading before my eyes.

Later that evening, dad must have got a call from the hospital. Mum was lying in a bed and her finger had been sewn back on. I wanted to be sick every time I looked at it but I couldn't tell her that. I couldn't spend too much time in the room with her either. She was uncharacteristically quiet. That scared me more than anything. If she'd shouted at me, I could have dealt with it but the silence; the silence killed me. She must have known that was the best way to hurt me too.

When dad burst into the room, I was flicking through a festive edition of *The Star* which featured oiled-up men in Santa hats and red thongs. Christmas might have passed but with those sexy Santas, every day was Christmas. He rushed to her side, a bunch of red carnations in one hand. I raised my eyebrows, thinking, *and it's a stereotype for gays to be melodramatic.* Fair enough if she had a heart attack, but she lost a finger, and she didn't even lose it because they stitched it right back on like Gran had done with a button on my Huggy Bear when I was three.

'Are you OK? Are you both OK?' he asked, his eyes trained firmly on mum.

Mum motioned for dad to lean in close and I could tell then that she was going to tell him. I rubbed my sweaty palms against my jeans. I was excited because dad would understand where mum didn't. I saw her lips move and I noticed dad's jugular vein throb with excitement. He ran across the room and I threw my arms wide for a hug. I never thought dad to be the hugging type. A fist came at me hard and fast.

'How could you?' he shouted. My head rocked back and hit the glass window. I tried to concentrate on my surroundings. I counted five stars. Hands grasped me by the lapels of my leather jacket and launched me across the room.

'RICHARD!'

I heard thundering footsteps. Two nurses burst into the room. The nurses tackled dad as he lunged at me. I wasn't confident they could keep dad down though. Dad was a weapon when he wanted something and in that moment, he had an I-really-want-to-beat-

4

the-crap-out-of-you look in his eyes. For the second time that day, I could taste tears on my tongue.

I watched as mum reached new levels of hysteria and dad exploded, and I experienced my worst fear – fear of snakes – times a hundred.

'You disgust me!' His voice rang out as security arrived and dragged him down the corridor. I sat huddled in the corner, doctors examining my head and asking if I was OK. Mum asked if she could have a moment with me. The medical staff obliged but they didn't go very far, and there was now a security guard stationed outside, as if I had a whole collection of crazy, messed-up relatives waiting with crowbars in the car park to beat the shit out of me.

I couldn't move. I just sat there like I was fused to the clinically white linoleum floor, the bag of ice the nurses gave me pressed tightly to my bruised eye. I could feel mum watching me but I wouldn't look up.

'Cal.' That word stirred something in me. I jumped to my feet clumsily, sprinting for the door. 'Cal, wait!' I ran and I ran, but I stopped at a door. I stepped into the cleaner's cupboard and sat in the corner, sobbing into a dirty blackened rag. No one followed me. Maybe they realised what a mess I was. Maybe they didn't know what to say to a kid whose dad just gave him a black eye. I stared at the chemical cleaners and bedpans. Someone probably should have locked the door. I gave myself ten minutes to calm down. I drew my hood over my head and slipped into the corridor. I made it to the lift. A nurse spotted me and frantically gestured for me to stop, but the door had already closed. There were only two women in the lift; a middle-aged woman who shrunk in on herself and the other, who must have been born when dinosaurs roamed the Earth. I knew they wouldn't give me any trouble. I admired the older lady's black thigh-high boots.

The cheesy elevator music filled the silence. The woman turned her head towards me. Click. Click. The sounds of her last two vertebrate shattering. 'Are you that Justin Believer?'

The door pinged open. I fumbled in my pocket for my phone, trying to distract myself. My fingers closed around slick plastic. I removed it from my pocket, eyeing the single square of chocolate that had melted into the wrapper. I glanced around me before licking the chocolate from the plastic.

I arrived at our flat on autopilot. I felt the void.

No Mum.

No Dad.

No Kayleigh.

Chapter 2

A BAD EXAMPLE

I think Em knew I was gay before I did. I met up with her the next day and when I told her, she shrugged. She didn't care. It didn't change anything between us.

She insisted we celebrate. We passed through the metal detectors at Heaven nightclub. One of the bouncers patted me down thoroughly after inspecting our fake IDs – courtesy of Em. He didn't like it when I said, 'a little more to the right'. He didn't like it one bit. Em slapped me in the back of the head and hauled me away. We walked down the steps, Em teetering like a demented penguin in her wedges as she tried to lean on Duncan – Em's new "friend". She paid for me to get in.

We hadn't realised it was a foam party. In the middle of the main room, there was a pit with two foam cannons pumping sudsy bubbles into the crowd. I later learned that some of the guys were pumping foam of their own beneath the bubbles.

I was starting to sober up a little, enough to remember how to order a double Captain Morgan and Coke at the bar. I downed it before he gave me my change, asking if I could get another. He wasn't impressed.

Duncan bought us jägerbombs and when I asked him what a jägerbomb was, Em retorted over the booming bass, 'just drink it and stop asking questions.'

We danced. Em told me over the phone the next day that I looked a bit like the Hunchback of Notre Dame on speed. In contrast to my sober dancing, I took that as a compliment. I don't remember much of anything else but luckily, I had seven snaps on Snapchat waiting for me this afternoon when I finally woke up.

Snap #1: Em was right. I look like the coolest hunchback in the club.

Snap #2: I'm knocking back a row of drinks that Em has called a "jäger train".

Snap #3: I'm throwing up in the toilet.

Snap #4: A very dismayed toilet attendant.

Snap #5: More dancing.

Snap #6: Though I can't hear the conversation, I'm chatting to a guy and he's cute.

Snap #7: I'm kissing that same guy. Correction, I'm licking his face like it's a chocolate sundae.

I vaguely remember leaving the club with the cute guy from the snaps. I'm not sure where Em was at the time but judging by the barrage of texts on my phone the next morning, I must have sneaked off. I went into McDonalds with Michael – I think that was his name, or maybe it was Micah? Miller? Liam? – and when he bought me a double cheeseburger, I knew it was love.

I didn't have a towel and my clothes were soaked through. I must have ventured into the foam pit at some stage. I headed for the night bus when Michael/Micah/Miller/Liam asked me if I wanted to go back to his place. He flagged down a taxi and took me to a suave apartment with scented candles and a jagged vase filled with tiger lilies – even a freaking leather couch. It put our pleather two-seater to shame.

He asked if I wanted anything and I told him a glass of water. I fought with the doorknob and entered Michael's/Micah's/Miller's/Liam's bedroom. From the window, I could see the Shard, glinting in the sunrise and setting the skyline on fire. I wish I had a camera. My phone died in McDonalds. Slowly, a small glow filled the room. Dimmer lights. I turned around and Michael/Micah/Miller/Liam pressed his lips to mine. We fell onto his bed, his hand fumbling with the button on my skinny jeans. Topshop skinny jeans are like guy-kryptonite. It took us a full two minutes before we removed them. Stripped down to our boxers, we dived under the blankets, his warm sweaty skin sticking to mine.

We touched and kissed – it was perfect. My first kiss! Well, my first kiss that I remembered. It was everything I thought it would be.

Sensual.

Intimate.

Personal.

Every inch of my skin was brimming with heat and energy, my mouth tingling from all the places his tongue had touched. His sheets were so soft and they smelled like musky cologne. I rested my head on his chest. I looked up at him but his eyes were already closed.

I woke up to the pitter-patter of water coming from the shower. I heard a creak and the water stopped. A door shut somewhere else in the apartment. I didn't know he had housemates.

'Danny?' a male voice called, young-sounding. Shit. 'Hello?' The voice sounded closer now and then, I was staring at a shorter guy with dark hair and bushy eyebrows. 'Who are you?'

'Who are you?' I retorted because my brain was on autopilot, trying to piece everything together. Panic set in.

'I'm Danny's fiancé. What are you doing in my apartment? Who the hell are you?' Crap. He opened the nearby closet and removed a golf club. He took two steps closer and the bathroom door creaked open. Danny stepped out with an oh-fuck look on his face.

Danny tried to pacify him but he swung the golf club around the room, knocking over a lamp. Danny grabbed the golf club and they wrestled for control. I searched frantically for my clothes. I scooped them into my arms but I couldn't find my second Converse.

'Vinny, I can explain.'

'I'm going to kill him. I'm going to. *Kill. Him.*'

Vinny ran at me. I undid the latch to the window and jumped. Luckily, the drop was only about six metres. My feet bore the impact but I hobbled through the pain, failing to multi-task spectacularly as I attempted to slip one leg into my jeans.

I had all my clothes on by the time I got to Bermondsey tube station. The ticket assistant threw me a funny look, but I ignored her as I scanned through the barriers with my Oyster card and waited on the platform. I bit my lip. I refused to cry in public.

Chapter 3

SEXPLOITATION

After a forty-minute tube ride home, I realised that Danny wasn't exactly boyfriend material. *I* wasn't boyfriend material. I was the "other boy": Danny's Number Two. I folded my arms across my chest, attempting a hug and failed.

Two tall police officers were talking to mum in serious tones on the porch when I arrived home looking like a homeless boy. I quickly popped a stick of gum into my mouth to disguise the alcohol. Mum clocked me as soon as I moved out of her blind spot. Her lips thinned, her jaw tightening.

'Here he is now,' she smiled through gritted teeth, pinching my shoulder a little too hard. 'Cal, this is Inspector Milnes and Officer Daniels. They want to ask you some questions about what happened at the hospital.' Mum did this strange wink-blink thing with her eyes but I wasn't sure what it was supposed to mean.

'Are you having a stroke?' I asked her.

'No,' she deadpanned, inviting the police officers into our living room. She quickly re-arranged our cheap throw cushions to disguise the cigarette burns on the couch. Mum didn't smoke but dad did. She disappeared into the kitchen. I could hear the clinking of spoons against cups.

'Now Cal, I know it must be difficult to talk but we need to ask you what happened at St. Andrew's. Is that OK?'

I gulped and nodded. It wasn't like I could say 'no'.

Inspector Milnes removed a digital recorder from the inside pocket of his jacket and placed it on the stained coffee table. 'We need to record your statement, in the event this goes to court.'

Court? I nodded. I didn't know how to say 'no'. I didn't know if I *could* say 'no'.

Inspector Milnes clicked the recorder and a red light shone. Inspector Brendan Milnes and Officer Robert Daniels interviewing the alleged victim—'

He jerked the recorder into my face. It took me a second to catch on. 'Cal Adams.'

'—at his home in Leytonstone on Sunday the 1st January 2020 at 2.37pm. So, Cal, tell us what happened on the evening of the 30th December 2019.'

My mouth opened. I was worried that no sound would come out and they'd be sitting there looking at a supernaturally sweaty boy fidgeting with his hands. Instead, the whole story flowed from my lips, more eloquently than I thought I was capable of.

'But he's never done it before,' I added. 'He's never laid a hand on me or my sister. I've never seen him hit mum either.' That was true but I had heard him shout at her. I'd seen the steely look in his eyes when he was in one of his moods. I wasn't sure why I kept that a secret.

There was a click and the recording stopped. Mum entered the living room seconds after, making me wonder if she had been listening from the kitchen all that time.

'Tea,' she chirped, setting the tray down on the coffee table as Inspector Milnes picked up the tape recorder. 'I'm afraid we're all out of biscuits. We haven't done the weekly shop yet, have we, Cal?'

On our shoestring budget, I wanted to add but I knew to keep my mouth firmly shut. 'Yeah.' I forced a feeble grin.

'I'm afraid we can't stay, Mrs Adams, but we'll be in touch.'

'He won't go to jail, will he?'

'I'm afraid we're not in a position to discuss that right now, Mrs Adams. We'll get Cal's statement to the station. These things can take weeks, months even. As soon as we hear something, you'll be the first to know.'

Officer Daniels fixed his hat in place and followed Inspector Milnes out the door, leaving a huge void in the living room. Mum walked them to the door. I could hear her cheery voice wishing them a safe trip. She returned to the living room, where I stood, like my legs were roots that hooked underneath the scarred floorboards.

How did we get to that point? I remembered mum being the

light of my life. When I was three, and I scraped my knee on the stones chasing Em at Abbotts Park, mum picked me up in her arms and kissed the pain away. When I was six, and Mrs Lynch told me I couldn't be in the school play because I had two left feet, mum went down to the school and I got a starring role as a tree. I was always on stage and mum told me I stole the show. I remembered the summer days when she drove me and Em to the beach, and we built sandcastles and ran away from the tide, yelping when the waves nipped at our feet. Back in the days before mum sold the car.

When had everything changed? I tried to think back but I hit a wall.

Mum watched me, an undecipherable look on her face. She rubbed at her red-rimmed eyes. Ten feet between us in our tiny living room suddenly felt like a chasm. It felt like a transatlantic body of water separating us. Mum was operating in a different time zone, a different world. How had things got so bad?

'Wee, wee,' Kayleigh shouted from upstairs and mum sighed, her shoulders slumping. She lowered her head and shuffled out of the room.

Who was this shell of a woman?

Where was the mum I knew?

I closed my eyes against the beading tears and dug my broken nails into the palms of my hands. That helped. That always helped.

Later that evening, I told Em about Danny because I told her everything. When she found out, she slapped me. I guess someone had to at some stage. At least it was someone I loved. We went to Westfield shopping centre to look at dresses that Em was never going to wear in a million years. Glam for Em meant wearing a pair of dark jeans, a cream blouse and a bracelet she got from Primark that she insists is Swarovski. I told Em she should get her green wrist checked out. She fidgeted with the bracelet as she told me that it was just her pigmented skin.

We spent an hour in Topshop and H&M, and eventually made our way to the seasonal markets. Em bought a pair of black thigh-high boots for forty pounds. I subtly snapped the seller's face when Em asked how many knives she could fit down the side before it became uncomfortable. That's what I love about Em. She never takes things too seriously, until she does and then you know you've crossed a line.

We ambled down a narrow street, lined with stalls selling everything from plantain to power tools. Em bought a pair of grey-blue cords that were cut roughly at the ends and a black leather jacket with studs lining the shoulders.

The sellers wolf whistled at Em who flashed them a withering look that sent them scampering out back. No idea how she did it. Our final stop was at the fishmonger's where Em got some saltfish for her nan.

Later that evening, I noticed a piece of paper in my bag. I unfolded it, reading the note written in loopy script:

Call me

Underneath, a number was scrawled across a crumpled receipt. I stared at the words, fingered the ink like it would suddenly come alive and unlock some deeper meaning. I folded the note into four, deposited it in the top drawer of my bedside locker and closed my eyes.

I didn't tell Em about the note. I knew she'd freak out and tell me I was crazy for even thinking about meeting up with a stranger, but that's what interested me. I tried to picture him as a forty-year-old hairy psychopath with an equal love of kittens and butcher knives, but then he kind of just morphed into this cute boy with black hair and dark eyes. I couldn't help but give it a shot. Deep down, I knew it was crazy, but I had to try. It could be like that movie *Serendipity* where the guy and the girl just miss each other every time, but finally re-unite in a spectacularly dramatic scene and kiss. What if I didn't encounter him again? What if he floated right out of my life?

I tapped the keys, typing and deleting my masterpiece. In the end, I kept it simple.

> Me: Hey
> Mystery Boy: Hey, who's this?
> Me: Who's this?
> Pause.
> Me: You gave me your number?

I wasn't sure why I included the question mark. It wasn't a question. I didn't buy a Sharpie, write the damn note and slip it into my own pocket.

> Mystery Boy: Oh yeah, the cute boy from the market.

17

I blushed.

> Me: So . . . what's your name?
> Mystery Boy: Al.
> Me: Hi Al, I'm Cal.
> Al: Cal and Al. Rhymes.
> Me: It does.
> Al: Why don't you drop by the market later and
> we can grab a coffee?
> Me: Sure.

I wasn't supposed to do much that evening; clean my room maybe but I had days to do that. There'd still be a room to clean tomorrow unless there was a sudden apocalypse and if that was the case, why would I bother cleaning my room?

> Al: Great, I'll see you in an hour.

An hour? I checked Kayleigh's *Dora the Explorer* watch. I had thirty minutes to shower, do something about the crow's nest atop my head, brush my teeth and change clothes. I raced to the bathroom, twisting the doorknob but the door wouldn't open.

'Someone in here,' Kayleigh shouted.

'Kayleigh, I need to use the bathroom.'

'I doing a poo-poo.'

Oh Lord, Kayleigh's poos were toxic. The minutes ticked by but eventually, she walked out of the bathroom with her trousers around her ankles. I pulled them up, hugged her quickly and locked the door. I stripped out of my clothes in record time, washing in the time it takes to write a Facebook status and drying myself in the time it takes to tweet. I ran into my room and tried on different t-shirts with my skinny jeans. I settled on an all-black outfit and started working some vegetable oil through my hair. It had been a year since we had enough money to afford hair gel.

I glanced at Kayleigh's watch. No time to brush my teeth. I popped a stick of gum into my mouth.

'I love you,' I shouted at mum's locked bedroom door. I was still angry at her but telling her I loved her before I left the house was second nature. I waited a beat. Silence. I didn't know what she did in there but in the late hours, I could hear her crying. I didn't know what to say so I never brought it up.

I arrived at the tube station and looked in my wallet. Pennies. I sped past the station and the shops, not slowing down until the markets were in sight. I ambled around the corner.

Me: What do you look like?
Al: Come to the fishmongers.

I weaved through the stalls and walked between the fruit and veg stand, and the fishmongers. I tripped over a loose lace and face planted the ground. I rolled over and when my vision cleared, I saw a boy looking at me, eyebrows arched and dark hair curling around his ears. That would only happen to me. He helped me to my feet. I couldn't help but notice how abnormally large his biceps were when he tensed his arm. He wore a grey tattered apron that cut off at the shoulder and a pair of dirty black-and-blue Vans. He had a lot of stubble. That was the last thing that really struck me before I clocked the worry in his eyes, like he was about to be mauled.

'Cal?' he asked.

I nodded because I was too mortified to speak. I was as red as the gala apples at the stand across from us.

'Alan, are you annoying strangers again? Get back here. You've got fish to gut.'

A woman in a matching apron and curly greying hair appeared behind him. Her eyes were a subdued blue, like the sky on an overcast day and her hands were knobbly and wrinkled. Something sparked in her eyes and silently, she turned on her heel and disappeared out back. Weird.

'Are you hurt?' he asked, rubbing circles into my grazed knee. I swear, he was like freaking Livewire from the *Superman* comics because electric currents ran through my veins. I smiled and so did he.

He handed me an apron and my face must have been a question because he said, 'come on, I'll show you how to gut fish.'

Yip-pee.

I spent an hour learning how to gut cod and sea bass. I threw up in my mouth four times and vomited into a bucket of fish heads once when Al went to serve customers. I could have done without that. I'm the same boy who can't wire a plug or operate the self-service tills at Poundland to save his life. He told his gran that we were going for coffee but we took a detour through the shopping centre. Not Westfield but the shoddy shopping centre across from Stratford rail station. I mean, why would anyone visit it when you have something shiny and new like Westfield?

'I thought we were going to Starbucks?' I asked.

'Eventually.'

He took me by the hand and it only registered that we were in the toilets when he bolted the cubicle shut. We were wedged beside each other. I looked at him, unsure of myself and self-conscious but he was already shoving his hands into his pants. The stench of beer and urine hit the back of my throat. Al loosened the buckle of my belt and put his hands on my hips, pushing me against him so our bodies were touching. He guided my hands down his belly and into his pants, showing me what to do. It felt good. I'd only ever kissed a boy. I'd been touched by a boy but this was different. He shushed me after a while and kissed me fiercely. My hand and boxers were sticky as he moaned. He shoved some tissues into his boxers and discarded them in the toilet. He unbolted the door and left before I could ask what the hell happened.

I did my best, cleaning myself up while my mind raced. The euphoria started to wear off and confusion seeped in. I flushed the toilets and ran like crazy. I'm pretty sure people stared but I blocked everything out. I made it back to my house, slipping in and up the stairs like a ninja. I changed clothes and stuffed my dirty clothes into the wash basket.

I stepped into the shower and welcomed the hot jets of water that burned the memory from my skin. I opened the lid of mum's super scrub and worked it down my arms and under my nails.

I breathed in the citrus smell, relishing the way it burned the acne dotting my shoulders. Tributaries of water soaked my hair and ran down my body.

Al's face worked its way into my mind; his hands on my hips, in places I didn't want and ways I didn't feel comfortable with. Nausea hit and I slipped onto the floor, water pounding my head. I brought my knees to my chest and let my tears mix with the water. If you couldn't see the tears, they weren't real.

My phone vibrated as I towelled off in my bedroom.

Al: You were great. We should do that
again sometime.

I ignored it, dropping my phone into the bottom of my sock drawer. I collapsed into my bed, wedging my head between two pillows and pressing down hard. Curled up in a foetal position, it started to settle in what had happened with Al.

Did I want it to happen?

Did I enjoy it?

Would it have happened anyway?

Was I overreacting?

It wasn't . . . bad. I mean, I enjoyed it. I liked how it felt but was I expecting it? No. Did I want it to happen? Further down the line, maybe. I shuddered when I thought about it.

I felt stupid; embarrassed by my inability to say 'no' and leave. I was angry with myself for hoping he'd be this really nice guy and maybe, he'd want to be my boyfriend. He told me he'd get us

22

coffee but he made me gut fish before giving me a handjob with fishy fingers. He didn't even have the decency to wash his hands. I was stupid enough to let him. Going forward, I told myself I'd speak up. I'd meet in public places and never allow myself to be put in a vulnerable position again. What happened with Al could *never* happen again. I started a list of *Guy Turnoffs* and I scribbled 'engaged/married' and 'fishy hands' as numbers one and two. I didn't see how my dating prospects could get much worse.

'You did what?' Em exclaimed, slapping her bare knees, mascara tributaries running down her face. 'I don't know whether to . . .' She couldn't finish the sentence before another fit of giggles burst out of her mouth. 'Seriously though,' she sniffled, regaining her composure, 'what the hell were you thinking? He could have been an axe murderer.'

I felt that it was the wrong moment to tell her that if an axe murderer wanted to kill me, he wouldn't have gone to such elaborate lengths to write a note, slip it stealthily into my rucksack and have a text conversation.

'What were you thinking?'

'I thought he might have been a cute boy. A boyfriend.' I felt a hundred times stupider just saying those words, baffled by my own ridiculous logic.

'Fishfingers,' Em shrieked uncontrollably. Glad someone found it so goddamn funny. I had a feeling that I was never going to live this one down.

'Em, does it – does it count?'

'Count? Count for what?'

I fidgeted with a loose thread on my jumper. 'Am I still a . . . *virgin*?' I stage-whispered.

'Unless it's up the Bourneville Boulevard, it doesn't count.' I cringed, feeling heat rise to my cheeks.

'Emmy, Dunc's here!' Em's mum shouted up to us. Thank God.

'Send him up.'

'Keep the door open.'

Em rolled her eyes. 'In case we decide to have wild frenzied sex twelve feet from my parents.'

Duncan arrived and upon seeing me, he rushed over and hugged me tightly, kissing me once on each cheek.

'God, Duncan, he's gay, not French.'

'You told him?' I'm not sure why I was surprised by this and much less, why I was hurt by it. 'Did you tell anyone else?'

'Cal, he's my boyfriend. Of course I told him, but I swear, I haven't told anyone else.' She mime-zipped her lips and threw away the key.

I wanted to let it go. Em was there for me more times than I could count but I couldn't quite let go of the hurt. It was mine to tell. A part of me. I'd met Duncan a few times. I didn't know him; not like I knew Em. Em telling Duncan, I felt like I never got to be the one to say it or decide how I would say it. Nothing changed. Duncan still treated me the same except for the occasional hug which I found uncomfortable and intrusive.

I left shortly after. I stayed in my room, minimising contact with mum. Saturday afternoon, I heard her speaking to a solicitor on the phone. *Divorce* rang in my ears before I carefully closed my door and sank into my bed, the springs biting into my back. The police were still investigating the matter at the hospital. I knew I'd be just fine without him. I didn't need his time. I didn't need his money. I didn't need *him*.

It was only when I was lying in bed late at night that Em's words registered. *He's my boyfriend*. They were finally official. I took out my phone and tapped out a quick 'congratulations' with kisses. God, I really was a crap friend.

I returned home Sunday evening, feeling upbeat. Mum held my Christmas exam results in her right hand, looking grim, and I knew immediately that the words that would leave her lips would burst what little zen I'd managed to scrape from the weekend. I failed English. This wouldn't have been so much an issue if I hadn't failed my last two exams too. That wasn't particularly interesting but it interested me because I was about to spend eight of my Saturdays at a two-hour group study session with a tutor mum found on the internet.

'It'll be fine, Cal,' mum tried to reassure me. 'I've spoken to him over the phone. He's a well-respected professor at King's College.'

'He could have had a knife in the other hand,' I murmured.

'What was that?' she replied, resting a fist on her cocked hips.

'Nothing,' I murmured.

Dad had been spending time with his brother, Vinny, ever since the "incident", as mum referred to it. I wasn't sure I bought that. Mum handed me an envelope when I got home. I'd been granted a temporary Protection Order. I wasn't sure what it meant but mum explained that dad couldn't come within one hundred metres of me at our home or in public places.

She'd also had the locks re-fitted. She didn't mention the obvious which was who it was meant to keep out. I hadn't forgiven mum but I was starting to slightly warm to her again. She freaked out. I got it – she cut her ring finger off – but still, those words didn't just roll off the tongue. *My son is gay*, announced with disbelief and shame. That disbelief and shame had to come from somewhere.

Mum hadn't directly spoken about dad and for that, I was grateful. I wasn't ready to talk about it. My bruised eye healed but the internal scars were wide open and festering. The week was full of tomorrows and it was the tomorrows that kept me going.

Chapter 4

EXPERIMENTAL BAKING

Someone shouted 'hoot hoot for the fag patrol' as I entered the Food Tech classroom, brushing the pencil parings Gareth and John had dumped in my hair during English. We were making coffee cake. If there's anything better than cake, it's COFFEE cake. Well, there's chocolate, but coffee is a close second.

'Find a station and get to work!' Ms Radley clapped her hands.

When I saw Electra Jones examining her acrylic nails, leaning lazily against my usual desk, I scanned the room for another spot. One spot left and yay, right next to Cameron Evans.

I left my bags in one of the three cupboards lining the right wall and sidled up to my new spot. I watched as Electra spotted Cam and made a sudden beeline for it. I broke into a jog, beating her by mere metres. Cam brushed his brown surfer hair out of his eyes and looked at me as I dropped my notebook and pen onto the tabletop.

He smiled at me. It wasn't his trademark, all-consuming crinkling-of-the-eyes grin but it wasn't forced either. Deep breaths.

'Are you . . . OK?'

At least I didn't sigh.

I nodded frantically, making a sound that reminded me of the slow opening and closing of a goldfish's mouth. Dad poured my goldfish – Zim and Zam – down the toilet when Kayleigh was born. Budget cuts, apparently. Dad lost his job when work began on a new shopping centre in Essex. They'd over-projected their costs and dad suffered for it. Mum babysat occasionally but not a lot – not enough to put actual food in my lunch box. Zim and Zam were the first in a long line of casualties.

'Crap, I forgot my coffee. Can I borrow some of yours?' Cam spoke to me. Cameron Evans actually *spoke* to ME. I did a victory dance in my head until I remembered that I forgot coffee beans too. More like, I couldn't afford coffee beans.

'Sure.' I pretended to look through my rucksack, hoping that I'd have a fairy godmother looking out for me, picking up on my feeble attempts at telepathy and deliver a bag of coffee beans. Nescafe. Carte Noire. Heck, I'd take the cheapest coffee beans she could find.

I slapped my forehead. 'I'm going to kill my sister.'

'It's OK. I'm sure Electra won't mind sharing.'

'Do you need some coffee, Cam?'

Electra leaned over the counter, her hair pinned up in a glossy brown beehive. She'd spent the Christmas holidays in Bermuda and it showed. Her tanned skin glistened under the harsh lighting, making me appear even more sickly pale.

Cam looked at her but I couldn't see his facial expression to gauge on the scale of Ecstasy and Electra, whether it was a 1 for, 'just give me the damn beans', a 5 for 'I wouldn't mind feeling my bangers on your mash', or 10, 'which cubicle did you say?' I coughed. Electra handed us the beans and sidled back to her table.

I could probably afford to learn a thing or two from her; how she managed to get her hair so shiny on dull winter Mondays and her hazel eyes sparkled when she smiled. I took a sliver of satisfaction knowing I could out-bake her any day of the week.

As if on cue, the oven timer pinged and I pulled our cake out golden brown. I grinned when Electra's set off the smoke alarms. When Ms Radley cut through our cake and tasted it, she commented on how moist it was. When she cut through Electra's with her chainsaw – just kidding, sort of – she told her she'd been to A&E once already that year and she wasn't looking to set a new record. That wiped the smile off her face but Cam didn't speak to me much. Sadly.

'I don't know why you picked Food Tech,' Em remarked distastefully, watching Ms Radley waft a tea towel against the cloud of smoke billowing into the corridor. We both ignored the massive penis carved down the side of my locker while we twisted the combinations. Em knew but so far, no one at school did; well, I hadn't confirmed it. I got a hard time as it was since they equated quiet as being synonymous with gay.

'Free food,' I replied, holding out my Tupperware container with a chunky slice of coffee cake.

'Have I ever told you how much I love you?' She batted her brown eyes at me. I opened the lid and we sat on the wall in the yard, the two of us licking icing off our fingers and piggy-me, inhaling the crumbs out of the corners.

Em removed a lunch box from her rucksack and popped the lid, placing a Granny Smith apple and what looked like a ham sandwich wrapped in cling film on the brick wall. Raising one eyebrow, she asked, 'are you not going to eat anything?'

I stared at my untied shoelaces. 'I already did.'

'You mean, the cake?'

I nodded.

'Here.' She placed the apple into my palm, wrapping my fingers around its waxy skin.

I bit into the apple and when the juice hit my tongue, I got a sweet sensation overload. I angled my body away from Em, shame and embarrassment running through my veins like some sort of anti-adrenaline, bringing me down. I felt someone push me roughly off the wall and when I stood up, something cold prodded my exposed skin, just above my belt.

'Give me your lunch money.'

Em stayed where she was and in her most unimpressed voice, she announced, 'is that a butter knife?'

'It's a knife,' the guy repeated, as if we didn't know what a knife was. I played the words over and over in my head and even though my assailant was wearing a cap down low on his face, I still recognised the voice. Gareth Mead. One of Niall's lackeys.

'You know what they say about butter knives.' Gareth swivelled his head, his attention on Em. 'It's a gateway knife.' I burst into hysterical laughter and through my teary vision, I could see Em grinning.

'Are you making fun of me?'

'Darling, is the sky blue? Did Newton discover gravity? Did man walk on the Moon?'

'Who's Newton? Your dog or something?'

I couldn't help it. I laughed even louder. Em could cut you down in as little as ten words if she wanted to, her wit, infinitely sharper than a butter knife.

Em removed something from her bag and hopped off the wall. She ambled over, feigning innocence. Gareth's knife hand quivered. 'If I was going to use a knife, Gareth,' she said, brandishing a steak knife, 'I'd aim a little bigger.' He dropped the knife and backed away. 'If you ever come near my friend again, we'll see how sharp this knife is, you hear me?' He nodded like a bobblehead dog. 'I'll. Cut. Your. Fucking. Balls. Off.'

I'd never seen anyone run so fast and simultaneously look so manic, except maybe Mo Farah. Gareth certainly gave Mo a run for his money. Em can be terrifying when she wants to be.

'Are you OK?' Em asked.

'It happens.'

Em swung her legs out and leaped off the wall. 'It doesn't have to! Why do you always play the victim? You should stand up to them.'

'Niall is the captain of the football team. He's stronger than me, more popular. I don't have a chance.'

Em clasped her hands on my shoulders, forcing me to meet her penetrative gaze. 'Yes, Niall is strong. Yes, he may be popular, but you've got something he hasn't.'

'Holes in my school jumper?' I interjected, fitting my hand through the hole in the armpit.

'Stop that!' Em slapped my hand. 'Fight him with words! You're smart, Cal.'

'And get beat up behind the school bins at lunchtime? No thanks.'

'What happens when I'm not here? You have to be able to defend yourself.'

'Em, I know you mean well, but I really don't want to talk about it.' I could feel my eyes beginning to well up.

'Fine,' Em huffed, folding her arms across her chest, 'but if you're going to sit here playing the victim, I'm not going to stand by and watch.' She stormed off, slamming the heavy oak door behind her.

Chapter 5

EXCEPTIONAL EDUCATION

Mum finally made good on her tuition promise when I received my fourth F in English Lit. Facts and numbers, I could learn them, but with everything going on in my head, Shakespeare was speaking double Dutch. The plays we studied might as well have been written for aliens. The more times I read them, the less connected I felt.

Mum abandoned me for a shimmering spring display at John Lewis, leaving me to navigate my own way. I marched to my tutor's apartment, passing the British Library.

My tutor, Armin Van Claude, was a pathological stoner but surprisingly on-it. He had a bald patch in the middle of his head. His remaining hair was swept to either side and held in place with two bobby pins, making him look like a demented unshaven

Satan. He ushered me in with a grand sweep of his hands. The room was wide and spacious with a small corner cut off by a semi-transparent wall for a steel and chrome kitchen. Bold, irregular-sized paintings covered the walls.

Armin sat opposite us with a spoon in his hand, staring hard at his alphabet letter soup with the intensity a scholar might study Shakespeare – or, you know, that a stoner might look at a hash farm. He pushed some letters around and in a lazy monotonous tone, he said, 'I think it's,' and he held up the bowl, 'TIME TO BEGIN.' He didn't shout. In the middle of the overlapping, questionable circle of letters, he had spelled out his words.

My heart was beating about eighty beats a second before I walked in the door and now, I was pretty sure I was going to pass out. The room started to blur at the corners of my vision. That's when a hand rested on my knee, squeezing gently. I looked to my right. A boy with electric blue eyes smiled at me. I think I might have gasped. I almost definitely stared and it's possible that I drooled down the front of my very unsexy, Christmas jumper – with flashing lights for aesthetic value. Mum had put a washload on and even though it was early March, it was that or a tattered cardigan covered in holes big enough to fit your hands through.

'I'm Matt,' he whispered.

'Let's begin,' Armin announced, his fingers running over the spines of the books on a metallic shelf and extracting a copy of *The Tempest*. 'I assume you've all read the text so we'll skip right to the meaning behind the play. Who can tell me the importance of Caliban in the text?'

I glanced at the two couches for the first time – placed perpendicular to each other. I tried not to meet Matt's gaze, but out of the corner of my eye, I could tell that he wasn't looking at me and something sank in my stomach.

Aside from Matt, there were two girls in our group. One wore pastels and her hair was mousy brown, tied into Shirley Temple pigtails. The other girl had roughly cut, jet black hair that she blew out of her face every couple of minutes.

'Cal?'

Shit.

'He was a monster, right? All of Shakespeare's plays had monsters,' the black-haired girl interjected.

'I don't think that's quite accurate, Adi.'

'Sure it is,' she replied, wiping her palms on her black jeans.

'What about *The Merchant of Venice*?'

'Shylock.'

'Riiiiiigght. *Romeo and Juliet*?"

'The Capulets and the Montagues.'

Armin removed his black glasses and pinched the bridge of his nose. '*Hamlet*?' The hash should have mellowed him but right then, he looked like he was about to give up teaching us and go back to spelling messages in his alphabet spaghetti.

'Claudius.' Then, after a brief pause. 'Hamlet too. Definitely Hamlet.'

'But Hamlet avenged his father!' Armin protested.

'So he can take a life as long as he's avenging his father, that's fine?'

'No. Yes. Look, can we get back to *The Tempest*?' A smug grin twisted Adi's lips. I began to wonder how she knew so much about Shakespeare's plays. I failed English Lit all year long but this girl was a walking encyclopaedia of literary knowledge. Why was she here?

Mid-meltdown, Armin looked like a cartoon. I could almost visualise the animated smoke coming out of his ears.

'You're the teacher.' She shrugged but I could hear the sarcasm loud and clear.

The rest of the session passed relatively quickly and without incident, though Armin started to ask more closed questions. I didn't learn much about Shakespeare though. I spent the remainder of the class catching Matt staring at me. Then, I'd look at him. He'd look away but he always grinned. Adi made vomiting gestures when Armin turned his back on us to pour a cup of tea. For his sake, I hoped there was something stronger in his tea than Chamomile leaves.

Armin told us to prepare an essay on the importance of the supernatural in *The Tempest* as our hour session came to an end. I didn't want to think about it and I didn't. Instead, I was first out the door and down the stairs. I crossed the street and rounded the corner.

'Hey!' a male voice shouted from behind me.

I turned, Matt jogging after me. 'You forgot this,' he said, removing one of my gloves and dropping my Blokia into my open palm.

I stared at it, not quite sure how to respond. I knew how he wanted me to reply. He wanted me to thank him and I should have.

That should have been the first thing I did if I didn't suspect he was a thief. Even when I got what Em called "white-girl-wasted", I never lost my phone, but suddenly, when I'd been on high alert, I'd left it at Armin's? I hadn't looked at my phone once since I entered his apartment.

'Thanks.' It came out of my mouth like sandpaper chafing against my windpipe.

'I already saved my phone number. You know, Boy-Who-Likes-To-Think-He's-Cute.'

A smile played at the corners of my mouth but memories of Al flashed into my mind. Matt had charisma but then, so did Al. 'Is that why you stole my phone?'

He held his hands up in the air, palms flat against the air. 'Are you calling me a *thief*?'

I watched and waited.

'Stole is such an . . . *ugly* word. I prefer pilfered.'

'So, you robbed – *pilfered* – my phone so you could give it back to me? That makes no sense.'

'Actually, I robbed your phone so I could have a conversation with you. You weren't supposed to think that I stole it. You were supposed to be grateful and then I'd ask you out for coffee.' We stood in the middle of the street, people bustling us side to side. When I didn't answer, he continued. 'How else was I supposed to get you to go for coffee with me?'

'A normal person would have asked.'

His forehead scrunched up like balled-up paper. 'But where's the fun in that?'

'How could I possibly say 'no'?'

'That's the spirit. Christmas coffees on me.'

'But it's March.'

'Gingerbread coffees should be year-round,' he shot back and before I could say anything, he slipped his hand into mine. I squeezed gently and he squeezed back. I sat down next to the window and Matt asked me what I wanted.

'I'll have what you're having.'

He rose, winked at me and joined the queue. I slipped my phone out of my jeans pocket and started typing a message to Em but stopped mid-message. She hadn't told me about Duncan; when they met and became an official couple. Why should I tell her about Matt? I gripped the sides of the table as my breaths became shallow. I closed my eyes, focusing on the sounds of steaming milk.

I locked my phone and dropped it into my bag. I could do this. I didn't need Em and she didn't need me. She had Duncan after all. Matt returned shortly after and put my coffee down on the table. I stared at the coffee. I liked the smell but it was overpowered by sweet gingerbread syrup. 'Thanks,' I said, taking a sip.

'You've never had coffee before, have you?' I imagine I looked a bit like the time Aunt Jean served the family pheasant for dinner and told us we were eating, Esther, the family pet mid-meal.

'I wasn't expecting it to be so sweet.' I tried to act cool but I spat my second mouthful over my jeans.

'It is pretty sweet,' Matt agreed, 'though not half as sweet as me.' I wondered how somebody that drank coffee could have such a Hollywood smile.

He wiped the damp stain on my thigh with some wadded-up napkins. I couldn't explain away the growing bulge in my jeans so I laughed loudly, trying to distract him. I probably looked crazy, if the subtle movements of Matt's dancing eyebrows were anything to go by.

'So, what do you like?' I asked him, deflecting attention from my weirdness.

'Swimming, cricket and museums. I'm a bit of art buff. Mum's the curator of a private gallery.' I bet my face was a picture worth capturing at that moment. 'How about you?'

See, the thing is, I always wondered about honesty being the best real policy. I mean, if I went by that, the response would be, 'doing tequila shots with Em, drunk dancing at one in the morning and drinking games; especially Lizzie's birthday when we played musical chairs and I missed the chair and fell through her mum's glass table.'

I couldn't tell him the truth so instead, I said, 'I love reading.' Not a total lie since I read *Men's Health* and skimmed my fingers over the glossy pictures like I'd be able to feel the ripples in the models' abs. 'Cricket.' Cricket is kind of like self-defence except instead of pepper-spray, you use a wooden bat. My sports knowledge was limited. My cricket knowledge was questionable. On a side note, has anyone ever looked at a cricket player and thought, *I'd love to rip his cricket pads off and show him a thing or too?* Cricket is a very *unsexy* sport. 'Tennis.' I was about as good at tennis as Em was at beauty pageants. Not to say that Em is ugly; she's anti-paint-your-face-like-Tony-the-Tiger. 'And . . .' I struggled for something to say but over

39

Matt's shoulder, I noticed a wrinkly man in grey cords and a white vest, peeling back the adhesives on his book of stamps and affixing them to a stack of manila envelopes. 'Stamp collecting.'

'Stamp collecting?' God, he had amazing cheekbones.

'Stamp collecting,' I confirmed. I tried to think of all the ways I could make stamp collecting sound cool. 'It must be the thrill. The travelling. The rush of adrenaline. You know.'

He nodded but it wasn't a slight, that's-pretty-cool nod. It was more of a send-help nod. 'Cool,' he said with flatlined enthusiasm.

I could never get my head around this. When I was with Em and Lizzie, I was the most sociable person in the world. Lock me in a room with a cute guy, a round of cocktails and jetpacks, and I guarantee you that I'd find a way to cock it up. So, though it may have come as a surprise that Matt liked me, it was hardly a surprise that he looked ready to self-mutilate and escape what had become the most awkward coffee date ever.

Em once told me that the most beautiful thing about me was my smile. 'You could light up a room with that smile and as long as you're happy, keep smiling.' So, I did. I smiled. I wasn't sure what I was expecting but he looked a bit confused and horrified, like I was going to handcuff him to the radiator and cut off locks of his hair so I could make a voodoo doll.

'Excuse me,' I said and made a beeline for the bathroom. A message flashed on my phone.

Mum: Window shopping on Oxford St.
Text me when you're finished x

I stared at my phone and contemplated calling Em again. It was my problem though. I needed to focus. I could still turn this around. I pocketed my phone and ran the tap, letting cold water gurgle over my fingers.

I marched back to our table with renewed purpose, intent on winning Matt over. I walked around the corner and my eyes narrowed. Matt was gone. My coat was still hanging on the back of my chair. My schoolbag was still under the table. I scanned the table for a message, a note. Nothing. It took half a minute to realise I'd been abandoned.

My heart started to race as my eyes darted around the café. I hoisted my bag up on the chair, trying to mask my embarrassment. I rummaged through my bag, feigning purpose, biting my lip to hold back the tears.

'Hey.' I turned around. Matt. 'Don't take this the wrong way, but you seem like more of a classic latte kind of guy,' he said, holding out a mug to me. Matt fidgeted and I wondered if he was as nervous as I was? He looked at me and the other patrons melted away as I dissolved into the seat.

'So, do you like Scrabble?'

'Scrabble,' I echoed incredulously. 'Love it.' I *hated* it. I hadn't played Scrabble since I was eight when Em and I would try to spell out as many bad words as we could. Triple word score for "boobs", I reminisced. Something told me that wouldn't have gone down too well with Matt.

'Mum puts together a cheese board for our monthly game nights. We crack open a bottle of wine; dad, mum and me. Does your family do game nights?' Envy pinched my stomach as I realised that that was what a normal family should be. I should have been playing board games and watching movies with my family; not filling out police reports and minding my little sister because dad blew a fuse.

'Of course! You're looking at the Twister champ of East London.'

'Is that so? Crap,' Matt muttered, catching a glint of gold on his wrist. A watch. No. A Rolex. 'I've got to help mum with dinner in an hour.' He cooked. *Keep it cool, Cal.* 'I'd really like to see you again though. Maybe next Saturday?' I nodded because right then, words failed me.

We strolled to the tube station where Matt hugged me goodbye. I watched as he disappeared into the crowd of people and even then, I stood there watching the space he had been, thinking that for once, maybe things were finally beginning to look a little brighter.

Chapter 6

PERPLEXING EVENTS

'What do you see?'

'Red,' I replied instinctively.

I wasn't sure what Matt expected me to say. His mum was the curator of an art gallery. The closest I got to art was gluing dad's car keys to the countertop when I was four. What did I know about art?

'I think,' Matt whispered pensively, 'that it's a metaphor for yin and yang; man and woman; black and white. The explosion of colour is grey.' It didn't look grey to me. It looked red but I didn't voice my opinion. 'Everything else is one colour, one finite meaning but everything in between is . . . infinite.'

It sounded like nonsense but I tried to look impressed. This was what Matt liked. He was showing me his world. I didn't need to like it but I wanted to at least respect it.

'Should we get something to drink?'

I nodded. I'd had enough of art galleries to last me a lifetime. Matt put his hand in my jacket pocket. 'Are you trying to rob me again?'

'One time. It was *one time*!' Matt removed his hand and held mine, gently swinging it back and forth.

Nobody pointed.

Nobody shouted.

Nobody laughed.

It felt nice having someone want to show me off to the world. We exited the gallery and turned a corner, passing the window of a quaint café with tiny china sets for tea and scones. Matt stopped by the door, closing his eyes and leaning in close. I followed suit, our lips pressing together. Matt moved his fingers through my oily hair as our tongues met.

My heart pumped wildly and when I faced the café window again, the blood froze in my veins.

Him.

And her.

'Mum . . . Dad . . .?'

Mum, with her hands around her belly.

Dad sipping a cup of tea like nothing had happened.

Mum clocked me as the memories hit me like a freight train.

The feeling of broken glass embedded in the palms of my hands. The metallic taste of blood gushing into my mouth. The ache at the back of my skull. Dad's face twisted into a snarl. The *crack, crack, crack* of glass. The cries of the nurses, the squeak of their shoes slapping against the linoleum floors.

Adrenaline coursed through my veins and instinct possessed me. In Biology, at the beginning of the year, Ms Pearson covered hormones. I remembered her telling us that adrenaline was a "fight or flight" hormone.

Fight.

Flight.

Fight.

Flight.

Fight.

Flight.

Fight.

Flight.

I don't think I consciously decided but I could feel the energy buzzing in my fingertips, fizzing into my legs. My reaction was as natural as a bird taking flight when a predator approaches. I ran. I pumped my fists harder, forcing escape as quickly as my legs could carry me. I didn't know where I was going. Saturday shoppers stared. Let them stare. I stepped into a nearby alleyway sidestepping a taxi as the driver blared his horn. Sinking down onto the damp ground, I closed my eyes, wrapping my arms around my legs, pressing them closer to my body. The brick wall bit into my back. I liked focusing on that rather than reality. I struggled to catch my breath, running my fingers along the coarse concrete as I imagined my safe place: the Food Tech classroom. I could almost taste the bitter lemon on my tongue and smell sweet flaky pastry in the air.

My heartbeat wouldn't slow down but when I got my breathing under control, I removed my phone from my jean pocket. Seven new messages. I swiped right:

> Mum: It's not what it looks like!
>
> Mum: Are you OK?
>
> Mum: Cal, please talk to me.
>
> Mum: I'm concerned.
>
> Mum: WE'RE concerned x
>
> Mum: Just tell me you're OK.
>
> Matt: I hope you're OK :(

Typical mum. The first thing she wanted to communicate was her innocence. Matt's message, on the other hand, that one surprised me. I wasn't expecting it. In fact, I wasn't expecting to hear from him ever again. I pocketed my phone and faced the red brick wall, desperately trying to make sense of what I had seen and what I was going to do.

'Hey,' Matt called breathlessly. He marched over, hauled me up by the armpits and took my weight in a bear hug. I felt tears soak my cheeks.

'How did you find me?' I whispered.

'I followed you.' With Matt holding me, I felt the world stop spinning around me. When I calmed down, Matt released me and we made a beeline for the underground station.

We looked at our feet awkwardly. I didn't want to talk about my freak-out and Matt didn't pry, whether he wanted to know or not.

'We should go and see it,' Matt stated, vaguely nodding his head in the direction of a giant poster for *Kinky Boots*. I'd watched the movie once and it was alright. I didn't bother telling him that there was no chance I'd get lucky and find a fifty pound note blowing in the wind before then. 'Look, Cal, whatever happened is between you and your parents. I'm not going to ask you to tell me but I don't think you should go back there tonight.'

'I have a friend.'

'I'm sure you do, but they're not here and I am and I'm telling you now that you're going home with me. Not in a creepy psycho-stalker, handcuff-you-to-the-radiator kind of way.' A watered-down laugh escaped my lips. 'Unless that's what you're into.' He winked.

Matt swept me away, around the corner and down the high street. It felt like being swept into an X-Men comic, where anything was possible.

Chapter 7

EXIT STRATEGY

We got the tube to Notting Hill station, Matt talking animatedly over the *beep, beep, beep* of the closing tube doors and the whirr of the train's motor as we sped through dark tunnels. Matt told me all about his mum and how she'd probably assault me with questions, but that they came from a place of interest more than anything else. I nodded along, noticing that he hadn't mentioned his father, only because I was thinking about mine. My throat felt tight and scratchy. I wasn't sure I could have spoken even if I'd wanted to.

We came to a narrow road with a small line of houses; the roofs of which could be seen over an assortment of wooded gates. Matt led me to the cul-de-sac and punched a code into the keypad. The gates swung open. I clocked the CCTV camera over the keypad. Could Matt's mother see us? Was she watching us now? I glanced quickly at the wine-coloured Audi, parked on the gravel driveway next to a sprawling oak tree and sighed deeply. There were no flowers where I lived unless you counted the baby cactus mum positioned on the mantelpiece. The front door swung open as we approached. 'Brace yourself,' he whispered and it seemed to be more for his benefit than for mine. 'Thanks, Carmen,' he said, handing his coat to a short plump lady with dark hair pulled up in a bun.

He had staff! I gulped. I stepped across the threshold, burying my hands in my coat pockets. A grand mahogany staircase gleamed before us, diverging left and right. I followed Matt into a kitchen that was twice as big as our flat with its high ceilings and tiled floors. Tan mosaic tiles along the walls caught the sunlight and brightened the room.

A tall reedy woman, dressed in a black-and-white, pencil-skirt-blouse combo curled up on a tawny couch like a cat; relaxed but ready to pounce. Bitter coffee scented the air and she brought a fancy glass cup to her lips, sipping from it delicately. She frowned up at me, softening her features to flash me a ceramic smile that pinched the corners of her mouth, making her appear older than she probably was. I tried my best to smile, to disarm her with charm, but she didn't buy it. Matt's feeble cautions weren't enough to prepare me for this and suddenly, I saw sleeping on the street as a preferable option, though I knew Matt would never allow it.

I held out my hand to greet her but she visibly recoiled. 'Hi, I'm Cal. Matt's . . . friend.' I fumbled for words in a squeaky voice. Time stretched out, like school time, where minutes felt like hours.

'Mum,' Matt said. Was he chastising his mum?

'What? I haven't said anything!' she protested with theatrical innocence. She looked about as innocent as Kayleigh when she flushed mum's keys down the toilet.

The non-conversation was more interesting than the actual conversation; the not-so-subtle looks; the tension in his mother's shoulders; the square jawline; the disapproving click of her tongue – just once but enough for me to know that I wasn't welcome at Matt's house. I could interpret the subtext by the dagger looks alone. I relaxed a bit, knowing that Matt saw his mum the way I was seeing her.

She swept me into the foyer with icy indifference. I must have made a sound because she remarked, 'yes, *Fish of Paradise*! Isn't it fas-cin-at-ing?' She spelled out each syllable like I was a Mexican trying to learn English in a dodgy drugs operation. Matt and his mother exchanged another round of pointed looks.

'Mum curates a gallery in Mayfair. She loves art, particularly glasswork,' he added, motioning to the high-ceilinged foyer with its wide walls, the chandelier with lights like gemstones dripping down and a row of plinths, each with a bespoke piece of glasswork in a panoramic rainbow of colours.

'Is that salmon?' I asked. The smell made my mouth water. It had been three years since we were able to afford salmon.

'Congratulations, Matt, bringing Olivers into my home. I suppose we'll be operating a soup kitchen from the guesthouse fairly soon.'

'*Mum.*'

When I got scared or intimidated, I often thought about what Em would do and that usually got me through the situation. Somehow, I doubted calling her a bitch, would earn me a seal of approval.

'What a beautiful home,' I announced to no one in particular, when the awkward tension mounted. I couldn't take it anymore. I wanted to jump out the window and escape.

'It needs work but it's a start. Where do you live, Cal?'

'We live close to Canary Wharf,' I answered noncommittally, hoping she wouldn't probe further. I didn't feel like telling her about our ramshackle flat in Leytonstone which was a twenty-minute tube ride from Canary Wharf.

'Is that so?' She disappeared through the doorway behind her but not before casting a raised eyebrow.

She hated me. If I wanted to date Matt – and I really, *really* did – then I needed her to like me. I noticed that Matt's face was scrunched up and his eyes were narrowed.

Matt opened the sliding patio door. I heard a bark, followed by the sounds of a dog bounding across the floor, skittering into me as it tried to grip the tiles and slow its momentum.

'Matt! How many times have I told you about letting Duchess into the house?' Duchess. Figures who named the cocker spaniel.

'The vet said we need to spend time with her. We can't keep her outside all day and night.' Vet? What the ... My thoughts were cut off by a sound like cymbals being smashed together violently as I got to my feet. Duchess whimpered and bowed down low.

Matt's mother banged a pot with a metal spoon, inching closer to Duchess with deliberate steps. She got within four feet when Matt yelped 'stop' and Duchess vomited a green liquid over her tiles. Matt's mother lost it. All grace and poise disappeared as her face became a mask of feral fury.

'Get out. Get out, get out, get out! Get her OUT, Matt. OUT!' She grabbed the dog by the collar and dragged her out through the sliding door with laboured breaths. Matt pursued and me? Well, I did what anyone would have done in that situation. I ran.

I didn't care that it seemed like a cowardly thing to do. I didn't care that Matt's mother hated me in that moment and I didn't particularly care what Matt would think because he'd either understand or he wouldn't, and if he didn't, then maybe he wasn't the guy for me.

Matt's mother, Duchess – it got the cogs whirring in my mind. I thought about mum and why she was with dad. I'd pondered it since dad went psycho.

Mum wasn't that bad. She paid for my tuition and God knows where that money was siphoned from – almost definitely a loan and it was to help me. Given how pretentious Matt's mother was, I can't imagine the tuition was cheap either.

So I ran, my footsteps hitting the concrete, my legs leading the way. The pitter-patter of rain didn't stop me. Raindrops hit me harder and harder, like bullets ricocheting off my skin. I had a lot to think about. I stopped under a bus shelter and slid my phone out of my jean pocket. I tapped away at the screen quickly, listening to the rhythmic *plink, plink, plink* of the rainwater on the roof.

Me: I'm OK. I'm OK and I'm staying with Em tonight.

I owed her that much. She may not have been the best mother in the world but she was far from that ice queen I left behind. She didn't respond. I respected that. I didn't have anything particularly good to say to her. Forty-five puddles, two ponds and a lake later, I arrived at Em's front door looking like I'd just led a scuba expedition. Em answered the door, deliberately hesitating with her arm blocking my path.

'What?'

'Nothing.'

'Just say it and hurry. I'm soaked.'

'You're not going to get any wetter.'

She ambled into the sitting room with her tacky pink robe and its fur trim collar – the one I got her for her sixteenth birthday.

Em had a mug of hot chocolate and a couple of bourbon creams waiting on a plate beside her. Best. Friend. EVER. That also meant that she knew I was close to a breakdown. She rested her hand on mine when I sank into the blue suede couch beside her. I loved her for that. She didn't say anything. She knew I'd talk eventually, when I was ready.

'I met a boy. He took me to an art gallery but on the way out . . .' I got all squeaky so that 'out' sounded more like 'oot'. I cast my eyes to the wooden floor, breathing hard and blinking fast. I wouldn't cry here. I couldn't. I launched into the story, my voice rising and falling so that my tone of voice oscillated between Alan Carr and Danny Dyer. Em nodded every now and again. The story came gushing out of me but I held some of it back. I didn't tell her about how Matt made me feel like fireworks were exploding inside my belly whenever he held my hand or our first kiss.

'It's completely messed up,' I concluded, circling back to mum and dad. 'You're telling me.'

'I should be mad but I can't find it in me. I'm just – I'm just hollow. I'm on the cusp of crying just *thinking* about it.'

'I'll be right back.' Out of all the things I thought she might say, that was not one of them. She returned in seconds, carrying two shot glasses and a bottle of whiskey. She poured the glasses to the rim. We clinked our glasses and downed it. Em ah-ed with satisfaction. 'We need a little something to help you through this. Heck, we need something strong to help *me* through this.' I laughed because if I didn't, the alternative was to cry.

'Your dad is a dick.' I nodded. 'I know it's tough to hear but maybe you're not ready to lose another parent. Maybe you can't be mad at her because you can't lose her *and* your dad.'

'Yeah,' I mumbled.

'I love you though. You're stuck with me.'

Am I though? Do you really love me? Or do you just tolerate me now that you're with Duncan?

'Now,' she said, pouring out two shots and handing me one, 'would it make you feel any better if we drank this bottle of whiskey?' I nodded, blinking back the tears. 'Cheers to the queers.'

'We do have the best shoes.'

'I quite like my shoes,' she shot back, demonstrating her red shoes with their white straps, beaded eyes and pincers on either side.

'Are those lobster heels?'

'Crab heels.'

'Em has crabs,' I hooted. She punched me on the shoulder and we downed a third round of shots.

Chapter 8

EXTREME REACTION

I woke up the next day to fifteen new text messages, ten missed calls and a raging hangover. I knelt and when the room stopped spinning, I leaned a hand on Em's open drawer and stood. The empty bottle of JD caught my eye. I heaved and vomited into the drawer. Em rolled over, disgusted.

'Did you just vomit in my drawer?'

'I'm sorry,' I said, tears burning my eyes.

Em planted her feet on the carpet and marched towards me. She inspected the contents of the drawer and laughed. 'It's cool. It's just Duncan's jumper.'

'Won't he be mad?'

'Probably, but you've done him a favour. I hated that jumper.'

I should have asked about Duncan but I was too busy wrestling with my own thoughts.

Mum.

Dad.

Kayleigh.

School.

Matt.

Each one was like a saucer I was juggling in the air and I was always waiting for the earth-shattering crash.

Em scooped up the jumper with a plastic bag and dropped into the wheelie bin outside her house. We slid into our seats at Em's kitchen island. I inhaled the bitter scent of coffee and freshly baked chocolate croissants. The scene from Matt's house suddenly surfaced in my mind but I pushed it to the back of my brain.

'Morning, Cal,' Em's mum chirped in her red-and-white flannel apron. She patted Em's shoulder before setting down a pot of coffee in front of us, followed by a plate of croissants. I tore at the corner of my croissant, drooling as the flaky pastry melted in my mouth. Em poured coffee from the percolator. Breakfasts at Em's house were the best, unlike the wartime rations that mum served us. Lumpy porridge and water – orange juice *from concentrate* if she went wild with the shopping budget.

Em spat out her coffee dramatically over the chrome countertops. 'What the hell?'

'It's decaf, love. You're still seventeen. You shouldn't be drinking that much coffee.'

'We have an espresso machine.'

'That's for adults.'

'That's bullshit. Caffeinate me.' She held out her mug.

'Emily!'

'Matilda.' Em crossed one leg over the other. I muffled a laugh.

'I'm calling your father.'

'Good. Call Amani.'

'You're being very immature right now.' Em knew her mother hated talking to her father.

'Good.'

Em's mum hesitated, sighed and grabbed Em's mug. She placed it under the nozzle, flicked the switch at the side and clicked a coffee pod into place. I loved the hissing sound as the machine forced the coffee into the cup, followed by the steamy gurgle. It reminded me of the whirring of our boiler at home.

'Cal, would you like some *real* coffee?' Em asked me.

I wanted some. I really, really did but when I looked at how much Em had broken her mum down already, I really didn't have the heart to say anything. I shook my head, scooping two teaspoons of sugar into my coffee when her mum wasn't looking. 'No, thank you. I'm good!' I exaggerated my grin and her mum smiled. She collected the laundry from the washing machine and grabbed a basket of pegs as she made her way outside.

'You should go easy on her,' I whispered.

'Are you serious? Kettle, pot – black much?'

'This is not the same thing and you know it,' I shot back, as she slid another croissant onto each of our plates.

'Could have fooled me,' she retorted, making her way upstairs.

I followed.

I watched her mum from the window, wishing I'd offered to help as she struggled to pick a peg up off the ground. 'Em, I know she stopped you seeing your father; I get that you're angry but he destroyed your mother's life. He cheated on your mother.'

'Don't go there, Cal,' Em cautioned.

'With her best friend.'

'Cal.'

'*And* had a kid with her.'

'*Cal*!'

'He's known where you lived for years now and he hasn't made contact. Years of vouchers for Claire's Accessories says it all. She's doing the best she can.'

'I know, OK?' she shouted, slamming a snow globe against her desk. A fissure spread down the middle but neither of us addressed it. I walked over to her, coaxing her head onto my chest. 'It's not fair. He's with his new family in Tobago and I'm . . . *here*.'

'None of this is fair,' I told her, reflecting on my relationship with my father. 'Not on your mother. Not on you. You can't take all that anger out on your mother and you can't keep bottling it up.'

'I know,' she mumbled, staring at the ceiling so her tears wouldn't fall.

Em face planted her bed and I lay down beside her. We stared at the ceiling, which her dad had painted baby blue when Em was four after she refused to come inside the house, shouting about how she wanted the sky to be the first thing she saw when she woke up. Courtney Love and Joan Jett posters covered the wall above her bed.

'Do you miss him?' I asked her, taking a picture frame from her bedside locker. Em's skin wasn't as dark as her father's. Standing next to him at Legoland, she looked happier than I've ever seen her with her mother.

'Every single day.' She braced her hand on the bedside post. The colour went from her knuckles and her jaw squared. 'And I hate myself for it,' she whispered. I put my arms around her, hugging her to me; an embrace that wanted to take away just a fraction of the pain that lived deep under her skin. My phone pinged. 'Do you want to get that?'

'Will you be OK?' I released her.

'If you check your phone? I think I'll survive.

I swiped across the screen.

> **Matt:** I hope you're OK :-(
>
> **Me:** I'm fine. Sorry for leaving.
>
> **Matt:** I'm sorry about mum. She can be a bit odd with new guys.

'What are you smiling about?' Em remarked. Shit. Was I smiling?

'Nothing.'

'Does "Nothing" have a name? Matt maybe?'

'May. Be.'

I told Em all about Matt's mum and the messages he sent; how he held me when I saw mum with dad; how the feeling of his arms around my body stopped the cracks from spreading. He stopped me from having a complete meltdown and he never asked what it was about. He never probed. He just held me. He was there for me.

Em tapped her nails along her jawline. 'From what you've told me – and let's be honest, you tell me *everything* – Matt seems like a catch.'

'He is. I just wish his mum wasn't such a bitch.'

'If you recall, Duncan's mum wasn't too keen on me when we first met.'

'Didn't you almost kill her cat?'

'How was I supposed to know the chicken had a bone in it? Besides, it's an ugly cat.'

She flashed me a picture of the cat. It was an ugly cat. I couldn't disagree with her there. 'So, you're saying I should – I don't know – try to impress her?'

'God, no! Focus on Matt. He likes you. Every guy comes with a drawback.' I wondered if she was thinking about Duncan's mum's ginger tabby too.

Em was right. Matt was kind and, for some reason I couldn't fathom, he cared about me. My own dad wanted nothing to do with me. Matt was beautiful.

'If you need some help with his mum . . .' Em drew a line across her throat.

'I don't want to kill her.'

'Who said anything about killing her? I was going to rough her up a bit, maybe push her down the stairs. Jeez, Cal, your mind does wander to the darkest regions.'

I rolled my eyes, already wishing this moment would never end.

'Seriously, Cal,' she said, taking me by my Mickey Mouse ears and planting a slobbery kiss on my forehead, 'Matt seems like a nice guy but if his mum doesn't see what Matt sees – what I see – then maybe you should forget about him. I know every guy you've met so far has practically featured on *How to Catch a Predator*, but there are so many great guys out there. Enjoy your tequila teens.'

I let Em's words sink in. I really tried to absorb them, but I couldn't because she was wrong. I had no control over my family life; over dad and his anger management issues or mum and the bubble she'd retreated into. School life was a like a game of Battleships; I always expected the blow and sometimes it never came, sometimes it was exactly as I expected but other times, it was worse. That left my love life and look how that was turning out. I wasn't exactly Cupid's poster child.

It was nice for Em. She had Duncan. Her mum made sure she had food in her belly and money in her pocket. She went to school and no one picked on her. They *feared* her. I wanted to be feared if it meant I could stand up for myself. I wanted to go to school, shedding the fear like snakeskin and live each moment as it came, but I was me, and things like that never happened to boys like me.

I was lying in bed, making a conscious effort to work towards a better grade in English. I had *The Norton Anthology of Poetry* propped up on two limp pillows. I read through a poem called *Elm* by Sylvia Plath. I started to read through her biography, unaware of her depression and the attempts to "normalise" her. What the hell is wrong with people? I read it twice over, focusing on the metre and the imagery. Finally, something clicked and it started to make sense.

I have suffered the atrocity of sunsets.

Scorched to the root

My red filaments burn and stand, a hand of wires.

I felt her pain, the darkness deep inside her that she couldn't change. I shuddered at the electroshock therapy references.

My phone rang, jarring me from my thoughts. I reached across to the windowsill. Matt. My thumb hovered between the green and red phone icons. If I spent the week rejecting his calls and had to sit beside him at Armin's on Saturday, it would be beyond awkward. I tapped the green icon.

'Cal?'

'Yeah.'

'I'm sorry.' Pause. 'I'm sorry about mum. If I knew she was going to be like that, I—'

'You what?' I knew I was being unreasonable. Em's niggling doubts chipped away at the back of my mind. He'd never done me any harm. He bought me a coffee after our first English session together. He was there for me when I witnessed mum with dad and had a breakdown at Westfield which only made me feel worse.

'I don't know what I'm trying to say but I like spending time with you, Cal, and I want to see you again.'

I hesitated, biting down on my lip. I could hear his laboured breaths, like he'd just run a marathon. 'What about your mum?'

'What about her? If I liked everyone mum liked, I'd be surrounded by snobs.'

I smiled.

'Cal, are you still there?'

I waited a beat. 'I like you too, you know.'

'I never said I liked you.'

'Yes, you did,' I insisted.

'Nah-ah.'

'Uh-huh. You said you wanted to see me again.' I looked at my reflection in my window. I had a dopey grin on my face.

'Whatever. I'll text you during the week. We'll sort something out.'

'Sure thing.'

'Goodnight, Cal.'

'Night, night.' I scolded myself as soon as the words came out of my mouth. I sounded so childish. I didn't hang up the phone and neither did Matt by the sounds of it.

'You have to hang up sometime,' Matt teased.

'Same time?'

'Sure. On the count of three. One, two, three.' Pause. 'You're still there, aren't you?'

'So are you!' I fired back.

'This is never going to work.' I could imagine him shaking his head. 'OK, I'm hanging up, but this means nothing.'

'Fiend.'

'Night, Cal.'

He hung up. 'Night, Matt,' I whispered to myself.

A knock sounded on my door. I waited a beat. 'Cal?'

Mum? Had she been outside all this time? Had she heard my conversation with Matt? 'Yeah?'

'Can I come in?'

'K.'

She opened the door slowly and closed it behind her gently. She shuffled towards me, the maroon stained carpet muting her footsteps. I watched as she plopped onto the bed – not the most graceful of movements. She picked at her nails, not meeting my eye. I'd been dreading this moment.

'Did you want something?' I hated how incensed I sounded but she betrayed me. I couldn't bring myself to forgive her. Dad attacked me and she met up with him behind my back. Was I supposed to forget any of that happened?

She looked at me. Immediately, I could tell she'd been crying. I guess dad wasn't the man any of us thought he was. 'I know you saw me on Saturday, with your father, but it wasn't what it looked like.'

'Really? Because from where I was standing, it looked like you were both pretty cosy, sipping tea from china cups.'

'I wasn't— I'm not—' Her lips moved but I wasn't hearing an explanation. Better still, I wasn't hearing an apology. 'You weren't what? Spit it out.'

'I-I-I—' she stammered.

'You-You-You—' I realised it was a shitty thing to say as the words left my mouth.

'I'm pregnant!'

The words tumbled out of her mouth. She immediately cupped her mouth with her hands, like she didn't want any other secrets coming out. The words hit me like a freight train. *I'm. Pregnant.*

It took me a minute to comprehend what that meant. Mum was having a baby – another child that would be born into this fractured family. I wasn't sure what mum wanted me to say. Congratulations? Lovely? Great news? Did she want a hug and a kiss?

'Cal?'

'Get out.'

'Cal, I'm—'

'Get. Out,' I whispered through gritted teeth.

It was a horrible thing to say to a pregnant woman; especially my own mother but I couldn't help it. She could barely juggle two children. How was she going to manage with three? The fact that she'd told dad before me was the icing on the cake.

I stood up, bracing my hands on the windowsill. The room went helter-skelter as I stared up at the ceiling. I breathed in the crisp air from the open window, wondering how many more little bombs lurked in the dark, counting down the seconds until they blew our family further apart.

Chapter 9

EXQUISITE MOMENTS

I'm.

Pregnant.

Pregnant.

Pregnant.

No. I was not letting mum ruin the one good thing I had going for me. I marched purposefully through Waterloo station, phone to ear as pigeons swooped around me, descending on discarded sandwich crusts and empty coffee cups.

'What platform are you near?' Matt asked.

'Platform one.'

'OK, walk up towards platform nine-and-three-quarters.'

'You're an absolute geek,' I teased.

'You didn't know that?' He popped his lips at the end.

I looked up: platform five, more than halfway there. I felt butterflies fluttering around in the pit of my stomach. 'There's a lot to know.'

'You're smiling.'

'That's not creepy at all.'

'You're cute when you smile.'

'Cute but still creepy.

'Gotta go. Cute boy at ten o'clock.'

'You better be talking about me!' I raised my voice but the line went dead.

I scanned the platform barriers and then cast an eye to my right, at Foyles bookshop and the line of food outlets lining the opposite side of the station. There was a crowd of schoolboys or maybe scouts being guided by three adults, a few families but mostly couples dramatically swinging their hands back and forth.

Matt stood behind them. He smiled when he saw me. Damn, that smile. He kissed me on the cheek and instantly, I felt myself blush.

'There's a bakery in the market. Best brownies in town,' he promised.

'That's a bold promise,' I countered as he slipped a hand into my back pocket. I did the same. It made it more difficult to walk, especially with his guitar whacking my elbow.

'Matt, why did you bring a guitar?'

'Have you got something against guitars?'

'It just feels a bit . . . odd.'

'I'm not going to answer that,' he replied, sweeping me into the Southbank market.

I wanted to press him to answer, but I was immediately distracted by a cloud of spices and a small stall that displayed quirky brownie combinations.

'What would you like?'

'I can't decide,' I answered, ogling the cakes.

'Between which ones?'

'Death by Chocolate, White Chocolate Surprise, Salted Caramel and Mint Aero.'

'So, all of them,' Matt quipped. 'We'll take these four.' Matt pointed to the four I'd selected, before I could respond.

'Are you sure?'

Matt nodded, accepting the box from the vendor. 'Now, let's get some coffee.'

Matt made a face when the coffee shop told him they didn't do gingerbread syrup. We sipped our lattes, passing restaurants and pubs as we emerged by the Thames. Matt sat on a stone bench, patting the space next to him.

I stared at a boat passing along the river while Matt traced patterns across my denim-clad knees. I grinned stupidly. I reached across him for a napkin, certain that I had chocolate staining my mouth and teeth. He grabbed me by my t-shirt and dragged me towards him, our bodies crashing together. I ran a hand through his hair and he pulled away, pretending to be insulted. He winked and I laughed. While I had my mouth open, he pressed his lips to mine.

'Yum, chocolately,' he announced, licking his lips. I slapped the back of his head.

The Thames and the couples walking hand in hand disappeared. It was me and him.

Kissing him didn't feel like enough.

Not close enough.

Not warm enough.

He lifted me off my feet awkwardly, bear-hugging me. He released me and I sat down on the bench, staring out at the London skyline. Matt bent down, undoing the zip of his black guitar case.

'What are you doing?' I asked, gently knocking my feet together.

'Playing you a song.'

Matt began strumming the guitar softly at first, his voice low and husky. His fingers crashed down on the strings, his voice rising louder and more distinct. Matt smiled knowingly. I glanced behind me. He'd attracted a crowd of tourists who spoke in animated tones, jabbing their fingers at Matt. Then, the cameras came out. He didn't falter once during the *click, click, click* of the camera onslaught.

Surrounded by the group of tourists, I saw an elbow, a shoulder and then I lost sight of Matt. I could imagine the expressions to match his words though. I closed my eyes, listening to the words and the notes he shouted with a fire I'd never heard before. He wrote me a love song. He strummed out the final notes on the strings and through the space between two elbows, I saw him slip the guitar into its soft case.

'Cal?'

'I'm in the middle.'

'There you are!' Matt beamed, kissing me on the lips. Flashes went off in our faces. I felt like Bambi on ice. He was so smooth, so self-assured and when he laced his hands through mine, I felt the calluses on his fingertips rub up against my skin. I followed Matt along the banks of the Thames, unable to find words to convey how I felt.

'Close your eyes.'

I complied. A light breeze gusted into my face. I heard a clip as he undid the button of his Hermés satchel and rustled through it. 'Are you digging a hole to China in that thing or—'

'Oh, shut up and open your eyes.'

The last rays of the setting sun temporarily blinded me. It took a minute for me to focus on what was in his hands. Paper. Printed paper. Tickets? He gestured for me to take them. I held the smooth paper in my hand. *Kinky Boots.* He'd gotten us tickets to *Kinky Boots.*

'Matt, I . . .' The words died on my lips.

The brownies.

The song.

The theatre.

'Thank you' didn't seem like enough. As I tried to think of something worthy and thoughtful to say, he kissed me, taking my breath away. I wish I could have freeze-framed that moment forever. A snap. A photo to keep by my bedside to remind me that good things do happen to good people and that I can be happy.

Matt pulled back and placed a hand on the nape of my neck,

massaging it with tender fingers. 'You don't have to say anything. Now come on, let's walk along Southbank.'

He took my hand and swung it back and forth. Back. Forth. Back. Forth. When our hands shot forward, I felt like I had wings; like I could soar over the Shard, dart around the Gherkin and keep on flying for as far and as long as I wanted.

Sunday matinee. *Kinky Boots*. Matt and I. I couldn't have asked for more. I picked at a hangnail, gnashing down on it between my incisors as I counted down the tube stops to Tottenham Court Road. The skin tore and stretched down the side of my nail. I watched the blood bubble out of the wound, placing my index finger and thumb either side and pressing hard, relishing the pressure and distracting myself from how nervous I felt about the whole thing.

The train pulled into Holborn station and I brought my finger to my mouth, sucking up the blood. Matt would be waiting at the next station. I didn't want to get blood on his shirt. I wasn't sure why but I enjoyed the metallic taste of the blood. I clenched my fingers hard around my cut finger and held the bar next to me with my other hand as the train slowed down. The doors shot open and I jogged up the escalators, every step taking me further away from mum and the house. I told her I was spending time with Em. There was *no way* I was taking Matt back to my Lego flat.

Matt waited at the top of the escalator, like Ryan Phillippe in *Cruel Intentions*. I jumped into his arms and he swung me around in a circle. He placed a hand on the small of my back as I recovered from a dizzy spell. We held hands even as we passed through the station barriers and out into the night-time air, crisping my face with its coolness.

'The front row was sold out but luckily, mum pulled a few strings and got us on our own box.'

'Your mum got us a box? Does she know you're taking me?'

Matt laughed. 'Of course she knows. See, I told you. Mum isn't that bad. It just takes a while for her to thaw.'

Matt handed the tickets to the patron. I had my doubts that his mum had done a complete one-eighty but I bit my lip. If I was going to date him, I'd had to endure her company at least once a year, twice if I had to spend Christmas at his house.

We ascended the grand red-carpeted staircase and emerged onto the balcony. Chatter exploded throughout the theatre. I didn't know where to look. There was one other balcony across from us. As I tried to make out who might be in the seats, Matt squeezed my knee.

'You've been awfully quiet. Is everything OK?'

I shook my head, dazed. 'I'm fine.' That wasn't strictly true. My relationship with mum felt like continental drift. Every day that passed was like another metre between us and I was beginning to wonder if we'd ever repair what we had. I didn't want to tell Matt that. 'I'm just a bit overwhelmed. I've never been to the theatre before.'

'Well, that's going to have to change right this minute.'

'Do you not think I'm a bit . . .'

'A bit what?'

'Out of place?' I looked down at my best pair of chinos, stained where Kayleigh had managed to spill milk on me just as I was leaving the house. My knock-off Converse were black with dirt and dust. I felt even more underdressed sitting beside Matt in his blue blazer, crisp white shirt and tie.

'Cal Adams, I'm telling you now that you are beautiful to me just as you are and you shouldn't care what anyone else thinks.' The problem was I did. I really did. 'And for the record, you're not out of place. You're never out of place when you're with me.' I burrowed into his chest and he put an arm around me.

I felt him move his body to the right. 'The show should be starting in a couple of minutes.' I closed my eyes for a minute, basking in the chatter, the stage lights, the grandiosity of the theatre and the sheer extravagance of it all. 'Do you want to look through these?' Matt questioned, removing a pair of gold binoculars you'd see royalty view an opera through from his inside pocket. I took them from him, holding them by the stick. 'Er, Cal? People usually looking through the small holes.' I pulled back, realising why the stage looked so microscopic. You couldn't take me anywhere without embarrassing myself. I righted the binoculars, viewing the stage and the spectators.

'Matthew, darling! What are you doing here?'

I looked behind us, at Matt's mum decked out in a head-to-toe, cream gown with a swirling fiery pattern branching out from the midriff. Her hand, weighed down with ostentatious rings, held a champagne flute. I didn't look at her for long because beside her was a tall lean boy with dark features. I studied his face carefully. He couldn't be much older than me. What was she playing at?

'Mum, what are you doing here?' If looks could kill, Matt's mum would be in a coffin six feet under.

'Seeing the show.'

'But we're on a date,' he retorted through gritted teeth.

'Well, the more the merrier, right? You'll hardly know the two of us are here.'

'Two of us . . .' His voice trailed off and as he clocked the boy behind her, the colour drained from his face. 'What?'

'Hey, Matt,' the boy announced, shyly shuffling up to him and hugging him tight.

'Alfie.'

'Yes?'

'It's just – what are you doing here?'

'Imelda invited me out to see the show and you know I had to come. Remember when we watched the movie together?'

Matt nodded carefully, like sudden movements might make his head implode. I watched the scene with confusion at first, but a bitter jealousy had boiled my blood and I was getting closer and closer to pushing Matt's mum over the edge.

'This is my *boyfriend*, Cal.' Matt made a huge show of kissing me on the lips, a lengthy kiss that felt off compared to our kiss at the tube station. I wasn't sure how I felt about that but it did ease some of the jealousy gnawing away at my insides.

'Nice to meet you, Callum,' Alfred said, motioning to himself rather dramatically. Fitting that we were at the Adelphi Theatre. 'I'm Alfred.'

'Actually, *Alfie*, it's just Cal.' This was going down like the

Hindenburg. I glanced at Matt. He had none of the easiness about him that he normally had. His muscles were rigid, his movements stiff and he was visibly sweating.

'I'm going to get us some drinks. Can I get you anything, Cal?'

'Just a Coke, please.' I pecked him on the cheek, to let him know I was there for him and it'd be OK, even with Maleficent looming over us in the corner. Matt disappeared behind the curtain and I felt two pairs of eyes burning into the side of my head.

'I think I might nip to the lavatory, Imelda. Would you like anything while I'm up?'

'If you could ask Marty for a top-up, that would be perfect.' She left the glass on the side table and Alfred made his way down the stairs.

I rubbed my sweaty palms on my jeans. I had a vague notion of who Alfred was but none of this made any sense.

'I find it interesting,' Matt's mother began, twisting in her seat to get a proper view, 'that a peasant like you thinks he has a shot with someone like my son; a boy who goes to private school and is captain of the swim team; a boy who writes songs and plays four instruments; a boy who paints and plans to become a lawyer when he's older. You are completely out of his league and I'm here to show you how wrong you are to think that someone like Matt could ever fall for someone like you.' She stabbed a manicured, wine-coloured nail in my direction. 'And if you think that I'm going to sit here and watch my son throw all of that away and lower himself to your squalid lifestyle, then you'd better prepare for a long hard fight.'

'But he likes me, and I like him.'

She laughed scornfully, taking a long, deliberate sip from her glass before commenting. 'My son is a man and men get bored of their . . . *toys* after a while. He'll outgrow you. Do you see Alfred? Tall, ambitious, successful, charismatic and intelligent. Alfie's parents own the most prestigious law firm in London. My son may not know what he wants but I *do.*.' She focused her steely gaze on me.

'Is that what happened to your husband?' I retorted, unable to stop the words from vomiting out of mouth. 'He got bored?' I pursed my lips and held eye contact, until laughter floated up the stairs and Matt and Alfred pulled back the curtain. Matt took a seat next to me. I was hyperaware of Alfie's position between Matt and his mother. I tried to ignore it but a thick woody scent rolled off his shirt in waves and choked me.

'Got you a Coke and a Dairy Milk.' Matt winked.

I saw so much of his mother in him but so much kindness and warmth too that I pecked him on the cheek. We held hands as an announcement boomed through the auditorium, signalling the beginning of the show.

'Showtime,' Matt whispered and when the curtain rose, everything else faded into darkness.

Chapter 10

EXPLORATION

I relaxed into the red sofa while Matt drew circles into my ankles with his thumbs. With his mum at an exhibition launch, it was easy to relax and melt into Matt's arms. I scanned the cinema room. A candy floss and popcorn machine reflected the dim light. The opening credits to *Titanic* appeared onscreen.

'I like this film.'

'Really?' Matt remarked and in the flashes of light emanating from the screen, I could tell that his eyebrows were arched.

'A young Leonardo DiCaprio? You bet your sweet ass I like this film.'

Matt stopped massaging my feet and picked up a bucket of popcorn. He watched the film, his expression blank as he shovelled handfuls of popcorn into his mouth.

'What?'

'What, what?'

'You can't say *really* and go all silent on me.'

'It's nothing. Come on.' He offered me the bucket. 'If you're lucky, you might see Leo in the nip.'

'Bit late for that,' I remarked.

Matt swatted at my ankles, mock-horrified.

I bit my nails to stubs when Rose attempted to jump from the stern and breathed a sigh of relief when Jack intervened. 'Shit,' I exclaimed as the iceberg cut through the side of the boat.

'Are you crying?' Matt questioned me as Rose screamed for Jack. I watched as Jack froze in the water, holding on to life. I wanted someone to love me like that.

Irrevocably.

Unconditionally.

Passionately.

'No,' I sniffed, wiping the tears from my eyes, as the screen faded to black.

'Come here,' Matt said, collecting me in his arms and carrying me. He kissed my jawline, planting kisses along my face that tickled my skin. He let me down on his bed, towering over me, planting a soft kiss on my cheek. I cupped one hand at the back of his neck and rested the other hand at his waist.

His tongue slipped into my mouth and his hands rested on my hips, pressing down firmly. I threw my body against his, feeling our chests breathe in and out in unison. His hands caressed my hair, moving lower, tugging my t-shirt over my head. Matt tore his shirt open, tossing it over his shoulder. His chest was against mine, my skin against his. His hands trailed my chest down to my belly, making me smile. His fingertips burrowed under the waistband of my boxers, inching lower. They connected and – I shoved his hand away. 'I can't.'

Matt recoiled but I could tell he wanted to comfort me. 'Cal? What's wrong?'

'It's not you, it's just—' I choked on the words. Images of Al hit me like a bucket of ice cold water in the face. Touching me. The rush. The excitement. The fear. The anxiety. The insecurity. The revulsion. Because that's not what I wanted. I wanted to share that experience with someone I liked; someone like Matt and here I was, with the perfect guy and I couldn't let him touch me there without thinking about Al and how he touched me without asking.

Matt still looked unsure but he took a risk and pulled me into him. I cried into his jumper, covering it in snot and tears. 'Get it all out. We can talk about it when you're ready. Or we don't have to talk about it all.'

I felt obliged to tell him. No, I *wanted* to tell him. 'I was so stupid,' I blubbered. 'I never should have met up with him.'

'We were all stupid at that age, Cal.' I was glad he didn't try to tell me that it wasn't my fault. 'And he probably should have asked you but he's a dick. Just learn from it and move on. Besides, you have an absolute stud for a boyfriend. I can't see you making that mistake again.'

'Did you actually refer to yourself as a *stud*?'

'If the shoe fits . . .'

'You are so ridiculous sometimes.'

'That's why you love me.' He winked.

I kissed him – a peck on the cheek – and I was in his lap, pushing him back into the couch. My hands were on his wrists, pinning them to the cushion. Matt's eyebrows rose. He lifted his knees and I tumbled forward. I lost my grip on his wrists and his arms snuck around my body, holding me close. His teeth bit down softly on my lips, knocking me into an easy submission. I dissolved into the mattress, Matt above me.

His forehead creased. 'We can stop, if you want.' I shook my head. 'OK, but let me know when you want to stop.'

'If I want to stop.' I can't remember why I said it but it felt so right in the moment.

I rolled onto my side, relishing the heat of skin on skin, of his chest moving in and out in sync with mine. I shimmied out of my jeans, propping my head up with my elbow as Matt dropped his jeans.

'You're enjoying this, aren't you?'

'Immensely,' I responded, smiling broadly.

I closed my eyes and counted to ten, bracing myself for the worst when Matt's hand slipped under the waistband of my boxers. 'Matt, I think you should stop. I'm going to—' He didn't stop and neither did I, and it felt AMAZING. The shock of pleasure blindsided me and I jerked sideways, kneeing Matt in the face. He rolled over, falling from the bed and hitting the floor with a loud *bang*.

'Matt! Are you OK?'

'Nothing a cold press won't fix,' he replied, holding his jaw as he leaned on the bed.

'Matthew. Matthew, honey!'

'Shit.'

'You said she wouldn't be back until midnight!' I tried to inhale through my lips but it wasn't working. Matt rested his hands on my shoulders as I hastily cleaned myself with a cream towel.

'Relax. This house is huge.'

I slipped into my shoes and pulled my t-shirt over my head. I hopped into the hallway, struggling to get my left foot into my jeans. My fingers shook as they pushed the buttons through the holes. We sped by the cinema room, taking the circuitous route to the west wing of the house. All the time, I heard Matt's mum shout up the stairs, closing in like a shark that could smell fresh blood. We jogged down a narrow staircase and Matt led me to the side entrance.

'I'll call you later. Sorry about this.' I could tell by his frown that he really was sorry. He kissed me once on the lips and shut the door. I walked home on jelly legs, adrenaline pumping through my veins.

> Matt: I'm sooooooooooo sorry but I hope you had fun?
> Me: OF COURSE I had fun.
> Matt: Night, Cal ☺
> Me: Night ☺

'How's your freakshake?' Matt asked me.

'Calorific. How's your water?'

'Delicious.' He took a mouthful and savoured it, over-egging imaginary flavours.

A new dessert bar, *Freakout*, had opened in Stratford. I'd never heard of it but Matt insisted on taking me. I sucked the chocolatey goodness through the straw, dislodging brownie pieces and chocolate chips. I ran my finger around the rim of the glass, collecting the chocolate sauce that trickled down the side.

I looked over at Matt. He picked at a loose thread in his jumper. With a jolt, I realised he hadn't made eye contact since we sat down. Even outside, he'd been wearing shades.

'Matt, is there something you want to tell me?'

I placed a hand on the curved, teal couch, hoping he'd reach out but he didn't. His eyes were far away, his forehead scrunched up. Usually, it was cute, but there was nothing cute about it then. I discreetly rubbed my palms on one of the ruby-red pillows, trying to ignore his weirdness.

'I want to ask you something.'

'O . . . K.' This didn't sound good.

Without meeting my gaze, he said, 'it's pretty close to prom. I mean, my prom. I've booked the limo and I have a spare ticket. I have the suit and I've already paid the photographer and—'

'Matt,' I interjected. As cute as his babbling was, I wanted to ease his nerves. 'Are you asking me to prom?'

Matt took a deep breath. 'I wanted to ask . . .'

'Yes?'

'. . . if you think a wine or maize cravat will match my eyes more?

I'm joking,' he amended. My hand was clenched dangerously tight around his glass of water. 'Cal.' He ah-hemmed. 'Would you like to go to prom?'

'I'll think about it.' He kicked me under the table. 'Of course I'll go to prom with you!' I laughed. 'Is that why you're acting so weird?'

'Yes.' He frowned. 'No.' He waited a beat. 'There's something I need to tell you.'

'Are you pregnant?'

'No.'

'Have you suddenly developed feelings for . . . *women*?'

'No. I—'

'Have you got a metal testicle?'

'No, I – why would that matter? I was supposed to take Alfie to prom and . . .'

It took a moment for the cogs in my head to start churning again. Alfie. Matt's ex. 'So Alfie's not going to prom anymore?'

'He's not going to prom as my *date* but it's his prom too, Cal, and I can't blank him.'

'Are there any other skeletons in the closet I should know about?'

'No, we've only buried one body over the years.' I glared. 'Seriously, no secrets. Hand on heart.'

'What happened with you and Alfie? How did it end?' Half of me was curious, the other half threatened.

'I was hoping you wouldn't ask that. Alfie cheated on me with a girl at school. I saw the pictures before he told me and when I confronted him, he told me that he loved me. He told me I was special and that he'd never do it again.'

'So you believed him?'

'Actually, I broke up with him.'

'But you still love him?'

'No. I don't love him but I do care about him. I don't think you can date someone for three years and suddenly not care about them. I'll always care about him but I could never love him again like I did.'

I didn't know what to say to that. If Alfie hadn't cheated, they'd still be together. They'd be the perfect couple. Matt's mother clearly loved him. His Twitter account was full of pictures of him on the debate, the swimming and cricket teams, and all the wonderful bloody cakes he could bake when I stressed about whether we'd have electricity for the week. Maybe Matt deserved better than me. Maybe he deserved someone that could give him everything he needed. What could I offer him?

'Hey.' He snapped his fingers. I hated when people did that but I didn't let my irritation show. 'Penny for your thoughts.'

'I was just thinking about prom,' I lied, realising there was something I needed to tell him too. 'I don't have a suit.'

Matt's face brightened up, the skin crinkling around his eyes as his pupils widened. 'I have a suit. It was supposed to be Alfie's but... Anyway, it might be a bit long in the arms, but it should fit.'

That, I was not expecting. 'Are you sure?'

'Well, I doubt mum is going to be wearing it around town anytime soon. Personally, I think it'd look better on you anyway.' He winked. I laughed, trying to suppress my niggling thoughts. Better than his mother or better than Alfred? 'I need to go to the restroom. Be right back.' He pressed his lips to my cheek and disappeared through a side door.

I eyed his phone on the table. It vibrated once, twice. I ignored it. It wasn't any of my business. Three times. Curiosity got the better of me. I slid the phone closer to me, turning it around. I hit the button on the side.

Alfie.

3 new messages.

I could have unlocked Matt's phone. I saw him tap the code in enough times. It would be so easy but I needed to trust Matt. I needed to crush my worries. Matt was here with me. Not Alfie. If he wanted Alfie, he'd be with Alfie.

That didn't mean Alfie didn't want him though.

> Alfie: I miss you x
>
> Alfie: I still love you x
>
> Alfie: [Photo]

I didn't want Matt knowing I'd seen his messages. I couldn't see the photo without unlocking the phone. I clicked the button again, darkening the screen. I slid his phone across the table, placing my hands on my jittery legs.

I tapped my fingers rhythmically.

Breathe in.

One, two, three, four.

Breathe out.

One, two, three, four.

Memories of the theatre hit me.

He'll out-grow you and do you see Alfred? Tall, ambitious, successful, charismatic, intelligent.

'Ready to go?' Matt offered his hand.

I plastered a smile on my face, pushing my worries to the back of mind. Despite the sweet aromas wafting through the dessert bar and the feel of Matt's calloused hand on mine, I couldn't help but wonder, was there something he wasn't telling me?

Chapter 11

EXECUTIVE DECISIONS

'Are you going to tell your mum about the prom?' Em asked.

'I don't know. I haven't really spoken to her since I shouted her out of my room.'

'Maybe hold out an olive branch?'

'Why don't you hold out an olive branch to *your* mum?' I fired back.

Stony-faced, Em chose to ignore me. 'I'm not saying that I'm on her side but she might have been in shock at the hospital. She did just chop off her finger. She's your mother whether you like it or not. You can make it difficult on the both of you but the only one that loses out in this scenario is Kayleigh and the baby, and really, was there ever going to be a good time to drop the baby bombshell?'

I hated when Em rationalised things. I picked at a hangnail until it bled, sucking up the blood.

'That's disgusting. Go wash your hands. There's plasters in the cupboard above the sink.'

I did as she said. I twisted the tap and squeezed blood from the wound, enjoying the pinkish swirl of the water circling the stone sink. I put my finger under the tap and washed the cut. I reached into the back of the cupboard, fumbling around for the plasters. My fingers closed around something cylindrical and small. I removed it and brought it close to the light, examining the label.

XANAX. 30MG. TAKE ONE AT BED TIME.
NO MORE THAN TWO IN A TWENTY-FOUR
HOUR PERIOD. CAN CAUSE EXTREME
DROWSINESS.

I listened for footsteps outside the door. I flushed the toilet and bolted the door as quietly as I could. The cap came off easily, two tablets falling into my palm. I broke a tablet in two, placing half on my tongue and the other half in my pocket. I twirled the tap and gulped some water, swallowing against the chalky taste. I splashed some water onto my face and quickly dried it in the towel.

'I thought you'd fallen down the toilet and into Wonderland,' Em quipped.

'It's called beautification.'

'Someone should tell that to your face.'

'Mean!'

I thought about telling mum. I wondered how she'd react but I realised that telling her involved far too many complications. Matt would meet mum. He'd see where we lived. I couldn't decide what to do.

'How are things with your mum?' I questioned.

'Fine.' Em's tone was poisonous.

'You should give her a chance.'

'You should mind your own business!' Em snapped. I flinched. 'I'm sorry. It's just . . . there's a lot going on.'

'Do you want to talk about it?'

Em shook her head. 'Do you remember this?' Em opened her top drawer and pulled out a homemade Valentine's card from when I was seven. It displayed a crudely drawn bee with the caption, 'BEE MY VALENTINE' above it.

'I can't believe you'd torture me with this nine years later. If I knew that, I never would have given you that damn card.'

'If you think that's bad, you're going to hate these.' She pulled out a stack of cards, held together with a brown, elastic band.

'Put them away. Please!' I plead, hamming it up like they were my kryptonite.

'So, you sent me this one when I jumped out of a tree and broke my arm.'

'Why *did* you jump out of that tree?'

'I was convinced I was Supergirl. Still am. Seemed like a good idea at the time. You made me this one for my eleventh birthday. Look at that craftsmanship.' She literally rubbed the card in my face, the hardened glitter glue chafing my face.

'Put it away. It's ridiculous.'

'It's cute.'

'If I had the money, I would have bought you a decent card.'

'I like your cards. Anyone can buy a card but making one takes a certain level of ineptitude.'

'Oi!'

'Just making sure you're still with me. No, it takes a lot of time to make a card. It's one of the reasons we're friends.'

Friends. Was that what we were? The word tasted like poison on my tongue. Em was my best friend. She was the constant in my life but our friendship felt so far away from how it used to be. Em was closed off, isolating herself. She was so edgy around me; happy to dish out advice but when I asked about her family, she'd shut down. She met Duncan. She didn't need me anymore. I wondered what had happened between us, when things had started to fray like the elastic band in Em's hand.

I rolled the Xanax pill along my window sill with my thumb, staring out at the cloudy skyline. Em's words burrowed under my skin. Anger at mum simmered in my belly alongside guilt. She was pregnant and I snapped at her.

Last night, I went downstairs to fill a glass of water. I found mum dozing on a table of electricity and water bills. With dad gone, I never thought about her. We struggled before. Without him, what must it be like for her now?

Matt would show up at our front door tomorrow, decked out in a suit. I needed to tell her but anger warred with guilt. Mum.

Dad.

Em.

I inhaled a deep breath, opening the door and darting into the kitchen.

Chop. Chop. Chop.

'Mum, I need to tell you something.'

Chop. Chop. Chop.

'What is it, sweetie?'

Chop. Chop. Chop.

'I'd prefer if you put the knife down first,' I cautioned, eyeing the butcher knife in her right hand.

Mum laid the knife down carefully on the chopping board. 'We wouldn't want to lose another one, would we?' She wiggled her fingers at me. I smiled, happy that we were at a place where we could at least joke about it.

'I'm going to prom tomorrow.'

'Prom? With who?' Mum asked, incredulous.

'With my *boy*— partner.'

'You have a partner?'

Was it really so hard to believe? 'Yes. His name is Matt.'

'And how long have you and Matt been dating?'

'Three months.'

Mum stood up, motioning for me to stand. I obliged, unsure what was happening. 'I'm so happy for you!' she whispered, hugging me tight.

'Mum! The baby!'

'The baby is fine, Cal. Do you – do you want to feel it kick?'

Did I?

I nodded. Mum sat down in her chair, angling herself towards me. She lifted her navy jumper and guided my hand under. It felt so odd, touching her bare belly. She left it there for thirty seconds, saying nothing. I felt something pound against mum's belly twice.

'He likes his big brother.'

'It's a 'he'?'

'I think so. It feels like a boy. He kicks as much as you did in the womb.'

'That's . . . I really didn't need to know that.'

'You know I love you, right?'

'Right.' My voice was brittle. I wonder if she noticed.

'Is there anything you want to talk about, Cal?'

How are you going to support a baby without Dad?

Did you know I'm being used as a human punching bag at school?

Does Dad hate me?

'Nope,' I answered casually, swallowing against the lump in my throat.

'I'll get some snacks in tomorrow.'

'Thanks, mum.' I hugged her, eyeing the pile of bills stuffed atop the kitchen shelf.

Chapter 12

UNEXPECTED EX

Matt knocked at the door. I hastily worked vegetable oil into my hair, praying it would cooperate. I bounded through the hall but mum beat me to the door, dressed in a sparkly, shimmery green dress that complemented Matt's navy tie and wine-coloured blazer. I buttoned my blazer and fixed my wine tie.

'You must be Mrs Adams,' Matt greeted, handing my mum a beautiful bouquet of roses and a yellow gift bag.

Mum didn't know where to look. Under her make-up mask, I swear I could see her blushing. The roses were the most vibrant things in our flat. 'Can I get you anything?' she asked, setting the gift bag and roses on the table, next to a medley of popcorn, Wotsits and Maltesers sitting in sad, white polystyrene bowls.

'I'm OK, thank you. We have to leave in a few minutes.' Mum's face dropped. 'I'm sure we have time for a few photos.'

'Yes!' Mum beamed, pulling a Kodak disposable camera from the drawer. I was fairly certain Kodak cameras were in museums and who knew, maybe mum's might be worth something in another year or two. She ushered us into the sitting room and positioned us in front of the boarded-up fireplace. Matt looked at home standing next to me, his hand resting on my shoulder. I fidgeted with my hands until Matt took them in his. We smiled through the flashes and the draught that blew in under the door.

'Why don't I take one of you and Cal?' Mum looked surprised but she obliged. It was weird. She didn't quite know where to put her arms. She was Matt's polar opposite. Matt calmed me down and gave me clarity while mum sent my pulse skyrocketing. We stood side by side like estranged relatives. The faint click of the camera sounded and right on cue, Kayleigh started to shout.

'Chocolate! Chocolate!'

'Excuse me.' Mum left the room and I fell into Matt's arms.

'I'm sorry.'

'For what?'

'This.' I gestured around the room, thinking of what he must think of mum and our flat.

'Cal, do you think I care about where you live? It's about you and your family. Your mum seems nice.' *Compared to mine.* He didn't say that but he might as well have.

Thump. Thump. Thump.

'You're about to meet my sister.'

'I'm scared.'

'You should be.'

Kayleigh slid into the room, sucking her finger as she took a good look at Matt. 'Who you?'

'I'm Cal's friend. Matt.' I wasn't sure why that annoyed me. Kayleigh was young and it was a bit early to teach her about love. I watched as Matt removed a netted bag of gold coins from his pocket.

'Money!'

'Not money. Chocolate.' Matt widened his eyes obsessively. 'Do you want to know a secret?' Kayleigh nodded her head frantically, her eyes on Matt instead of the chocolate coins. 'I love chocolate too,' he stage-whispered, even though mum and I could hear. 'This is my favourite chocolate.' He tore through the netted material with his fingers and deftly pulled apart the gold foil and popped a chocolate disc into Kayleigh's hand. Kayleigh began licking the chocolate disc until it somehow smeared her cheeks and hands.'Want to see my pwon-ies?' she asked , pulling him into the kitchen.

'He seems like a really nice guy,' mum observed, watching Kayleigh laugh next to him, playing ponies. He picked her up and zoomed around the room. Kayleigh threw her head back, kicking and screaming. I nodded, because I still found it hard to speak to mum, refusing to face what was right in front of my eyes. 'I'm happy for you. I mean, I'm happy you're happy. You seem happy.'

'I am,' I said, turning my back to her and running towards Matt and Kayleigh. 'Hey Kayleigh, can I steal Matt away? We need to go to the prom.'

'I want to go to the prom.'

'Maybe next time, when you're a bit older.'

I could tell Kayleigh was going to sulk. 'Here,' Matt said, removing the red rose from his blazer pocket. He slid it behind her ear and took her to the grubby mirror. 'Now you're a princess.' Kayleigh giggled and kissed Matt on the cheek. I wiped the chocolate stain from his cheek, smiling. Kayleigh hugged his leg and ran over to me. She hugged me and whispered in my ear, 'I like Matt.' My heart melted. Why had I been so worried about Matt meeting my family?

'Champagne?' Matt took a bottle of Dom Perignon from a bucket of ice. I nodded. He set two flutes on the side table as the limousine pulled away from the kerb. The pop was louder than I expected and I looked at the fizz of the champagne as it filled our glasses. We clinked glasses and lapsed into comfortable silence.

I peered out of the window, lost in thoughts as I looked at trees and concrete houses that eventually blended together into a blur of grey.

'How are things with your mum? Any progress?'

'I felt the baby kick yesterday but . . . we haven't spoken much.' Matt's silence said it all. I noticed he was biting his lip. 'What? What?' I repeated, when he wouldn't speak. I wasn't sure why I sounded so defensive. Mum and Kayleigh loved Matt. He was taking me to prom. He hadn't judged our flat and he loved me. I was happy.

'I don't think now is the time to talk about this.'

'Well *you* brought it up.' Where had the pointed edge come from?

'Let's leave it. We can talk about it tomorrow.'

'No, we can talk about it now. Tell me.'

'Well, your mum seems sweet. I mean, I know she's hurt you. I can see that but maybe you need to forgive her and move on. For you.'

'It doesn't work like that, Matt.'

'Your mum is carrying your baby brother or sister. I know you're angry with her but I can tell by looking at her that she's suffering and if she's suffering, the baby suffers and your family, Cal, your family suffers. Most importantly,' he continued, reaching out to brush my cheek with his fingertips, 'you suffer.' I recoiled. 'I don't want to talk about this.' Because I couldn't – not with him – not with all these thoughts that had been festering in my brain for months. He was so grounded and reasonable. My thoughts were irrational. I knew I was bring unreasonable. I started to pick away at the scab. Mum. Dad. School. Where did I start? I couldn't forgive mum because I couldn't forgive myself. No, that wasn't true. I switched off my thoughts, focusing on the champagne fizzing on my tongue, but it was no use. Wild thoughts plagued my mind like phantoms. The blistering pain overwhelmed me like a tsunami and it all came rushing back.

I was in the hospital, my head cracking against glass while dad loomed over me.

I sat in the classroom, fists pounding against my skin, leaving bruised kisses across my body.

I looked into my grimy bedroom mirror – really looked at myself – and the reflection leering back at me asked the question that haunted me.

How could anyone ever love you?

I faced away from Matt, closed my eyes and inhaled, struggling to remember what tonight meant. Tonight was Matt's prom. I was his date. He booked a hotel room for us so we could sleep side by side, in each other's arms instead of worrying about when his mother might be home. I thought of all the good things that could come from this night and though my heart raced and my mind conjured up nightmares, I tried to relax into the leather seats. I relished the bubbling fizz of the champagne on my tongue. Air passed through my lips. The car smelled like pine and Matt's musky aftershave. It should have been perfect.

I felt an impossible barrier building between us and I wasn't sure how to break it. Dark thoughts clawed at my mind and I suddenly craved a release. I thought about the Xanax and how easy it would be to swallow the other half of the tiny pill and forget about all of this. Forget all the pain that this year had brought.

I jerked forward as the driver jammed on the brakes, champagne sloshing around the glass. I looked at Matt, making sure he was OK but he looked as unruffled as ever. His mouth opened and he stopped. He withdrew a handkerchief from his blazer pocket and leaned across, dabbing at the champagne stain on my blazer.

'Here,' he said, undoing the buttons, 'let's take this off.'

He started to rub at it vigorously and I wondered if this had more to do with the blazer or me. I placed a restrictive hand on his. 'Matt. Matt. It's OK.'

'It's not. It's not OK. I wanted this to be perfect.'

'It is perfect.'

'NO! It's *not*.' It was the only time I'd ever heard Matt shout; a booming authoritative voice that unnerved and excited me simultaneously. 'I wanted this to be perfect and it's not. I needed it to be perfect. For *you*.'

'It's – wait, perfect? For me?'

'Yeah,' he sniffed. 'I just wanted . . .'

'Are those tears?'

'No.' He wiped his arm across his face.

'They're tears.'

'Big manly tears,' he argued.

I laughed. He stopped and watched, bewildered. His eyes were red-rimmed and watery. 'Matt, this – all of this, spending time with you – *is* perfect.'

'You're not just saying that?'

'Do I look like someone that would just say things?'

'Thank you.'

I climbed into his lap, tugging on his tie as I squeezed his waist with my thighs. If I felt his lips on mine, his hands on my body, I knew it would drive away my demons. Maybe I wouldn't have to force my smile. 'Now come on and show me how manly those tears are.'

He smiled, laying me down on the seat. His teeth nibbled my ear and tiny pulses of pleasure exploded in my blood. He kissed me like he'd never get to kiss me again and it was beyond perfect – beyond anything I deserved. All I could hear was the soft purr of the engine as we thundered closer to Harrow.

A misty shroud of rain fell as the limo pulled off. Matt squeezed my hand tightly and we ascended the stone steps together. Above us, I could make out the soft twinkling of stars.

'Wait,' Matt instructed. The unmistakable sounds of a trumpet and saxophone floated out of the building. Matt put his hands on my waist. 'Hop on my feet.' I did as he asked and linked my hands around the back of his neck. His lips were inches from mine, our chests breathing in and out, yearning to touch. The soft glow of the nearby lamps highlighted his sharp cheekbones. He never looked more beautiful with his slicked-back, brown hair. Matt stepped side to side, lulling away my nerves. I tilted my head up and he kissed me. I could have skipped the prom and stayed like that all night, frozen in time. W when my

friendship with Em was rocky, my family was fractured and school was a living nightmare.

The sound of wild applause jolted us from the moment. I felt Matt's lips curve upward into a grin. 'Shall we?'

I followed Matt down the red carpet on trembling legs; from the champagne or the kiss, I couldn't be sure. The photographer asked us to pose beside a cream backdrop. Matt pecked me on the cheek as the flash went off. I rubbed my eyes and we continued into the hall. The ceilings were huge. The floor was black-and-white, chequered marble and there were narrow, floor-to-ceiling windows lining either side of the hall.

'Vol-au-vent?' a passing waiter asked, bowing. I took one and chewed. Matt declined. Guys and girls flocked over to Matt, shaking my hand and kissing my cheeks. They gushed, telling us how cute we were in our matching suits. A couple noted Alfie's absence which made me paranoid. I glanced around the room, but there were too many people and I couldn't be sure if he was there.

Matt secured two glasses of champagne from one of the passing waiters. I didn't question it. We linked our arms and took a sip from each other's glass.

'Shall we dance?' I stepped closer and we entwined our hands, placing his spare hand on my hip and rocking me back and forth on the outskirts of the dancefloor. Matt twirled me around and caught me. I knew he was excited as he leaned over my shoulder, kissing my neck, pressing his body closer to mine. I liked that I was doing that; that he wanted me as much as I wanted him. I pushed his face further into my neck, momentarily forgetting where we were.

He lowered his hands to my waist. I opened my eyes, unaware of when I actually closed them and noticed a couple of the girls staring. I nudged Matt in the ribs. He released his hold on me and I turned to face him.

'Calm down, soldier,' I teased.

'Can you blame me?'

'It's your prom. Come on, you need to be good.'

'Good is overrated. I can't wait for tonight.' He leaned in close. I could feel his breath on my neck. He knew what I liked but it wasn't working then because panic was already pulsating through my body. I laughed and pulled away, trying to act natural.

'I'm going to find the toilet.'

'Second door on the right,' he instructed, pointing down a wood-panelled corridor. I raced down the corridor, pushing the heavy wooden door. The toilet was empty so I entered the furthest cubicle and sat on the lid, pulling my legs to my chest. I breathed in and out but so fast that I almost induced a panic attack. I thought about all the things that could go wrong. I took out my phone.

I called Em, listening to the dial tone. *Pick up, Em. Come on.*

'Hey ...'

'Em!'

'. . . sorry I can't some to the phone right now but I have a life. Leave—'

I hung up.

Blood pounded in my veins and my palms were clammy. Was tonight the night? Did Matt expect me to put out? I unbolted the cubicle door, just as the bathroom door swung open. Alfie smirked. His teeth were whiter than I remembered. He sauntered over to the urinals. I pressed the soap dispenser ten times too many and lathered my hands.

'All set for tonight?' I looked over at Alfie. He zipped up his fly and washed his hands in the sink next to me, nudging me with his elbow. 'The post-prom promise.'

'What?'

'Matt booked the honeymoon suite.' Gauging my expression, he continued. 'You mean he didn't tell you? About the Hilton?'

'Of course, he did,' I lied. He told me he booked a hotel. He never told me he booked a honeymoon suite at the Hilton.

'Cool.' He reached into his pockets and handed me a ten pack of condoms. 'Better to be safe than sorry.' He took some paper towels and dried his hands. 'Matt can go all night, if you know what I mean?' He winked, exiting abruptly.

My hands clamped down on the sides of the sink. Had Matt spoken to Alfie about me? About us? I tried calling Em again. No answer. I reached into my inner pocket, removing half a Xanax tablet. I popped it into my mouth, leaned into the sink and gulped the water. I swallowed, already feeling better.

I re-entered the hall, cutting through the dancefloor. I froze, nudged forward by people doing the Macarena and one guy who aggressively elbowed anyone in his way.

Alfie stood beside Matt, trying to grab his hands. Matt pushed him away but his expression looked torn, like he wasn't sure if this was something he should be doing. Someone grabbed me from behind, forcing me into a dodgy version of the dance. I glanced over my shoulder. One of the pretty blondes Matt spoke to earlier. Was she one of Matt's friends? I couldn't remember. She pushed me forward and hugged my hips. Everyone jumped and switched directions, but the awkward angles of my arms had my elbow sticking out and I felt it connect.

'MACARENA!' the crowd chanted. I stopped, shaking off the girl's grip. I massaged my elbow, realising with dread that the music had stopped. I scanned the dancefloor and the circle of people framing me.

A teacher cut through the crowd of students, bending down to help a girl in a hazardous, puffy white dress that made her look like a marshmallow. Beads of red dotted the front of her dress. Blood. I stood there stupidly, anchored to the spot and unable to move my lips to apologise.

'Hey,' Matt whispered, snaking his arms around my waist and

pulling me to him. 'Are you OK?' I nodded my head a fraction of an inch but it must have been enough. He didn't ask me again. 'Come on, let's see if she's OK.' The plaid-coated teacher was in the process of dispersing the crowd when we approached. The girl was resting in a chair, leaning forward like she might be sick at any moment. 'Hey, Daria.' Matt flashed a sympathetic smile. 'Cal wanted to come over to see how you were. He was really worried.' Daria looked up. Was her nose always that big?

'Yeah.' My voice was hoarse. I cleared my throat and tried again. 'I'm so sorry. How are you feeling?'

'I'll be OK.' The tremor in her voice was unmistakable. In the background, the DJ blasted Whigfield through the speakers.

'If there's anything I can do, let me know. And by the way, your dress is beautiful,' I lied. The only place that dress might have looked beautiful is in a landfill.

'Come find us for a dance when you're feeling better,' Matt chipped in.

'Thanks,' she replied.

Matt led me onto the dancefloor. We hugged, waiting for everyone to stop bopping to *Saturday Night* before executing a slow two-step back and forth to Ed Sheerhan's *Thinking Out Loud*. The lights dimmed and the candelabras in the corners of the room soothed me. I thought back to our first English lesson with Armin, wondering what Matt saw in me.

'Having fun?'

'Yes.' I told him what he wanted to hear through the storm of questions whirling around me.

Why did I always manage to get myself into these situations?
What did Matt see in me?
Why was he talking to Alfie and what was he talking about?'
'Everything OK? You're holding on a bit tight.'
'Sorry.' Seems I couldn't do anything right.
'Should we get a drink?'

'Sure.' I knew as soon as the champagne hit the back of my throat that I probably shouldn't be drinking, especially with half a Xanax fizzing away in my stomach, but I locked away my voice of reason and lived in the moment. I tipped the glass back, finishing it in three mouthfuls. The tinkle of glass cut through the hall. Nobody but Matt and I seemed to acknowledge it. I clocked the teacher at the front of the room, his face flushed. He tapped the spoon against his glass a little too aggressively and it shattered in his hand. He didn't acknowledge it, just stood there with a teaspoon in one hand and half a glass in the other.

'Now that I have your attention: dinner will shortly be served in the dining hall. Please make your way into the hall and take your assigned seats.'

The music cut out and we followed the crowd through a set of double doors and into a smaller, more intimate room. The tables were like shining gold islands in a sea of wine carpet. Matt took my hand and guided us to our seats. An assortment of gold and wine candles were positioned in the centre of each table, giving off cinnamon notes. Great. What was the worst that could happen? I took my gold napkin and laid it down over my lap, minimising potential embarrassment. Matt poured us each a glass of water.

Waiters darted around tables, setting up stands for their trays next to each table. They disappeared into the kitchens and re-emerged with trays laden with plates, accompanied by a fishy aroma. I could feel the champagne bubble and boil in my stomach. I wondered if I could get away with pretending I wasn't hungry.

I watched our waiter set down the plates in front of each of the guests, clocking the empty space across from me. I counted the people at our table. Nine. Had someone come to their prom alone or—'Sorry about that,' Alfie announced, sitting beside the blonde girl I'd elbowed in the face. Daria. 'Oh, hey Matt.'

Matt flashed a tight smile.

'Prawn cocktail. Remember when . . .' Alfred began. The words died on his lips. I wondered what he was going to say and why he stopped.

I stared down at the prawns on my plate. I knew I should be grateful. They were marinated in a tangy sauce but I couldn't get over how much they resembled dead animals. I mean, when you order roast chicken in a restaurant, it doesn't exactly come out looking like a dead animal carcass, even though you know that's what you're eating.

I stabbed the leaves decorating the plate with my fork and attacked the cherry tomatoes and grated carrot. Matt didn't pick up on the fact that I hadn't touched the prawns, but that didn't stop Alfie driving his truck of obnoxiousness through the silence.

'Not a fan of prawns?'

'Not really,' I answered, hoping that would be the end of it.

'It's funny, you think someone that comes from a family of

peasants would gobble up anything you give him. I mean, it's not like you can afford to turn your nose up at a perfectly good meal.'

I wasn't sure what to say to that. My mind drew blanks. I was so used to being pushed around at school that I stayed silent. I never voiced what I really felt and thought. Seconds passed and everyone at the table held their breaths. You could cut the tension with the shitty butter knife that Alfred was using to clumsily slice his bread roll in two.

I thought about grabbing the plate and dumping the prawns over his head, and telling him to eat them if he loved prawns so bloody much. I thought about reminding him that Matt was here with me, that he'd got some sauce on his tie, but all of those short-term throwdowns wouldn't be enough to resolve my long-term insecurities.

Instead, I rose from the table and addressed Matt, 'if you'll excuse me.'

'Cal, don't—' Matt commenced but I was already half-running back into the hall and down the corridor to the toilets. 'Are you fucking kidding me?' Matt snarled at Alfie, just as I exited the dining room.

Chapter 13

AN INEXPLICABLE END

I locked myself in a cubicle, tears falling before I'd lowered the toilet cover. I felt so inadequate standing next to Matt as it was. Alfie was a constant reminder of what I wasn't. Rich. Beautiful. Smart. Alfie, who knew what Matt liked; knew how to push the right buttons. The box of condoms bit into my leg as I sat on the toilet, making me feel nauseous.

The door slammed open. 'Cal?' I counted to five, hoping he'd leave. 'Cal, I can hear you.' He knocked on the door. 'I know you're in there.' He'd come to find me. Of course he had, because even though I was an emotional mess, Matt still cared. Was I his charity case? His good deed for the year? Did he genuinely care? Was everything finally coming together?

'You don't have to be here? Go enjoy your prom.'

'It's our prom. If you're not having fun, I'm not having fun. Now, come on. Open the door.'

'I don't know what you see in me but Alfie . . .'

'Alfie is a dickhead and we are *done*. I'm not going to let him and mum tear us apart. You mean too much to me. Cal, don't cry, not when I can't hug you.' I heard him flip the toilet seat down one cubicle over. He grunted. His fingers peeped over the wall separating us and then he was there, his face hovering in the dim light like the Cheshire Cat. 'Hey.'

'Matt, get down. You're going to hurt yourself.'

'No, I'm – ouch.' He banged his head on the ceiling tiles. Flecks of dust rained down on me. I coughed, closing my eyes against it. He slid over, manoeuvring into the corner. He placed a shoe on each wall and slid down. 'Hey.'

'Hey,' I repeated, rubbing the grey dust from his hair. 'You're crazy.'

'Crazy about you,' he fired back with a goofy smile.

'Did you rob that joke from a Christmas cracker?'

'How dare you! My jokes are hi-larious.'

'You're so cheesy.'

'You *gouda* done worse.'

'Dear Lord.'

'*Brie* mine?'

'Will this ever end?'

'As far as cheese-related jokes go, that was my last one.'

'Dodged a bullet.'

'I have plenty more jokes though.'

I pressed my lips to his. 'Please don't.'

He backed me up against the wall, which wasn't hard, pinning my hands to the cold cream tiles. He nudged my neck to the right and carefully kissed the exposed skin. I bit down on my lip hard. Matt was a drug that lifted my insecurities with one kiss. He drew circles in the palms of my hands and when he lowered his trail of kisses above my collar bone, I wrapped my arms around his waist, pulling him closer. His kisses were gentle but passionate, like the kiss that woke up Snow White or restored Ariel's voice so she could call out to Eric.

His fingers burrowed under my blazer, unbuttoning my shirt. His fingertips were like nodes sending electrical currents pulsating through my body. I leaned into him, craving more. I heard a tear as he tugged at my shirt. I didn't care and I wasn't sure he noticed. His lips were on my collar bone, his tongue flickering across my skin. I pushed him away. Matt looked at me through laboured breaths.

'You should go back to your friends.'

'I don't care about the prom. I'd rather be tucked into bed next to you, watching a movie. I'm happy when you're happy and I know you Cal, you don't want to go back into that dining room. I don't blame you. I wouldn't want to go back either if I was you. So, let's run.'

'Run?'

'Yes, run. Are you with me?' He held out his hand. I took it and he opened the door. He stopped by the row of sinks and I looked at him, a question in my eyes. 'This toilet is filthy. I think we should wash our hands.' I laughed a pain-in-your-belly giggle that made my eyes water.

'Soaped and washed. We're ready to go.'

We held hands, pushing through the door and thundering down the corridor, through the hall and up the slope to a church. The sky was dark now with a scatter of glittering stars under the lamplight outside the church entrance. To our right, I glimpsed headstones. We stopped after the church and stepped up, leaning over the railing. 'Oh Rose, how did we ever get so lucky?'

'Why do I have to be Rose?' I retorted.

'Because you're so pretty and delicate.'

I laughed. 'Though not quite as delicate as Daria.'

I hit him on the shoulder, awkwardly twisting my arm around. 'That wasn't funny.'

'I thought it was funny.'

I couldn't see anything below us except darkness and some faint shapes in the distance, but that was OK because Matt was by my side and he was all I needed.

'Come on,' Matt said. 'Race you down the hill.'

'I can't see my hand in front of my face, let alone the hill.'

'You'll be fine. I'll even give you a head start.' And a push. I tripped over my own feet as I pounded the concrete in shoes that cut and blistered my feet. Matt shouted after me but I couldn't hear what he said. I could hear him panting behind me. He stood on my heel and I tumbled forward, Matt pursuing me. Stone scraped my hands as I tried to stop myself. I veered off the path and into a bush.

'Cal?' I groaned. 'I'm sorry.' Another groan. A light shone through the branches. 'Marco? Marco?' Another groan. 'Marco.'

'Polo,' I shouted.

'Found you.' He hoisted me up onto my feet, pointing his phone at the ground. 'Let's get you back to the hotel.' Matt ordered us a taxi. I couldn't remember the last time I was in a taxi.

The hill was bigger than I thought. It took us about twenty minutes to make our way to the main road and by then, the taxi driver was waiting for us – and he did *not* look happy. He turned up the radio when we got into the car. I was foolish to expect a cheery bubbly greeting. *Don't Go Breaking My Heart* came on through the speakers. We mumbled along to the lyrics, getting most of the words wrong. I can't imagine it endeared us to the driver. The only part of the song we successfully managed was *woo-hoo* and I can't say that was in tune.

'You look a bit shocked,' Matt remarked as we pulled up to the hotel. 'I've never stayed at the Hilton before.'

'Enjoy it.'

He flashed the receptionist a smile and pressed the button on the lift. The 6th floor. I prayed for a city view. 616. Matt tapped the key card and shouldered the door open. The first thing that caught my eye was the enormous white bed, scattered with red rose petals. I wanted to dive onto it but realised that that probably wasn't the best idea. I walked over to the full-length mirror and picked a twig out of hair.

'We should probably shower.' He pulled off his t-shirt and I ogled. There was no other word for it. 'I'm not just a piece of meat,' he spat out dramatically, cocking his hip. He stepped in close and tore open my shirt.

'You can pay for those buttons,' I said haughtily.

'Make me.' Then, we were kissing. Outside, cars crawled down Oxford Street and pedestrians made their way home. In our own little bubble, I was standing next to my boyfriend, wondering again, how I got so lucky. We stripped off and got into the shower. The door just about closed. I was sure Matt was trying to be sensual and sexy but every time he rubbed me down with the bar of soap, it tickled and I burst into a fit of giggles, swallowing a mouthful of water.

Half an hour later, we donned the complimentary robes provided. They were softer than anything I'd ever worn. I dove onto the bed next to Matt, whose wet fringe stuck to his forehead.

We entwined our legs under the sheets and I wondered if he was as excited as I felt. I ran my hand up his thigh and discovered instantly that he was. He rolled over to face me. His mouth framed my bottom lip, pausing there so I could take in the feel of his stubble on my skin, the spicy scent of his cologne and the feel of his warm calloused hands on mine.

The robes lay discarded on the floor. Matt leaned over me, his hands on the back of my neck, my back and my hips. I was sitting in his lap, unintentionally teasing him. Teasing myself.

Maybe it was the champagne or maybe it finally clicked. Matt was good for me and he seemed to think I was good for him. The only person that was going to ruin this was me and my insecurities.

I grabbed onto his hips and leaned forward, whispering into his ear. 'I'm ready.'

'Are you sure? There's no pressure.'

'I want to. I really want to.'

'Do you want to . . .?'

'Do I want to . . .?' I repeated.

'Do you want to top or bottom?'

I'd always wanted a boyfriend but I never thought about sex. I mean, I thought about boys but never thought about sexual specifics. 'Bottom,' I told him. I figured Matt would know what he was doing.

Matt kissed my neck, lips pressing across my collar bone and down my body, his tongue prodding the waistband of my boxers. I couldn't get close enough. The thought of what was about to happen made it all exciting, made me think that we'd be closer than ever.

Matt searched his trousers for a condom while I lay on my side, admiring his broad shoulders, his defined chest, his big arms – and not just the physical things. His kindness. His passion. His loyalty.

I relaxed onto my back. Matt rolled the condom on and hoisted my legs over his shoulders. My heart pounded wildly in my chest.

'If it hurts, let me know.'

I nodded, legs stiff.

I grimaced as he penetrated, twisting my hands in the sheets. I didn't expect it to be so painful. Matt towered over me, gently rocking back and forth, lips pulled into a smile. He leaned over me and his lips grazed my ear, pressing lightly onto my neck. His tongue was in my mouth, a sensory overload.

As painful as I found it, it was intimate, intense and beautiful.

Maybe a little bit icky. Sex wasn't as perfect and beautiful as *Sex and the City* made it out to be but with Matt, it felt right. The pain started to ease and I started to enjoy it. It felt more pleasurable. Matt was gentle and a pleasurable sensation flooded my body. Goosepimples covered my arms and though I could feel my body soaking sweat into the sheets, Matt and I were closer than ever.

'That was amazing!' Matt's head hit the pillow.

'Better than Alfie?' I clamped my hands over my mouth, trying to stop further word vomit. I prayed he hadn't heard me but I could feel his body tense under my fingers.

'Why would you say that?'

'B-B-Because he's – well – he's better than me.'

'Cal, if I thought Alfie was better than you, do you think you'd be the one lying here beside me in this bed?'

'But if Alfie hadn't cheated, you'd still be together.'

'I don't know, Cal, but what I do know is that he cheated on me and sat there with her tonight to get back at me for taking you to the prom.' Daria. Daria was the one Alfie cheated with. 'Can we not talk about Alfie anymore tonight? He's already pissed me off enough tonight and I'd rather not talk about my ex when I'm lying next to my actual boyfriend.'

'Sure.'

Matt rolled onto his side. I wanted to say sorry but it didn't feel like enough so instead, I let it lapse into silence. Matt turned off the bedside lamp. I didn't know whether to lean in it to him or not. I'd never seen him this angry before. I lay awake into the early hours of the morning, wondering if Matt and I were still together.

I stared at the white ceiling, craving his lips on my body and his hands on my face. Matt always found a way to make me feel like a shooting star.

I woke to blazing sunlight. Matt buried his face under the duvet and continued dozing. A vibration arrested my attention. I reached over to the bedside drawer and checked my phone. It wasn't me. I got out of the bed and walked around to Matt. His phone lit up and I could see new Facebook notifications piling up. Curiosity tugged at me. I knew I shouldn't look but Matt's phone was already in my hand as I thought about it. I tapped the code onscreen and unlocked his phone. I tapped on the notifications, not knowing what to expect. A flash of an image but it automatically anchored me to the comment. I scrolled to the top and worked my way down.

> **Katie Jennings:** Soooo cute. Good luck you guys ☺
> **Daria Dumont:** Wait, I'm so confused: are you guys back on again?
> **Clement Jones:** Get the D ;)
> **Clarabelle Lyons:** I knew it. I ducking knew it!
> **Annabel Darcy:** Send me a picture on the honeymoon ☺

What on Earth were these people talking about? I scrolled through the comments. There were over fifty. I swiped up to the photo and my heart stopped. Matt and Alfie were . . . They were. *Kissing.* I racked my brain, trying to think of a plausible explanation. It was posted two hours ago but maybe it was from a year ago, when they were dating. Yes, that had to be it, but I noticed that damn teacher in the plaid coat hovering in the background, gesticulating. Matt was wearing his navy suit and . . .I ran into the toilet, lifting the lid before the alcohol-soaked vomit splashed into the toilet basin. It burned my throat. I held on to the pain, shocked. My tear ducts were frozen.

'Cal? Is that you?'

I gripped the sink and when the mosaic tiles on the walls steadied, I washed my hands. I belted my trousers and took Matt's phone off the floor. I threw on my shirt and put my blazer over it, not bothering with the buttons

'Is that my phone?' I stared down at his phone. I sucked in a breath but it was like trying to breathe underwater. I looked at Matt, really looked at him and the faux concern on his face. He was chocolate gateaux, beautiful and sophisticated, and I was own brand swiss roll, plain and basic. How could I ever think Matt would pick me over Alfie?

I wanted to smash his phone against the wall but I couldn't. I tossed it onto the bed. While Matt examined it for damage and unlocked it, I slipped on my shoes, not bothering to tie the laces.

'Check your Facebook updates, Mr Popular.' I walked to the door.

'Oh shit. Cal, I can explain.'

'You gave me such a hard time for talking about Alfie but you didn't tell me you kissed him. You didn't tell me about this. I thought you liked me but this was all a joke to you, wasn't it?'

'Cal, wait—'

'You're worse than the bullies at school. They broke a lot of things but they never broke my heart.'

'Cal!'

I slammed the door and ran to the elevator. I stabbed the button and counted to five. When the elevator didn't arrive, I opened the door to the fire escape and sprinted down the concrete steps. I burst into the foyer and stomped through the exit. I took out my phone and Google-mapped my route home. I walked away from the Hilton, from Matt, and I didn't look back.

Chapter 14

EXILE

'Hey, how was the prom?' mum asked, fixing her blouse in our grubby mirror. I hadn't witnessed her in a suit in years.

'It was ... can we talk about this later?' I asked, my hand resting on the bannister.

'Of course, sweetie. Is everything OK?'

'No, everything is not OK.' I made it to my bedroom door when I stopped. 'Mum? If anyone calls, tell them I'm not home. Even Em.'

I didn't wait for her response. I climbed into my bed, still in my prom suit. I took out one of the Xanax tablets from the bottom of my sock drawer and swallowed it. I just needed to sleep.

I had all this light in my life and it was like the plughole had been opened and all that happiness washed down the dark, murky pipes. Matt was better off with his Oxford-to-be boyfriend. I couldn't compete with him and I didn't want to. Alfie could have him.

Was I a joke to everyone in my life? I pressed my face into my pillow, muting my tears. They came all at once as I drowned in a tidal wave of pain. If I couldn't hear them, maybe they didn't count.

A bang jolted me from my sleep. I opened my eyes, blinking against the sunlight. My tongue was dry; worse than dry, it felt like I'd been sucking on a massive cotton ball all afternoon. I whipped off the covers and stared at the suit, trying to make my fuzzy mind remember how I got there.

It all came back like a punch to the chest. I lay there, focusing on my breaths. *In. Out. In. Out.* Daria and her bloody nose. The photo. The comments. My virginity. Matt had taken my virginity. No, I'd offered it to him on a plate. It was all too much and mum, Kayleigh and everything that had happened at school; it was mounting and I was trying to keep afloat in the ocean with cinder blocks tied around my ankles. My hand slid over the sheets, searching for my phone. I fumbled with it, dragging it closer. My limbs felt heavy. I wondered if it was a side effect of the Xanax or something else. Then, I remembered that I rolled down a hill and into a bush.

Another bang. I ignored it – probably Kayleigh stomping around in the kitchen, pretending to be a dragon again.

I had twenty-five notifications. Texts and missed calls. I deleted all my messages and blocked Matt's number. I went onto

Facebook and un-friended him. I wasn't angry. It happened. It happened to me – it was inevitable. I couldn't be happy. It was like a cosmic joke that everyone was in on. I pulled the duvet over my head and groaned.

'Are you going to answer the door or mope in your duvet fortress for the day?' Em shouted.

'Em?'

'Who do you think has been banging on the door?' When I didn't reply, she barged into the room. 'Get dressed and we'll get you some coffee.' Em's voice was like a blazing sun when you were extremely hungover. She opened both my windows and I shivered. 'Come on, we're going to the park.'

'Since when do we go to the park?'

'Since you decided to become a hermit.'

'How did you even get into the house? I told mum not to let anyone see me.'

'I walked in,' she replied matter-of-factly. 'I walked right by your mother and into your room. Now, get up before I start singing show tunes.'

'I'm up, I'm up!' I leaped out of the bed. 'Can you give me some privacy while I get changed?'

'Of course.'

'Em.' I motioned to the mirrored wardrobes that she viewed me through.

She closed her eyes and shrugged. 'Nothing I haven't seen before.'

I quickly changed into fresh clothes, spraying a bit of deodorant under my arms and splashing some water onto my face. 'Going out,' I called to mum, slamming the door behind us before she could speak.

'How are you doing?' Em asked as we veered left at the end of our street.

I thought about Em, how she hadn't answered my call when I needed her at the prom, how she was so quick to dish out advice but never accept mine. 'Fine,' I grumbled.

'Really?' she probed as we made our way through the gates of Abbotts Park. 'Because from where I'm standing, you don't look fine.' We skirted around the small pond that usually housed two ducks. I hadn't come here with Em since she discovered she had a step-sister. We sat at a stone bench; the same bench I'd listened to Em scream and cry on; the bench where I assured her everything would be OK; the bench was where we'd shared secrets and pain, where we grieved and loved. I should have known Em would take me there.

'Your mum told me. I'm sorry, Cal.' The ducks swam out of the reeds, quacking loudly. Em took a bag from her pocket and threw something to the ducks. I was too trapped inside my own cerebral hell to notice what it was.

'Don't tell me it was his loss, Em, not when it feels like this.' Like a black hole eating away at my chest.

'You don't have to tell me what pain feels like, Cal. I've been there before. We both have. You've been through worse.'

'He took my virginity.'

'Did you enjoy it?' Images blasted through my mind. The

passion. The intensity. The pleasure. Alfie and the betrayal. I stared at the ground, unable to speak. I couldn't meet Em's probing gaze.

'We all want our first time to be special but for every person that happens for, it doesn't happen for the next five hundred.'

'Were you one of the five hundred?' I asked instinctively, trying to re-direct the conversation. Em laughed. I didn't see what was so funny about it. 'Oh Cal, what a stupid question.' She wiped the tears from her eyes. 'I lost my virginity in the back of Ricky's Nissan Micra.'

I gawked. 'Ricky? Really? Dicky Ricky?' Ricky was a wannabe biker that went to our school the year before. He wore black leather jackets, regardless of the weather, and matching black boots. He got expelled twice and eternal detention for "violating the dress code". 'Classy.' A little of the pressure around my chest eased and I inhaled a deep breath.

'He kept referring to his leather seats as his love seats and I almost concussed myself on the roof. It could have been worse.'

'I suppose.' I picked at a hangnail. Em watched but she didn't say anything.

'Let's talk about you though. Did you enjoy it? I mean, before you found out.'

'It felt uncomfortable and sore at first . . .'

'Yeah, books and movies make it out to be *way* more romantic that it actually is. *He towered over her, pressing his magic wand against her. Sweat rolled down their bodies and his wand erupted in a blaze of sparks. She was already one with him, her willowy legs wrapped around his strong thighs. Her hands fingered his horcrux, his square jaw and the dimples that could have been carved into a statue. Myrtle fell onto the bed, a smile playing across her lips.'* She made exaggerated sultry eyes that made her look somewhere between Carmen Electra and Freddie Krueger. 'What even are willowy legs?'

My belly hurt from laughing so much. 'That was so good! Seriously.'

She shrugged, like it was nothing. She took another handful of – seeds? – and launched it at the ducks. They quacked happily. Em frowned. 'Can white rice kill a duck?'

'I'm not sure but it's not great for the pigeons.'

'Pigeons are greedy bastards anyway.' She deliberately tossed a handful onto the footpath.

'Mean.'

'They're rats with wings. Nobody likes pigeons. Find me someone that likes pigeons and I'll find you a unicorn.'

'I'm a unicorn.'

'You've certainly got the horn,' Em retorted.

'*That is* not funny.'

'It's hilarious. I'm hilarious.' My cheeks were sore from smiling, my belly tight from laughing but my chest still ached from a Matt-shaped hole. 'About Matt . . . I'm not going to sit here and tell you this is all going to be easy. It's never easy. It's never going to be easy, but you can't let this change who you are, why people love you . . . why *I* love you.'

'When I'm at home, with mum, I feel so . . . *alone.*'

'I'm here for you. You're not alone in this and I don't want you to ever think that you are. Understand?'

I nodded because I couldn't think of anything significant to say to that. I wanted to click my fingers and forget Matt.

'You're not going to forget this overnight and you probably never will, but you can find ways to move on. You're the one of the smartest people in our year. You're head and shoulders above the rest of your Food Tech class. I've seen the smoke,' she added, before I could interrupt. 'Don't let Matt dry out your sponge.'

'What?'

'I was trying to say something profound and baking-related. Cut me some slack.'

'Don't let Matt dry out my sponge? That sounds so . . . *dirty*.'

'OK, moving along. If you want to talk, I'm here.'

'Thanks.' I swallowed against the sour taste in my mouth. Em should have been there for me mid-freak-out during Matt's prom but she never picked up, never acknowledged the missed call. I couldn't help wondering if she had picked up, if I'd spoken to her, would I still have ended up with Matt at the Hilton?

'Now if you don't mind, I'm going to ask Siri if rice is detrimental to a duck's health.'

I smiled even though my heart was breaking all over again.

Chapter 15

EXCITING NEWS

We sat at the dinner table because mum had "exciting news". I knew it was good because we were using silverware and the good china. Mum crinkled the brown paper bag as she took out our food and handed us our meal in turn. Kayleigh viciously munched on her McNuggets beside me, making "argh" sounds and closing one eye like a pirate.

I waited for mum to say something more but instead, she took her knife and fork and started to cut through her quarter pounder with cheese. I did the same with my Big Mac and for the first time in a long time, there was pin-drop silence in our flat. Mum hadn't pressed me to find out what happened with Matt, even when we'd been getting gourmet chocolate cakes sent from

The Hummingbird Bakery and dozens of roses.

'Ice cream, ice cream, ice cream,' Kayleigh chanted, rhythmically banging her fists on the table. Mum watched from the corner of her eye. When I turned, she went to the freezer and began scooping chocolate into bowls.

'Chocolate, chocolate, chocolate!'

I picked at the chocolate ice cream she set down in front of me. She regarded me openly this time. I stared back at her.

'You said you had news.' My voice was quiet. After everything that had happened, I'd learned not to get my hopes up. She'd been tiptoeing around me for the last week and a half though, so I could hardly condemn her if she delivered a blow.

'Yes!' She clapped her hands together. 'I got a job as a receptionist,' she said but my mind was somewhere else. While I wanted mum to get a job – and this was great news since it meant I might have a proper lunch for school – it also meant she'd need someone to mind Kayleigh. Unless this new job paid thirty pound an hour . . .'That's great!' I beamed. 'When do you start?'

'Monday.'

'Amazing!'

'Yes . . . I was wondering, could you mind Kayleigh, just until I work out something more permanent?'

I looked at her, really looked at her. She was more like mum now than she had been since the incident at the hospital. She smelled of vanilla but black bags still hung like weights under her eyelids. She needed this – not the money, though we needed that too. She needed an escape. 'Yes.'

'Really?' I could tell she expected this to be a struggle. Two weeks ago, she might have got one.

'Really,' I confirmed.

'Thank you. Thank you, Cal. I promise, it's only short term.'

'It's fine!' I waved her off and it was. Mum's smile was genuine. Kayleigh smeared chocolate ice cream across her face. I could see the cracks in our family unit starting to mend. Things were finally taking a turn for the better.

'Em wants to spend the day with me. Would you mind?'

Mum beamed. 'Of course not.' I think she was just happy to see me leave the house, eager to see progress and ignore the fact that I was still crumbling on the inside.

We ambled past cafés and crossed a pedestrian bridge that arched across the underground railway tracks. I jumped down the steps on the other side two at a time.

'Cal.' I turned. Em was still standing at the top of the steps, her hands perched on the bar. From down below, I thought I could see tears in her eyes. I raced back up to her, the wind whipping my fringe into my eyes.

'Em?'

'Nan is . . . she's got a lot worse, Cal. She's not . . . all there. Sometimes . . .' Em covered her face with her hands. '. . . sometimes, she can't even remember my name.'

I placed my palms over her hands. 'I'll be there. You've got me.' Em looked over at me. 'Now, wipe away those tears before anyone finds out you've got human emotions.' I held her hand tightly in mine, reminding me of those times we used to skip through Abbotts Park, mum watching us with a cheek-to-cheek grin.

A row of squished-together houses stretched before me. Em stopped at house 39, producing a key from her inside her coat that she slotted it into the lock. She twisted right, waiting for the click before pushing the door open. I coordinated each step with a breath, inhaling and exhaling my nerves away. The door creaked open. I half-expected to see Em's nan but the hallway was empty.

'Anything she says, take it with a pinch of salt,' Em whispered, like we were in the lair of a sleeping dragon. I gulped.

We entered the living room to the left and it was everything I suspected it would be. Light purple carpet. Blue couches with navy and dark purple cushions. Bookshelves split into squares that ran across one wall. A set of oak tables. Her TV displayed a blue loading page. A large window, framed with purple curtains and traditional lace blinds, that hung low over the window and shielded us from view.

'Nan,' Em sing-songed, 'this is Cal.'

She looked up at Em with narrowed eyes. My heart raced. Did she recognise Em or was this one of her bad days? The *click, click, click* of her lighter arrested my attention. Em's nan was enshrouded in a fluffy pink dressing gown that, oddly enough, was in harmony with the bizarre colour scheme of the room. The lighter clicked again, resulting in a small flame. She leaned forward, a cigar hanging out of her mouth. She lit the tip and relaxed back into her armchair, puffing out a large cloud of smoke.

'How are you feeling, nan?' Em enquired.

'I'm looooooooooooosing my mind,' she said, cackling as she brought her index fingers either side of her head, twirling them in circular motions.

'Sit down, Cal. I'm going to get nan's meds.' Em disappeared into the hallway, much like I wanted to.

There was silence except for the crackle of the TV, the *puff, puff, puff* of smoke and the *tick, tick, tick* of a clock with cat eyes that darted mechanically from side to side, as if they were watching me.

'Come here, boy.' Em's nan patted the footrest opposite her armchair. On jelly legs, I walked over to her. 'Sit down,' she instructed and I did.

We stared at each other. Her white afro bounced around her ears whenever she moved. Her eyes were a fierce brown; the kind of brown that kept secrets you might never know. My heart beat faster, two beats for every tick of the clock. She leaned forward, removing her pastel pink silk gloves and with wrinkled skin mapped out in blue veins, her withered fingers reached out and touched my cheek. Something flashed in her eyes but I couldn't be sure what it was. I remained still. She sat back in her chair, slipped her hands back into her gloves and placed them on the armrests. She propelled herself out of the chair and marched over to her bookshelves.

'Cal, I have to pop to the shops and collect nan's prescription. Are you OK here for a bit?'

'Of course,' I replied tightly. *Take me with you.*

'I won't be long.' She buttoned her coat, slamming the door as she left.

'Tell me, Cal: do you like to read?' I watched Em's nan like a panther, half-expecting her to pounce at any moment.

I nodded.

Without turning to face me, she asked, 'what's your favourite book?'

It was true that I liked to read, at least before my life had become my own personal nightmare. Every day felt like twenty-four hours of purgatory. Sleep. School. Home. Matt. Dad. Mum. '*To Kill a Mockingbird.*'

'Good choice,' she said, a smile in her voice. She plucked a large hardback from one of the shelves. She turned and I could see the cover. Beautiful illustration. 'Scotch on the rocks?' She opened the book and removed a hip flask from inside. Instinctively, I rubbed my eyes. Was I seeing things? 'Even a terminal bird like me has to have her vices.' A wicked grin twisted her lips.

She went into the kitchen, returning with two tumblers, three ice cubes in each. She poured a caramel-coloured liquid into the glasses and handed me one. 'Cheers,' she began, gulping down her drink in one. I followed suit, almost choking. 'To the queers,' she finished, winking at me. She knew. 'Don't look so concerned. My great-grandson is an anal assassin too. I have a sixth sense for these things.' She tapped her forefinger against the side of her skull.

I savoured the burning sensation as Scotch splashed down my throat, involuntarily coughing. 'Pussy,' she muttered, pouring us a second helping. 'So, I guess they told you.' I nodded. Em never specified what her nan had but I had a vague notion. 'Good.' I knew Em's nan was losing her memory but I didn't know the full extent of her illness, how it affected her. It wouldn't have changed anything. I was in her house. I was drinking her Scotch. I was inhaling her second-hand cigar smoke. I already thought that she was mad but I was starting to like her as much as I feared her.

She brought the rim of the glass to her lips and the bell rang, a shrill *brrrrrrrrrrnnnnnnnnnggggg* sound. Placing the glass down on a coaster, she massaged the area between her eyebrows with her index finger and thumb.

'They'll leave in a minute. They always do.'

Brrrrrrrrrrnnnnnnnnnnnnnnnnnggggggggggggggggg.

Sixty ticks passed on the cat clock. I could taste the ashy air on my tongue, feel the cigar smoke stinging my nostrils and the lingering burn of the Scotch at the back of my throat.

Brrrrrrrrrrnnnnnnnnnnnnnnnnggggggggggggggggggggggggggggggggggggggggg.

'Oh, for the love of . . .' She picked up her tumbler and plodded towards the door. I followed. She opened the door a crack. I couldn't see who it was but I could hear their chirpy voices.

'Good morning! We're here to spread the good word of the Lord.' Mormons.

'I'm atheist,' Em's nan deadpanned.

'Maybe we can help you see the Light of God.'

'I prefer to find my light in a glass of Scotch.' She took her hand from behind the door and brandished the glass in front of them, bringing it to her lips like it was the Elixir of Life. She ah-ed, popping her lips.

'Alcohol is a void, a void that the love of our Lord, Jesus Christ, can fill.'

'Does his blood taste like Scotch?'

'Jesus offers love and salvation for those that would worship at his door.'

'Well, I'm afraid we worship the spirits at this door.'

I wasn't sure if they understood that she was referring to alcoholic spirits or whether they thought Em's nan was a Satanist. I liked to think a bit of both. 'Do you want to come in for a glass of Scotch? Brandy? Vodka? We can praise Lucifer together.' I stifled a laugh behind my hand.

'Good day to you, madam. Maybe Jesus Christ will find his way into your heart and guide you to his everlasting love.'

'There's not a lot of heart left – three heart attacks.' She held up three fingers, swirling the ice in the glass with her thumb. 'He'll have a tough job competing for my love of Scotch.'

'Good day to you.' This came as more of a shout – less sunshine-and-rainbows. Were they scared?

She closed the door and smiled when she clocked me in the hall, the skin around her eyes crinkling like scrunched-up, Christmas wrapping paper. 'They're persistent, I'll give them that.' We laughed and we were still laughing as I sat down on the couch and Em's nan fell back into her armchair. 'You haven't touched your Scotch,' she chastised me.

I drank the Scotch more slowly this time, keeping my eyes fixed on her. It lasted a second but I noticed it, a fear and vulnerability in her eyes like she'd just woken up in a strange dream and she wasn't quite sure where she was. She looked around the room and relaxed. It was the first time I was conscious of her illness.

I pushed it to the back of my mind, trying to ignore it. I'd been dreading her company, the idea that I would walk on eggshells around this elderly lady, but she was something else. I loved hearing how she'd confronted those Mormons – though I did feel slightly sorry for them.

I felt a pang in my chest when there was a scratch of a key in the lock. Maybe Em's nan did too. She removed a tin from one of the pockets in her dressing gown and opening it, she offered me a lozenge. I took one, sucking on it before rising to answer the door. It tasted of cough medicine.

She looked away, lighting up another one of her cigars, when Em entered the room.

'I've got your meds,' Em chirped. This was a side of Em I wasn't used to. She'd been falling apart on the walk to her nan's house and now, she was Little Miss Sunshine.

'Great. You can run off back to your life now. Good deed done for the year.'

Hurt flashed across Em's features. She tried to hide it but her shoulders were tensed, her lips pressed tightly together. I placed my hands on my knees, unsure how to proceed. I remained silent – just like Em's nan – through Em's attempts at conversation, which made the air thick with tension. I counted down the minutes on the cat clock, hoping this visit would end soon.

Chapter 16

ATTEMPTED EXTORTION

I rang the doorbell. 'Nobody's home,' Em's nan screamed. I waited a beat before pressing the doorbell again. 'For the love of . . .' She clocked me, squinting like she couldn't remember who I was. 'Em's not home,' she announced, pulling the door closer to her.

'I'm not here to see Em. I'm here to see you.'

She watched, taken aback. She turned on her heel and shuffled back into the living room. I stood there a moment, awaiting a prompt before following her inside.

I wasn't sure what to say. While I didn't know the name and symptoms of her illness, Em had warned me that her nan might have trouble remembering things. Did she know who I was? Was I a ghost to her? Was she able to recall my previous visit?

She watched me blankly.

'Um, Em's nan . . .' I said dumbly, realising I had no idea what to call her.

'Call me Peggy.'

'OK, Peggy. Is everything OK?'

'Hunky dory,' she fired back, her face vibrant and light. 'I was just thinking about my great-grandson. Maybe you'd like him.' I was taken aback by how nice that was, so unlike the real Peggy. 'You bum bandits are all the same to me.' She shrugged and there it was. *Click*, she was back in the room.

I walked into the kitchen and returned with two tumblers that I set atop the bookshelves. 'What are you doing?'

'Don't you want Scotch?'

'On the rocks, love.' That 'love' was about as close as I'd ever get to a 'thank you'. She flicked aimlessly through the channels. I wasn't sure why; it wasn't like we could see very much. I watched the concentration on her face, the way her eyes shone with a determined glint and her forehead furrowed. She groaned, taking the remote and throwing it onto the carpet where the batteries fell out and rolled under the couch.

I knelt, feeling under the couch. My hand gripped the first battery when she spoke.

'I wouldn't bother.'

'But how will you watch TV?'

'You can't watch TV when you're dead.' Her words chilled me, tremors shooting down my spine. Did Peggy speak like this around Em?

'What do you mean?' I retrieved the second battery and stood up, facing her.

'Never mind,' she resigned, her tone devoid of all emotion. The shutters in her eyes had come down. It frightened me. She brought her tumbler to her lips. Her hand spasmed and the glass smashed against the coffee table. Scotch trickled down the sides and soaked into the purple carpet.

I went into the kitchen, grabbing the nearest tea towel and a roll of kitchen roll. Peggy relaxed into her chair, her eyes filmy and faraway. I didn't prod her. Instead, I picked up the glass shards with the tea towel and deposited them in the bin. Peggy moved past me and lurched up the stairs. I pressed kitchen roll into the carpet, soaking up the Scotch.

The tell-tale creak told me that she was coming down the stairs. I watched her perch her hand on the door frame and my eyes nearly fell out of their sockets as I took in her thigh-high, black boots.

'What are those?'

'These are boots,' she replied matter-of-factly.

'I know what they are but why do you have them? Why are you wearing them?'

'Why shouldn't I wear them? Unless you're implying that because I'm old, I can't wear boots?'

'Well, no but—'

'I'm dying, Cal. I don't give a flying fuck what you or anyone else thinks and neither should you. I'm going to see my husband.'

'Your husband?' I echoed.

'The cemetery. You don't have to come.'

'I want to,' I told her. I really didn't but I wasn't going to let her go by herself.

We stood over a weathered, grey marble grave. *Hugh Lewis Warisham*. Trees bearing crisp autumnal leaves waved their branches back and forth to the beat of the wind. Someone had left red peonies on Hugh's grave. I wondered if that was Peggy or someone else.

'Hugh was an exceptional husband,' she remarked over the whistling of the wind. 'One of a kind.'

'Why did it end?' I asked instinctively, realising how stupid that question was.

'He was gay.' I examined her face for any signs of humour but her mouth was set into a fine line.

'Why were you with him, if he was gay?'

'It was the late 60s. A very dark time to be gay. I knew. I never told him. I'm not sure how you tell someone you love something like that. He asked me to marry him and I think he was more scared than anything and well, I said 'yes'. I didn't think twice about it. I loved him. I don't think I was in love with him, but I know he loved me, and I loved him. I guess that was enough. They'd just decriminalised homosexuality but gay men were still beaten up in the streets and called every slur under the sun. They were scared. Hugh was scared. It's hard to explain. You'd do anything for the ones you love, and I was never unhappy with him. We made some incredible memories together. He was my second husband, you know.'

'What happened to your first husband?' I realised I was picking at a scab but if I didn't ask now, in her more lucid moments, I would never know.

'He beat me, told me he needed to put a woman in her place – told me I deserved what I got. He wouldn't let me see my friends or family and if he did, he was always there. I couldn't leave the house. I couldn't ask for help and I wouldn't have known how to if I had the chance. I was so afraid. I'd wake in the middle of the night, hearing him snore and wonder if I could make it to the front door without the floorboards creaking. I never tried.

'Then one day, he tells me how stupid I am. He's drinking his beer and screaming at the TV. He comes into the kitchen, spitting and spluttering, asking me when dinner's ready. My hands are raw from chopping vegetables and he takes a pan, dumps the hot water over my back and hits me with it. I scream. He laughs.

'He fell asleep watching the football. I poured myself a glass of Scotch. I stood in front of him, downed the Scotch. My hands shook. 'Terry?' I called out. He looked at me, blinking, rubbing at his eyes. I smashed the tumbler over his head and I walked out the door. My family got my things from the house. I never saw him again.'

'That's horrible.' I wondered how much of this Em knew. Was she keeping all of this from me? Was she bearing it all by herself?

'That's life, Cal. There's good and there's bad and you have to take both or you get neither.' She bent down and traced the white letters with her fingers. 'He reminded me a lot of you. He was smart, loyal and funny. I think sometimes, if he'd be born at this time, he'd have been so much happier. You can do it, where he couldn't. You're sixteen years old. You're surrounded by friends that love you. You take care of your sister while your mum works. Most kids your age couldn't do that. That's an achievement, Cal.' She clawed at the soil and dropped a handful on his grave. 'I can't wait to join him.'

'Don't say that,' I protested.

'I'm tired, Cal, and I don't want to live long enough to completely lose who I am.' What could you say to that? 'Would you mind helping me up? My heel is stuck in the dirt.'

I offered her my shoulder and we took careful steps to the footpath, trying to minimise efforts lifting Peggy's boots out of the dirt. Her eyes were sharper, more alert, her movements lighter. I guess seeing her husband had been a cathartic moment for both of us. Hearing about her second husband, it made me realise that it wasn't me; it was Niall, Gareth – the bullies. It was my father, who wouldn't accept me for who I was. There would always be someone who didn't like you for ridiculous reasons. If Hugh had lived through the decriminalisation of homosexuality and the AIDS epidemic, I could steel myself for school.

Peggy fiddled with the key in the lock and nudged the door open with her foot. Whispers rushed at us from the kitchen, panicked in tone but indiscernible. Peggy stepped ahead of me and opened the door to the kitchen. I peered over her shoulder at the two masked men in balaclavas. They were tall and lean – teenagers maybe.

'Get down on the ground!' The taller of the two shouted.

'What are you doing in my house?' Mrs Robinson's voice was calm. I wiped my sweaty palms on my jeans.

'I said: get down on the ground!'

'Maybe we should—' I placed a hand on her shoulder.

'I will do no such thing.'

He brandished a butcher knife. I turned to run for help but Peggy grasped my wrist and held me in place. 'Wait.' She unclipped the pocket to her handbag and withdrew a pistol with a jerky hand. My mouth instantly dried. She aimed it right at his chest, her finger cocked on the trigger. She moved it to the right, between both thieves, and pulled the trigger hard. The gun shook in her hand and a bullet blasted into her cupboard, inches from one of the burglar's hands. I jumped, instinctively covering my ears. Peggy's eyes narrowed to slits. I noticed how her hands trembled.

'The next one goes in his kneecap.' She waved the gun casually at the silent thief, watching us with widened eyes. 'Let's try this another way. Empty your pockets and slide the knives across the room.' I eyed them, watching as they kicked their weapons across the room and removed petty cash and some jewellery from their pockets, placing it slowly onto the counter. 'Now, drop the bag.' The silent thief conceded. 'If you come into my home again, you're dead,' Peggy spat, venom lacing her voice. With her free hand, Peggy guided me to the other side of the room. 'You have fifteen seconds to leave my house.' Neither one moved. 'Ten seconds.' I saw the split-second hesitancy as both thieves eyed their steals and bolted for the door. The door slammed shut behind them.

'Cal, be a darling and pour me a Scotch.' She left and closed the door behind her. With shaky hands, I opened a new bottle of Scotch and poured her a glass. I grabbed a cloth from the sink and mopped up the excess I'd spilled on the countertop.

'I'm sorry about all of that.'

'You have a gun!' I shouted, stating the obvious.

'Yes.'

'How have you got a gun?'

'You shouldn't ask questions you don't want the answers to.'

'You have a gun.'

'Yes.'

'A GUN that you brought to a CEMETERY.'

'Yes.'

She walked over to me and took her Scotch off the counter. I watched her walk to the door. 'Go home, Cal.' The words reached my ears but my brain couldn't process them. 'I'll understand if he doesn't come back.'

I shouldered my rucksack and made my way home. I didn't say goodbye. I didn't tell her that I would be back because even I didn't know if I wanted to return. Instead, I wandered home. I opened the door to our flat and hugged Kayleigh as she latched on to my leg. I told mum I wasn't hungry. I removed my jeans and slipped into bed. I fell asleep to the sounds of little footsteps stomping around downstairs and mum's protests. In my dream world, I was safe.

Chapter 17

ELECTRICAL EXPERIENCE

Mum was surprised to see me heading over to Peggy's so soon after my last visit, especially on a weeknight. I was equally surprised. I hadn't forgotten what had happened but I found myself magnetised, unable to stop thinking about her. I wanted to see her again.

'It's nice that you want to spend time with Peggy but maybe you could spend some time with your sister too?'

I slammed the door in response. What did she think I spent my weeknights doing? Letting Kayleigh starve? Ignoring her? Letting the plates stack up in the sink? Every day, I made a pound stretch into five because, although mum had a new job and was trying to make things better and mend our fractured family, she didn't get paid until the following week so we were still living on rations. I still fell asleep every night listening to the rhythmic cadences of my growling stomach. Not to mention the baby that was on the way.

Em came around sometimes to help, an hour here and there, but even she left early enough to head out. I was so exhausted by seven o'clock I usually sat on the sofa, watching *X Factor* with Kayleigh singing along and massacring half the words – you know, in a cutesy, viral-video kind of way.

Visiting Peggy seemed to be my only escape. She never pried and if I wanted to speak, she'd listen. I wasn't sure how much to tell her about what happened at school yet.

I knocked on the door, waiting patiently until Peggy opened it. I got used to the flicker of confusion that crossed her face before she recalled who I was and let me into her house. Some days, she'd call me by name. Others, she didn't seem sure of who she was. I wondered if that was a Peggy-thing or an illness-thing.

I sat on the sofa as she brought in a juddering tray of tea, cups and biscuits. I watched her plop two sugar cubes into her black tea and a splash of milk before she whisked it around vigorously with a teaspoon.

'If you want to talk, Cal . . .' Peggy remarked, picking up on the worries that I struggled to mask.

She unmuted the TV and I watched *Coronation Street* with her, unsure what exactly was going on and more confused at my ridiculous attempts to understand why a son would try to kill his mother. In the next scene, one man fought another over a girl and usually, I'd come up with a witty quip or a sassy remark, but I hadn't got it in me. Niall had set up a new Facebook group under the guise of Shaniqua Boovalateesy, running polls on how much of a faggot I was, photo-shopping images taken during the year to humiliate me. Words bled out of my mouth and I couldn't stop. I told Peggy everything.

'Well, I think we need something stronger than tea.' She went to the cabinet and poured out two double measures of Scotch. I downed mine in one, savouring the fire in my throat and imagining it burning out what it was that everyone seemed to hate about me; burning away that part of me that made me different; the part that marked me out as a target at school. I was already dreading my final year of torture. I shuddered whenever I thought about it too much, remembering that school began again in one week.

I had no idea where she got it from but Peggy suddenly had a package wrapped in brown paper in her lap, her fingers resting cautiously at the sides. 'This is something my nan gave to her daughter and her daughter to my mother and well, I should pass this along to Em, but you need it more.'

'Seriously?' She nodded. I tore at the paper, excited as it tore apart in my fingers. Chocolate? A book? CDs? I really hoped it was chocolate. You couldn't go wrong with chocolate unless you counted chocolate-covered raisins which were vile.'A Blokia?' Seriously? I already had a Blokia and my phone looked like an iPhone next to this relic.

'Don't look so ungrateful. He who looks on the exterior of beauty fails to see its workings.' She reached across and held down the directional key. I watched the on-screen battery bar as two of the six bars lit up. The phone flashed for a second and then a shock electrified my body, liquefying my legs. I fell but landed on the carpet. Peggy rolled me over onto my back. 'I'm not quite sure if you can hear me but that little taser in your hand might keep those little bastards away when you go back to school.' I wanted to shout at her. Who does that? 'You teenagers.' She shook her head but I could see the amusement light up her eyes like a Christmas tree. 'It should wear off in an hour or so. In the meantime,' she turned my head so I could make out the staticky TV, 'let's watch *Corrie*.'

'Hey nan.' Oh shit. Was that ... Em?

'Now I know this is going to look bad, Em but—'

'What the actual fuck? Nan! You tased him?'

'I was teaching self-defence,' Peggy muttered sullenly.

How could this get any worse? Oh, I was drooling. Definitely drooling down my chin. Fab.

Em turned me over, her hands pressed into my shoulders, but I couldn't feel a thing.

The thing about being paralysed from the neck down is that it gives you a lot of time to think. I thought about mum's baby, about what dad was doing right at that very moment and if he'd get a sadistic sense of satisfaction knowing I was on the verge of swallowing my own tongue. I thought about Kayleigh and when she was older; would she understood who I was and what dad had done? Mostly, I wondered just what the hell Peggy was playing at.

I saw Em caress my hand but Peggy must have killed the nerves in my arms. 'Cal,' she said it extra loud like I was deaf, 'I'm going to roll you back onto your belly, in case you swallow your tongue.' I tried to thank her but it came out as a gurgle and I knew there was saliva streaming down my face. Sexy. I was sure Em had seen me in worse states so I didn't think much of it until she tilted my head to the side, mimicking my pose as she took a selfie.

So, for the next hour, I stared at the carpet, wondering if the stain next to me was caused by tea, coffee or something else entirely.

When it finally wore off, I couldn't look Em in the eye. 'You have nothing to be embarrassed about,' she told me but I wasn't convinced, mostly because she couldn't keep a straight face. I wriggled my fingers, shook out my arms and folded them across my chest. '*Nan* is the one that should be embarrassed.'

'I was illustrating a point,' she replied nonchalantly, batting away the comment with her left hand while her right hand swirled her Scotch on the rocks. She obviously didn't care if Em saw her drink. At least I knew where Em got it from. I always wondered; her mum seemed so quiet and meek, certainly not the partying type. Peggy though – it all made sense.

'Only a psycho would tase someone to illustrate a point.' I didn't bother reminding her of the selfie she'd taken.

'Blood of my blood,' Peggy fired back like a grenade.

I didn't really know what I could contribute to the conversation so I remained silent. I scratched at the coarse skin of my elbows, scanned the still life on Peggy's wall and forced the occasional cough. I mean, I suppose I could have attempted to run but the reality was me falling down if I put too much pressure on my legs.

Instead, I stood up slowly, leaning against the wall. Em jumped up to help me.

'I'm going to the bathroom.' The words came out of my mouth awkwardly, like I was talking around a Rubik's Cube.

'Do you need some help?'

'I'll be fine.'

I stumbled into the hall, buffeted by the wooden bannisters engraved with daisies. I glanced back. Em raised an eyebrow. I couldn't manage stairs in my state so I took three steps to the tiny bathroom nestled under the stairs.

I stared into the mosaic mirror. As beautiful as it was, it was about as practical as a pork chop in a veggie meal. I twisted the faucet and splashed cool water onto my face, washing away the saliva trails. I watched as water droplets dripped from my hair down my hooked nose and onto my t-shirt.

I didn't really care that Peggy had tased me. I mean, I knew in her own twisted way that it was all fun. I thought about the sort of protection a weapon like that could provide. Would it stop the taunts? The pencil parings being dropped in my hair? The "faggot" slurs? Would it help ease the physical abuse? Or would it make me look like a complete psycho? More of an outcast than I already was?

I emerged from the toilet, running my tongue around the corners of my mouth, probing for feeling. 'Why?' I didn't trust myself to form a full sentence.

'Ignorance is bliss,' Peggy said as if that answered my question. Em squeezed my hand once and I immediately felt calmer about the whole thing.

'She really enjoys your company.'

'I enjoy her company,' I told Em, eyes closed, elbows leaning on the pedestrian bridge railing as I listened to the sounds of trains rushing through London. 'Why haven't I met her before?'

'The real reason?' I nodded, knowing she could see me. 'It's complicated. Mum stopped taking me to see her when I was younger, around the time that dad . . .' That her dad cheated, impregnated her mum's best friend and set up a new home back in Tobago. 'Nan sent mum letters, asking to see me but mum couldn't get her head around any of it. Dad drove a wedge between nan and mum. When we found out about the Alzheimer's . . .' I opened my eyes, embracing Em as her tears dampened my hairline. 'You had so much to deal with, Cal. I couldn't put this on you.'

'I wish you'd told me. I wish I could have been there for you.'

Em dabbed at the mascara streaks under her eyes. 'Well, we're here now.' Was that spite in Em's voice or was I imagining it?

'Your nan is sick, Em. It's OK to be sad but you need to be strong around her. For her. You still have time.'

'Thanks, Cal.' I noticed how she wouldn't meet my eyes.

'At least I know where you get it from,' I whispered into her ear as she leaned in for a goodbye hug.

'I am *nothing* like her.'

'Kettle, pot – black much?' I shot back, jumping down the steps.

'NOTHING. LIKE. HER!' Em bellowed into the night.

I smiled. Being with Peggy was like being pumped full of helium, floating away, high in the sky, sunshine bathing my skin. She took away my pain, let me be myself.

I slotted the key into the front door, listening to Kayleigh butcher a Whitney classic. *I want to dance with Noddy* isn't quite the iconic classic. I closed the door quietly and walked into the sitting room.

Our tiny living room felt like such a cavernous space when you drained away all of the character. I climbed the stairs, smiling as Kayleigh trampolined off her bed and onto the floor. Mum caught me looking. I examined her face, glimpsing the crow's feet that hadn't been there months ago. I hugged her, telling her I was off to bed. I didn't want to lose that feeling. I didn't want to tarnish that magic.

I stripped off and pulled the covers over me. I rifled through my bag for my phone and jumped when I found the phone-taser. It was hard to stay mad at Peggy. She was who she was and she wasn't going to change. She'd given me so much though. She'd given me strength and laughter and the courage to be who I was. She'd never told me that it was all in my head. She'd never dismissed me or spoke down to me. She was the little ray of light at the end of the tunnel that kept me trundling onwards. I wish everything could have stayed exactly as it was. I wish I could have frozen that moment, locked those emotions in place and carried them around with me forever – but forevers were like unicorns.

Chapter 18

EXCRETION

It was the first day back at school after summer – same routine but a few months older. I showered since mum had the money to finally get the hot water fixed – *not* to say that I'd gone all summer without a shower. I squeezed gel from the bottle and massaged it into my hair, spiking it at the front.

We had the same teachers as last year, with the exception of our English teacher, Mrs Fahy, who had taken a year out. Replacing her, was Mr Benedict who didn't teach us about Shakespeare and Plath so much as he quipped the most random questions and preyed on the weak and plain stupid – which made English entertaining.

'Supposing you're a detective and you find yourself at a crime scene, how would you proceed?'

'Everybody get out a pencil and draw a picture of justice.' I drew a rather questionable portrait of Victoria Justice because she is FAB.

'If you had twenty-four hours left to live, what would be the first thing you'd do?'

It didn't matter how you answered or even if you had the best answer in the world. It didn't matter if you had the right answer to what was an entirely subjective question. Everyone that answered his questions was met with the same resounding roar: 'WRONG!'

Niall Marsden hiccupped at the back of the class. Mr Benedict weaved between tables, reading from the Bible – go figure – and full-on screamed at Niall. There was pin-drop silence for a full thirty seconds and Mr Benedict broke it, asking Niall, 'are your hiccups gone?' Niall nodded nervously. I relished it.

> Em: Hey, got sent home. Fever :-/
> Me: Hope you're OK xx
> Em: You give me fever . . .Me: Get some rest!

When the final bell rang, I cut across the field, behind the thick oak trees, when a pair of hands grabbed me by the waist. Another pinned my wrists behind my back. A third pair of hands grabbed my legs and when I thrashed, they hit me, leaving a burning sensation in my belly. They took me around the side of the school, to a seldom-used cage,. Walled with concrete, it stocked gas cylinders and crates. The bars were rusted and the shards of glass embedded in the top of the surrounding walls glinted in the sunlight.

I watched as the cage door opened and they threw me in. I held my back, pressing against the pain as I stood. Niall, Gareth and John stared at me, laughing, shouting at me that I was a "faggot", a "nobody". I could have shouted but words failed me. My throat felt like it had been scraped raw with sandpaper. I stood in the centre of the cage, unable to move. I watched as raucous laughter brought tears to their eyes and then Niall came up close, gripping the bars playfully.

'You gays love watersports, don'cha? Answer me!'

'I don't know.' My voice quivered.

'Say it, say that you love watersports. Say it!'

He picked up stones and started to throw them over the gate. Gareth and John lobbed over some broken glass too. I shielded myself with my tattered coat.

'OK, OK; I like watersports.'

'Louder and take that coat away from your face.'

I did as they said. 'I like watersports.' My eyes watered. I bit my lip hard. I wouldn't give them the satisfaction.

Niall laughed, opening his fly. 'You like this, don't you? Seeing my cock like this? You love it.' Then I heard it. I took an instinctive step back as piss caught my shoe and Niall roared with exaggerated laughter.

I kept my head held high. Urine burned my nostrils. He tailed off and zipped up his fly.

'Say that you like it. Say it and we'll let you out.'

I folded my arms across my chest.

'SAY IT!'

Niall was screaming now, his eyes manic and sadistic. I wondered where the hell the teachers were.

'Say. It.' There was nothing loud about it this time but his words were tiny bullets pounding against my skin, toxifying my blood.

'I like it.'

'Louder.'

'I like it.'

All three laughed and shouldered their rucksacks, leaving me behind.

'Wait! You said you'd let me out!'

'Oops,' Niall said delicately, holding his hands in the air followed by a slight shrug. The other two howled.

They walked away. I stared down at the puddle of urine at the cage entrance. One foot either side of it, I slid my hands through the bars and pushed back on the bolt but I knew it was no use. It had taken both Niall and Gareth to bolt the cage. I was already at a disadvantage but the bolt was on their side too. I scanned the cage, an idea forming. I stacked the crates on top of each other. I used the bars of the cage to balance on the gas cylinder before stepping up onto the crates. I stumbled and got an arm over the wall before the crates tumbled to the ground. I hoisted myself up and over. Glass shards cut my palms and ripped my school trousers. I winced but the pain was a pleasant distraction.

The drop was about seven or eight metres. I jumped onto the ground, bracing myself for the inevitable shock that would catch in my ankles. I leaned against the wall, fighting the stench of urine and the taste of sweat on my tongue. The wall was coarse against my hand. I bent down and removed a can of deodrant, spraying it over my shoes.

I zipped my rucksack and stomped down the gravel path to the main entrance, ignoring the calls from behind.

'Cal,' someone called breathlessly. 'Cal, wait up!' I marched ahead, trying to hold in the emotion and the pain, but it was like trying to catch raindrops. Cam stood in my way, solid and sturdy, a lighthouse in the raging storms but I would never be his ship.

'Hey, are you OK? I saw – Cal, what's wrong?'

'Nothing.'

'Cal, what did they do to you?' I stuffed my hands into my coat pockets so he wouldn't see my cut palms.

'They were just messing around.'

'Cal, you're crying.' He reached up to touch my face but seemed to think better of it. 'What did they do?'

I couldn't stand it. Pity. It was on his face, in the way he moved his hands, in his words – everywhere I went, people pitied me and I wanted to scream at them. I was trying to be me. I was trying but it wasn't working.

'Cal.' Cam rested a hand on my shoulder.

'What do you care?' I snapped. 'No one in this school gives a shit about anyone else. No one cares about me. No one wants to hear what I have to say so do me a favour and leave me alone.'

'That's not true.'

I wasn't sure if he said the words or if I confused the sounds with the whistling of the wind as it whipped my hair around my face. I didn't stop and I never looked back.

I kept my head low on Tuesday. Em was still sick and I didn't want to draw any unwanted attention. I ate my lunch in a bathroom cubicle, covering my nose against the stench of urine with the sleeve of my jumper. I struggled to stop old memories re-surfacing and with them, I lived everything again – images of dad and Matt flooding my mind. I pressed my hands to my temple, desperate to block them out.Things got interesting during my last two periods. I marched to P.E. like I was stomping towards the guillotine. I covered my body as best I could, self-conscious as always. Niall asked if I wanted to suck on his "big one". The guffaws started. Nothing changed. We played football. Gareth and Niall were captains. Gareth stuck me in goal; purposely, I reckon, so Niall could volley the ball at my face.

Ten minutes from match end, Niall sprinted towards me. Neither Gareth nor the team tried to tackle him. His football boots tore up tufts of grass. I stood frozen, unsure what to do. Five metres away and I covered my face with my hands. I cried out as Niall's boot connected with my shin. My face hit the muddy ground. My hands sank into the wet dirt as I tried to stand.

'Nice one, fagster. Do you let all the boys score in your goal?' Gareth hissed over Mr Ashley's whistle. He distractedly waved me away as I limped into the changing rooms. I entered the changing room and Niall was rooting through my rucksack. My clothes were strewn around the room.

'Hey! That's my stuff.'

'Hey, gay boy.' He removed the taser. Crap. 'What's this? A Blokia? You have a Blokia, fagster?'

'I really need that back.'

'I bet you do.'

'Seriously, Niall.'

'I bet you do. God, you must be desperate if you want this heap of junk back. You know what, I think I'll keep it.'

'NO!'

Niall laughed. There was no way I was getting the taser back, not when he was built like a tank, standing at six-foot-one and I was a five-foot-nothing kid that looked like the poster boy for poverty.

'OK, but don't press down on the grey square.'

'This button?' Niall's finger hovered over it.

'Don't touch it.'

'*Don't touch it,*' he mimicked in a high-pitched, girly voice and then he pressed it. He flailed, shuddered and hit the ground. It was far from graceful. I wonder if that's what I looked like when Peggy tased me.

I leaned over Niall and picked up the taser. I heard shouting and the claps of high-fives in the corridor. I ran for the toilets in the main building. I changed quickly and sprayed some deodorant under my armpits. The bell rang and I quickly made my way to Food Tech.

'Uh-oh, what did you do?' I looked up. Cam Evans. I glanced around the classroom. There were a half dozen seats to choose from, including one beside Electra and her too-small skirt. 'What?'

'You're talking to me?'

'Oh no, should I leave?'

'No.'

'Cool.'

'Cool.'

Then, in a whisper, 'I'm here if you need to talk.'

'Cool.'

'Cool,' he repeated.

I turned to face Ms Radley and grinned because the first day of term, she provided the ingredients and we never knew what we would be preparing. When she told us we'd be making cupcakes, I nearly died. I whisked the ingredients together and poured it into the cases. Cam slid the tray into the oven.

Cam wanted to decorate them like superheroes while I wanted to shape a liqueur design on each. In the end, Cam won. There was complete silence while we decorated our cakes.

'I love your Batman cupcake,' Cam commented when we finished decorating our cakes. Ms Radley helped herself to two of our vanilla and strawberry cupcakes. Electra decorated hers with fondant nails though she lost a few of her own nails while she was whisking the cake mixture. Ms Radley choked on one and it was more than a little entertaining watching Electra sweat while Mina Sorrows administered the Heimlich manoeuvre.

'You can have the rest if you want,' I told Cam.

'Are you sure?'

'Sure, I'm sure.'

'Wow, thanks. See you around, Cal,' he said, shouldering his rucksack and making his way to his next class.

What the hell was that about?

Boys.

I walked through the corridors, hyperaware that something was about to happen. I mean, I'd unintentionally tased the most popular – albeit stupidest – guy at school. Well, that's not strictly true. He tased himself but I doubted he'd see things like that.

The classes themselves were fine but each time the teacher left the room, I expected the worst. I made my way from class to class on shaky legs. I was too warm with my jumper on but I knew it was just nerves so I tolerated it. I think that was the worst thing: the fear. The beating I could handle, but it was the not knowing that made it worse.

The final bell sounded. I removed books from my locker and slipped them into my rucksack, glancing around me in the eerie silence. I was alone and vulnerable. Most of the other boys had run from the school at the sound of the final bell. I ran my fingers along the message engraved into my locker door, wondering what psycho spent his time carving it into steel.

I'M HERE . . .

I closed my locker door, thinking about Matt. Was he thinking about me? I shook my head, shaking thoughts of him from my mind. I sauntered through the corridor, feeling watched but every time I turned around, there was no one there. I exited the main gates and swung left. I sped up my pace, my hands clutching the handles of my bag. I looked over my shoulder.

There's nothing there.

Nothing there.

Nothing. There.

I heard footsteps. I stopped, glanced backwards. Nothing. *It's all in your head.* My legs trembled, adrenaline pumping through my body. I sniffed the air. It smelled musty or maybe that was me.

I broke into a run, counting my steps and that's when I heard shouts from behind. I urged my body into a sprint. I prayed someone would open their front door and help me but I didn't spot a car in any of the gardens.

My head pulsed. I took a sharp left and cut through a narrow alleyway. I never looked back. Twenty steps and I'd be through the alley and home free. Instead, hands tugged at my coat and I hit the ground.

There were three of them, their faces concealed by hoods and scarves. I counted to ten, praying they were just trying to scare me; that they'd laugh and walk away. They didn't walk away. I heard the figures panting, male voices whispering amongst themselves and then I saw a shoe coming straight into my face. I tucked my head into my chest so my skull took the brunt of the force.

I curled up into a foetal position. Kicks rained down from all sides. They stomped on my side. The barrage continued and finally, after what felt like hours, it stopped. I heard one of the boys hock up some phlegm and spit at me.

I rolled over onto my back, moaning; a sharp pain in my side. I got onto my knees and drew in a sharp breath. I felt my head. No blood. I breathed a sigh of relief. Using the wall, I cautiously stood up, leaning against the wall for support. Pain exploded across my abdomen. Did they fracture a rib? It hurt to breathe. I hobbled down the alley. Our neighbour, Mrs Peach, was minding Kayleigh and mum would be at work. At least I didn't have to worry about them seeing me in this state. I entered the kitchen, heading straight for the medicine cabinet. I popped two paracetamol tablets from the tub and dry-swallowed them. I pounded my fist against my chest, easing them down my throat. I grabbed a bag of frozen peas from the freezer and pressed them to my ribs.

I went upstairs and crashed on my bed. The images played over and over in my mind, making sleep impossible. I lay with my eyes open, counting down the seconds until sleep pulled me under.

Peggy answered the door. I hadn't seen Em there in over a month and it had been almost a week since she'd texted. Was she angry with me? I pushed the thought from my mind. 'Em isn't here.'

'I know. I'm here for you.' Em was still home sick with glandular fever.

'Don't worry about me,' she replied wearily, 'this old bird hasn't much life left in her.'

'Don't say that.' Peggy looked at me, dark circles framing her eyes. I wondered how much sleep she was getting. The wrinkles on her cheeks were deeper and for some reason, each one reminded me of the circles you see on a tree stump – each wrinkle designating a year.

'How did that taser work out for you?' she asked, swiftly changing the subject.

I told her about Niall and how he tased himself. I left out the changing room scene, glamourising the reality because that was what Peggy needed right then. I didn't want to spoil the moment and tell her how I was starting to believe the voices in my head; the ones telling me that I wasn't good enough; the ones that told me that I was an abomination.

I poured us both a glass of Scotch and we knocked it back, celebrating another day in paradise.

'Have you ever wondered what other people think about you?'

'Quite frankly, I couldn't care less what other people think of me. Why do you ask?'

I looked at my feet, picking at some loose skin beneath my fingernail. 'Everyone at school hates me. I mean, they don't like gay people and I don't understand.'

'Maybe it's your school. Hugh was gay. I've never been to so many discos or drank so many Cosmos in my life – and our summer holidays in Mykonos.' Mrs Robinson's eyes lit up. '*Wonderful*.'

'I guess.'

'You don't sound convinced.'

'I just don't get why they hate me so much.' I sniffled.

'People hate different. They hate what they don't understand so don't take it personally.' I tried to point out that it was hard not to take it personally. 'The best advice I've ever been given was to be "me", Cal, and do you want to know why?'

'Was this advice given by a bartender by any chance?'

'As a matter of fact, it was.'

'Well, I guess he wanted to welcome an alcoholic to the bar because Scotch was a premium and he was hoping for a tip.'

She howled with laughter. 'He told me to be myself because everyone else was taken. I didn't wake up this fabulous, Cal. It was years of telling myself that I'm somebody and I matter. I started to accept it as the lights closed in. You, Cal, you're a special boy and you shouldn't let anyone – *anyone* – take that away from you.'

'That's what Em said.' I said it so quietly, I was surprised Peggy heard me.

'That sounds like my Emily alright,' she mused. 'You've been visiting me for what – two and a half months now?' I nodded. 'I've seen a lot in my life, Cal, a lot of strange and wonderful and tragic things. I've watched the births of my grandchildren and the deaths of my sisters and hand on heart, you are one remarkable thing. Your compassion, your energy, your charisma – everything that makes you, you. When you start to embrace that, you'll be unstoppable and all the slur grenades and dead-arms in the world won't hold you down.'

'I wish everyone at my school would see that.'

'They might never see it, Cal, and that's why you need to be strong. You're going to get a lot of bullets coming your way but you dodge, duck, dive and know the right moment to take a stand. Know the moment when enough is enough.' I took in her words. 'Have you ever thought of telling everyone, of owning it?'

'I've thought about it but . . . I don't see why I should. I don't want to be a label. I don't want to be "that gay boy".'

'That's fair enough but maybe, you don't have to do it for them. Maybe you need to do it for you.'

'What if things get worse?'

'Cal, darling, you bum boys rule the world. Elton John and David, Neil Patrick Harris and what's-his-face, Tom Daley – the gays are taking over, you better believe it. Ever been to San Fran? Tel Aviv? Mykonos?' I shake my head. I'd never been past Essex. 'Full of gays. More cock than New York's Meatpacking District.'

'Maybe.'

'Do what you need to do but embracing yourself, that's a powerful thing, and no words or fists can tear that away from you.'

Chapter 19

EXPOSED

'I'm going to tear his fucking head off.'

Fists clenched, jugular popping – I knew Em would react badly but there was no getting around it. She'd seen the way I was hobbling along to school. It took us an hour where it would have normally taken half that time and she wasn't buying my story about a stray rugby tackle either. She'd pressed down on my ribs and I'd gasped. She lifted my shirt up before I could swat her hand away and saw the massive bruise across my ribs.

She demanded the truth. I tried to laugh through the tears in my eyes. I'd tried to tell her it was nothing but she saw right through me.

'Em, you'll get expelled!' I countered, feeble attempts at damage control.

'And what? They get away with it? They get to live their lives and make yours miserable? Why Cal? WHY?'

'Just . . . just let me deal with it.' Em stared at me, a piercing look that cut me up inside and made it even more difficult to breathe. We both knew I wasn't going to deal with this. I wanted to be a wallflower but I was a homo with crosshairs on the back of his head. It was too late to change that.

'This is getting worse, Cal. You *need* to tell someone.'

'It won't help.'

'Cal, they could have put you in A&E. This needs to stop. What happens the next time I have a fever or the flu? What happens when I'm not there and they go too far? Think about your mum, Cal, and if you're not going to think about her, at least think about Kayleigh and the baby.'

I made a noncommittal sound at the back of my throat, rubbing my sweaty palms onto my school trousers. 'What are you going to do?' I asked her.

'I don't know.' She was trembling. I'd seen Em angry before, but this was rage, and I wasn't sure what that would mean for Niall and the others. I didn't want her to get suspended again or worse, expelled.

'Please Em, for me. Just let this go. If things get worse, I'll tell you. We'll do something about it.'

'Don't let them beat you, Cal.'

I nodded.

I wasn't sure what this meant. I spent my first three periods listening out for the sound of sirens and screams. Em was a timebomb and there was no telling when she would explode. I didn't want to be there when she did.

I knew she was right. I needed to talk to someone but I couldn't. It wasn't like I hadn't tried before. Whenever I opened my mouth to speak to a teacher, my mouth went dry and the words stuck to the back of my throat like glue.

Cam dropped his bag by my feet in Food Tech, smiling.

'Everything OK?'

'Sure.'

'Have you got sugar?'

'Cam, why are you here?'

'Because it's Food Tech.'

'No Cam, why are you *here*?' I pointed to our table.

'Because I want to be.'

I stared at him. He stared right back. 'Is there something on my face?' he asked, wide-eyed and mocking.

I shook my head from side to side.

'Good.'

We worked in silence, Cam pulling funny faces every now and again. Was I Cam's charity case?

This week was Choux Week. We were making eclairs. I had decided to make lemon eclairs. While I grated lemon zest, Cam measured out the flour. 'Cal,' he'd said at one point and when I'd turned around, he'd blown a cloud of flour into my face. I coughed and laughed, dipping my hands in the bag and patting them against his face. I was surprised by the warmth of his skin. He looked even better caked in flour!

Electra eyed me from across the room. Was she jealous? I glanced over at Cal who licked lemon curd off his fingers.

Ovens pinged minutes before the bell sounded. I moved our eclairs into a Tupperware container and grabbed my bag from the cupboard. Someone elbowed me in the ribs as I exited the classroom. I hit the floor, unaware of everything else but the words that hissed all around me. I gasped, trying to control my breathing.

'Watch it, *freak.*' Niall looked down at me as he passed.

'Is everything OK, Cal?' Cam asked.

'Peachy.' I smiled through the tears and power-walked away before he could say anything else. I knew that I couldn't power-walk away from all of my problems and sooner or later, they'd catch up with me.Outside the library, I sat down on a bench and opened the Tupperware container. I bit into a lemon eclair, the zesty flavour and explosion in my life. After licking lemon curd off my fingers, I balled my hands into fists. I was *not* going to let *them* win.

Chapter 20

INEXORABLE BEHAVIOUR

Friday started off relatively normal. Em walked with me to school. We parted ways as we entered neighbouring Form classes. I knew as soon as I walked into the classroom that there was a shift in the air. Twenty-five students looked up at me – an intimidating scene.

I pulled back my seat and the whispers started. I pictured my skin like armour, their words bouncing off my skin. *Sticks and stones* . . . I watched as a rubber sailed by my head, missing me by mere inches. Something slid up to my desk. Then, I smelt it – the sulphurous scent of a stink bomb. I kicked it forward but the damage was done. The classroom reeked.

'Good morning cla—ugh.' Mr Murphy wrinkled his nose in disgust. 'What is that smell?'

'It was Cal,' someone shouted from the back, the voice lost to a chorus of laughter.

'Enough of this. Silence while I call the roll.'

'I heard Cal likes a good roll.' More laughter.

Mr Murphy ignored this and continued down the list. When he called my name, my worst fears materialised into reality. The whispers spun around me like a venomous cocoon while Mr Murphy burrowed his head in his book.

Fag.

Faggot.

Gay.

Bum boy.

Cock jockey.

Fairy.

Poof.

The names pushed me deeper. The bell rang but I could feel the words cut through my skin and bury deep under the surface. Em accepted me for who I was but it made me think: what about my neighbours? What about the school? Would they accept me? Was there something wrong with me? Was it OK to be gay? Was I committing some sort of social crime? I didn't mean to. Dad attacked me. Everyone at my school despised me. Was this my future? Should I have prepared myself for daily abuse for being gay? I wasn't sure I could change but maybe I could mask it.

I opened my locker to get my books and a dozen notes were folded atop my books.

I know your secret.

Nobody likes a faggot.

You're going to hell.

I don't want you looking at my cock in P.E. Go and die.

You like dick? I have a big one for you.

When everyone finds out what you are, I'll hand you the rope myself.

I couldn't read the rest. I leaned my head into my locker, gasping for air, gripping the sides. I could smell the used book scent mixed with overripe bananas and the faint metallic scent of the lockers but still, I couldn't breathe. I closed my eyes but the words were burned into my eyelids.

I counted to three, pressing my palms against the cool coarse surface of the lockers either side of mine. I blinked and the walls stopped closing in on me. I was in control again. I pushed the names to the back of my mind and stuffed the notes into my Biology book.

I made my way to Food Tech. Cam stationed himself next to Electra. He smiled when he saw me. I tried to smile back but he knitted his eyebrows together. I turned away. I wanted to be alone. I wanted to immerse myself in the recipe, lose myself in the technique. Susan was my partner and choux buns were her favourite. She didn't contribute much and that was fine with me. That's what I liked about Susan. I knew what to expect with her but I could only imagine what Niall Marsden was capable of. I dreamt the worst, but I knew he could hurt me in ways I could never conceive and frankly, that terrified me.

I watched Cam and Electra, Electra nodding her head in my direction and Cam following her gesture. Cam looked apprehensive, so unlike the confident guy I fell in love with in Year 9. I heard a *ding*, signalling the end of the baking time for our buns. I slipped my hands into the gloves and removed the tray from the oven.

Susan burned her mouth several times on the piping hot choux buns while I specifically told her to wait. She was now in the toilets, gurgling cold water to help with her blistering mouth. The bell rang and Cam stopped at my desk.

'Don't go to P.E., Cam.'

'What?'

'Tell them you're sick. Don't go.'

'Why?'

'Electra told me that Niall is going to play a prank on you. Just please, don't go.'

'I'll do what I like, Cam,' I shot back defiantly and I swear, I could see hurt in Cam's watery eyes. I could never pinpoint exactly why I snapped. Maybe my emotions were running high. Maybe I needed to vent but I never should have lost it with the one person at school – besides Em – that actually seemed to care about me.

'What?' I asked dumbfounded. Mr Ashley had pulled me aside. He fidgeted as he spoke, unable to meet my eyes.

'The other lads don't feel comfortable changing around you.'

'Why?' I wanted my voice to sound strong and resilient but knew that it was squeaky and small.

'There have been complaints that . . . that you've been . . . looking at some of the other boys while they're changing.' He held

173

his hands up in the air. 'I don't want to take sides,' he continued, already choosing his side, 'but I have to go with the majority and look, you've got a changing room to yourself.'

Mr Ashley toed the door open with a boot. This wasn't a changing room. This was a joke. There were two changing rooms here and with twenty-five students crowded into those, they'd give me a cleaner's cupboard that smelled overwhelmingly of disinfectant. Memories of the hospital surfaced but I pushed them to the back of my mind.

'I'm sure you'll be fine in here. It's much quieter and quite roomy,' he added, as if somehow shucking all responsibility. He nodded and left, whistling as he strolled down the hall.

Was this actually happening?

What sort of teacher made a student change in a cupboard?

Did everyone hate me just as much as Niall?

Tears threatened to spill down my cheeks but I bit down on my lower lip hard. That's what Niall wanted. He wanted to break me. He wanted to take pictures and humiliate me in front of the world. I closed the door, moving a ladder so it rested against it. If someone came in, I wanted to know about it. I wanted to be ready.

Em's words resounded inside my mind.

Don't let them beat you, Cal.

I was trying – I really was – but I couldn't seem to find a way to make any of this right. I couldn't be the son my parents wanted me to be, the friend Em needed me to be and with the whole school gunning for me, I was finding it more and more difficult to get through the school days.

Football was ruthless and Mr Ashley seemed oblivious to the sly tackles that came my way. At one point, Niall had an open shot at the goal but he hesitated, knowing I'd try to intercept. He kicked the ball and nicked my ankles. I fell onto the wet mud, slipping twice before I was able to get my balance. I counted down the minutes.

When it was finally time to finish, I was the first to leave the pitch, making a beeline for my exclusive changing room. I grabbed my bag and ran for the main building toilets. I removed my boxer shorts from my bag and couldn't believe the holes that had been cut out at the back. I slipped them on, knowing that I couldn't tell mum what happened. I was down to five pairs now.

Niall wasn't in my remaining classes but that didn't stop the undercurrent of whispers, the names that rebounded around the room and the office stationary that whistled by my face. I hated Niall. I hated the way he made me feel, like I was nothing and nobody, but most of all, I hated that I believed him. Mum hadn't addressed the elephant in the room and I was beginning to think she resented me too.

Then, there was dad. Mum had prepared me, told me I would have to attend his hearing soon. I walked home with Em, deflecting her questions but no matter how hard I tried, I knew she'd already heard most of what happened, the name-calling at least. Luckily, she didn't know that I was being forced to change in the cleaner's cupboard.

'Don't let it get to you, Cal. Don't let them take anything from you.'

'Thanks.' We hugged. 'See you tomorrow?'

'See you tomorrow,' she smiled.

I trudged along, my footsteps heavy as I approached our apartment block. Someone sat on a wall, reading a book. I walked past them, listening to the birds whistle in a nearby tree.

'Cal.' The voice made the blood freeze in my veins. I stopped, unable to move, but I didn't have to. He walked in front of me, hands clasped in front of him.

'Matt.' I mouthed the words. I couldn't find my voice. I didn't know what to say. What was left to tell him? Matt didn't want me. If he did, he never would have cheated; never would have chosen Alfie over me; never would have lied.

It had been weeks since I'd last heard from Matt. The presents had slowly stopped and Matt took the hint – or so I thought.

Once upon a time, Matt made me feel ecstatic. Being with him was like going to the circus for the first time or enjoying a chocolate sundae. Safe. Comforting. Exciting. All the things I wanted it to be and more. We'd hold hands and kiss. He played me music.

He'd lied to me, taken my virginity and humiliated me. He broke my heart.

'Cal, I didn't want to surprise you like this but I've tried to call. I've texted. You're not going to Armin's lessons anymore and I need to know . . . I need to know you're OK.' He reached out to place a hand on my shoulder but thought better of it.

I surprised myself, my body acting on autopilot. I tried to fight back the tears but it was no use. I bawled in front of Matt and some part of me craved comfort. Em wasn't around and though she told me she was there for me, the unanswered calls and pictures with Lizzie and Duncan said it all. School was hell. I missed human touch. I missed how Matt used to hold me and it felt like all the fissures inside me were closing over. I missed . . . Matt. I held out my hands and Matt cradled me in his arms.

I didn't care that he saw me cry. I didn't care that he saw me being weak. I had all this emotion building up inside me – choking the breaths from my body – and I just needed to let it out.

Even through my t-shirt, I could feel the heat of my Matt's palms on my skin. Matt knew me in ways I didn't know myself. The simplest of moments were the most special. Walking through Southbank felt like I was walking on the moon once I was with him.

Slowly, reality started to filter in and my mind caught up with my body. I remembered Alfie, his mother, the messages on his phone and worst of all, the kiss. I pushed him away, covering my face with my hands.

'Cal—'

Some part of me knew I was being unfair. Letting him in and pushing him away within a few breaths was cruel, but I couldn't forget the past. I couldn't forget how he made me feel. I couldn't forget that the handsome, charismatic, compassionate boy in front of me was the same boy that broke my heart.

'I don't know what to say. Let me explain?' He sounded so unsure, so unlike the Matt I knew.

'I can't do this right now. I can't—'

'I'm sorry, Cal. I really am. I want to explain but . . . I can see now isn't the time. Maybe . . . maybe when you're up to it, we can talk?'

I nodded, unable to look at him.

'I miss you,' he murmured.

I heard his footsteps crunch against the gravel as he retreated across the street. I glanced over my shoulder, ensuring he was out of sight before I hunched down on the ground. I placed my head between my knees and let the tears flow, unable to stem the wound that had been torn open.

Chapter 21

EXIT WOUNDS

I checked my watch for the third time: 1.28pm. Em was late – really late. I stood up, pacing back and forth, stretching my arms over my head. Where was she?

Ducks quacked loudly, reminding me how much of our history Abbott's Park shared with Em and I.

Our first picnic.

Our first time riding a bike.

Our first time flying a kite – even though mine got stuck in a tree and mum had to promise me chocolate ice cream to soothe my wails when we left the park, kite-less.

I checked my phone for an update. Nothing. My fingers picked at my nails, tearing skin. I winced, secretly enjoying the distraction.

I pressed down on the fresh wound, watching the blood bubble on the surface.

A scream arrested my attention. Em raced towards me on rollerblades, laughing hysterically as she latched on to Duncan. A twinge of resentment pinched my stomach.

Peggy was losing her mind.

I was losing my grip on reality.

Em was skating through life breezily, with Duncan in tow.

'Cal!' she cried out, using the black iron bar framing the bench to stop herself. Her brown skin glistened with sweat, catching the Sun's rays. I bit down on my lip, watching Em squeezing Duncan's hand tightly in hers.

'You brought Duncan?' I snapped, unable to mask the venom in my voice.'He's my boyfriend.' I felt Em's guard immediately go up.

'He doesn't even know your nan, Em.'

'She's *my* nan, Cal – *not* yours – and Duncan is my boyfriend.'

I slumped onto the bench, hands folded across my chest. Em said she'd always be there for me. What about now? I needed someone to talk to – about the bullying and the thoughts whirring around in my head.

'What did you want to talk about?' Em sat down next to me, her body angled towards me, knee resting on the bench.

My mind raced. I scratched my skin hard. 'Never mind.' Pulling my coat closer around me, I stormed off. I heard Em's skates pound the concrete behind me but I couldn't slow down.

'Cal, wait!' I sped up, unable to face her. 'Where are you going?'

I glanced over my shoulder, Em skating robotically after me.

Duncan glided along beside her, linking arms. I felt her hand on my elbow. 'To see Peggy.'

'I'll come.'

I turned on her. 'You haven't been to see her in weeks. What's changed all of a sudden?'

Em wouldn't meet my gaze. 'I think I'll leave you two to talk,' Duncan remarked, skating back towards the pond.

'Are you happy now?'

'Are you serious? Am I happy? Yesterday, someone cut holes in my underwear, I was pushed down in the middle of the main corridor and Mr Ashley told me I had to change in the cleaner's cupboard because apparently, I'm making everyone uncomfortable. So, go on, Em, ask me again am I bloody happy?'

'I can't help you if you won't help yourself. You're enabling them. You're letting them win.'

'That's easy to say from the outside when you're not living it! No one is picking on you because you're gay. No one is telling you how wrong you are,' I screamed.

'Not everything is about you being gay!'

That cut deep. I could tell that Em instantly regretted it but she said it. The words left her lips and they were out there, pushing us further apart.

'I didn't mean—'

'Don't. You meant it or you wouldn't have said it. Even with all this going on – with everything at home and the bullying at school – I still make time for your nan. Here you are, skating around the park with Duncan. At least we know where your priorities lie.'

'Haven't you thought that maybe, there might be a reason I haven't been to visit? No, because you're so caught up in The Cal Show.'

'You never talk to me. You never open up. You deflect my questions. You dish out advice but you never accept it. It's very easy to tell someone how to overcome an obstacle when you're not facing it, Em.'

'You want to know what's going on? Mum kept me from her. She knew. She knew that nan was losing her mind. She lied to me, Cal, so, if you want to stand there and tell me what you think you know, then go ahead but *don't* pretend you're family. She's *not* your family.'

My stomach cramped at the poison in her words. She was right though. Peggy wasn't family. I couldn't be certain she would remember me from one day to the next.

Em rolled along, arms held out like a robot to balance. She clutched gates and walls desperately, shimmying along the street, while I stormed ahead.My heart raced as we stood outside Peggy's house. I could hear Em behind me. I knocked on the door, waiting for Peggy to answer. I knocked again, more insistently this time. The jingle of keys jarred me from my thoughts.

I moved to one side as she slotted the key into the lock, pausing. 'I didn't — I shouldn't—'

'This isn't about us now. This is about Peggy. We can talk about this later.' She nodded, twisting the key in the lock.

As Em pushed the door open, the acrid smell of cigar smoke made me wrinkle my nose. The house felt like a cavernous space, empty somehow. I heard the creaks of neighbouring floorboards, the *drip, drip, drip* of water and the hum of the boiler. Goosepimples sprouted on my arms.

'Nan?' Em marched into the sitting room, cutting through the silence. I followed. 'Nan?' Her voice was an octave higher than usual. I emerged into the sitting room, jolted into action by Em's scream. Peggy sat in her armchair, slumped with an empty bottle of Scotch in her grip. She looked ghostly and serene, her white hair covering her forehead, her eyes closed. Was she sleeping? I knew the answer already.

'No, no, no, no, no, no.' Em took her hand, feeling her wrist for a pulse. 'I can't get a pulse. Cal, I can't get a pulse,' she said, panic twisting her voice into a high-pitched shrill. I reached down and took Peggy's hand. Nothing.

'Tell me she's going to be OK. CAL, TELL ME SHE'S GOING TO BE OK.' I looked at Em as she melted into my arms, tears hitting my neck. I bit my lip, holding back my tears. I had to be strong. I couldn't speak. I opened my mouth but no sound came out. I shook my head solemnly. 'NO, she can't be . . . SHE. CAN'T. BE. *DEAD.*'

I took my phone from my pocket, tapping 999. 'London Ambulance services.' The operator asked how she could help. There was nothing she could do to help. This was all formality.

'My friend's nan, she's not breathing. She's just lying there.' I led a hysterical Em into the kitchen where she slumped onto the tiles, back leaning against the washing machine.

'Calm down. How old is the patient?'

'Seventy-five.'

'Male or female?'

'Female.'

'Have you felt for a pulse?'

'She hasn't got a pulse.'

'Can you try one more time? Press your index and middle fingers to her neck.'

I took her hand once more. 'No,' I whispered, tears trailing down my cheeks.

'Place your hand in front of her mouth. Can you feel any air?'

'No.' Every confirmation that the life had left Peggy felt like a knife twisting around inside my stomach, cutting me from the inside out.

'Paramedics are on the way. I'd like you to remain on the phone to answer further questions. I'll pass this information over to the paramedics.'

'OK.'

Em continued to wail in the background, crying into her nan's nightie. 'What about her cheeks? What colour are her lips?'

'Her cheeks are . . .' It was hard to tell what colour her cheeks were under all that blush. 'Her cheeks are pink bit it's blush.'

'What about her lips?'

'Aquamarine.'

'Aquamarine?' the operator echoed incredulously, temporarily slipping out of character. 'Lipstick. She's wearing lipstick.'

'Her posture? Is she lying down or sitting?' My heart twisted inside my chest.

'She's sitting. Her head is slumped to the side.'

'OK, thank you. Don't move her. The paramedics will arrive shortly.'

'The paramedics are on the way,' I relayed to Em.

She looked at me, something worse than pain weighing her down. Grief, I realised. Em leaped to her feet, opening the cupboards. She took a pile of plates from the shelf, howling as she smashed them, chipping Peggy's tiles.

'Em. Em, stop.' I placed my palms in the air. I had no idea what was running through her head. I held my hand up as another plate hit the floor. A stray shard rebounded, slicing my hand. I winced but the pain distracted me from my own pain.

Mum.

Dad.

School.

Peggy.

Matt.

The voices in my head telling me I wasn't good, that I would *never* be good enough.

Em slumped to the glass-strewn floor, shaking me from my thoughts. I bent down, lifting her from the ground, half-dragging, half-carrying her to the other side of the room.

Sirens tore through the air. I stepped out of the house, waving my hands wildly. I felt so far removed from the scene, a spectator to their tests and the final curtain that they laid over Peggy.

Em sat there, tears soaking into her t-shirt as she stared at the kitchen wall. I picked up my phone and called Em's mum before answering the paramedics' questions. One exited and left a stretcher parked near the door. Together, they carried her out and wheeled her into the back of the ambulance.

I sat beside Em, combing her hair back from her face as she lay in my arms, cradling her close to me. The paramedic spoke into her walkie-talkie. 'DOA, over.' I clasped my hand across my mouth, silencing the tears. Em needed me.

Em clung to me like a limpet to a rock. I was the only thing anchoring her. I thought about the slurs and the abuse I faced at school. Where was Em for me? Gallivanting about with Duncan? I pushed those thoughts to the back of my mind. Em needed me. That was all that mattered.

Em's mum burst into the room. Em didn't look up. She sat down beside her. I tilted Em's weight onto her, giving them a moment. On jelly legs, I climbed the stairs to the upstairs bathroom. I pulled down the toilet lid, sitting down. The rose tiles, the blue and purple towels – everything seemed to remind me of Peggy. I took the hand towel from the rack and pressed my face into it, the cotton muting my wails.

It was hard to digest that Peggy was gone. I would never be able to ask her for advice or listen to her stories. We'd never drink Scotch and watch TV together. Her laughter, her quips – it was gone. *She* was gone. The only person I could talk to was gone and she'd left me here.

Alone.

Em hadn't said a word.

Not when her mum showed up, hugging her tight.

Not when Duncan lifted Em from the house into his car.

Not now, the light shining on her face as we lay side by side.

Everyone was there for Em but who was there for me? I'd been there to help her, to support her. Em was surrounded by people that could help nurse her grief but who was going to help me with mine? Peggy was gone. Mum was working and practically oblivious to what was going on in my life. Em . . .

The sweet processed scent of roses suffocated me. Rain shot down from the sky like armour-piercing bullets, banging on the windowpane like fists trying to smash entry into Em's room.

'She loved you, you know,' I whispered. Silence. I worried that Em couldn't hear me over the elements raging outside.

'How would you know?' It wasn't an attack – more curious, like she was trying to seek validation.'She told me. She showed me old photos, told me stories.' Em turned over, staring right through me and into my soul. My words must have hit something because Em kicked off the covers, climbed over me and leaped out of the bed. 'What are you doing?'

Em pulled a large box from the bottom of her wardrobe, celebratory cards and photos cascading around her. Tears filled her red-rimmed eyes as she peered into each one, searching for something no one could give her.

'Do you remember this?' She held up a photo of us when we were five, Em wielding a brush as a weapon.

'How could I forget?' I retorted. Em hit me with a sweeping brush twelve years ago but I could still feel the lump above my ear. 'You were destined to be a badass. I feel sorry for Duncan.'

'Remember when I cried and said I didn't mean it?' I nodded. 'Yeah, that was a lie. I saw the attention you were getting from my mum and I was jealous. I was so jealous and I remember this feeling, this instinct to hit you and I did. Our mothers came rushing out to your wails and I realised that I'd gotten you even more attention so I cried too as mum shouted at me.'

'You did?' I exclaimed, but I guess I already knew that deep down, so I just smiled.

'I want to climb into these pictures. I want to go back to when mum and dad were together and my family was whole, when friendships were easy and the only thing we had to worry about was whether we'd get a chocolate bar after dinner or not. I can't deal with this. I can't do any of this, Cal.'

'Hey, it's going to be OK.' I rubbed circles into her back with my palm.

'It's not though. None of this is right. I couldn't put things right with my nan before she . . . I keep messing up.'

I placed my hands firmly on her shoulders so she couldn't move. I met her eyes, ensuring she could see me, see the lengths I would go for her. 'Peggy got to see you before she went, Em. She got to spend time with you, got to talk and laugh with you. She got to see you as I see you.'

'No, Cal,' she snapped, 'she got to see how great *you* are!' Em clamped her hands over her mouth but it was too late. The words were out there, coated in poison. I thought I knew everything about Em but I was wrong. The Em I knew never would have said that, never would have lashed out. Who was the girl sitting in front of me? Something surfaced in my mind. Sadness. Anger. Shame. Nothing I recognised. It was a darkness that scared me. The atmosphere in the room changed abruptly and I felt like I was suffocating.

'I'm going to the bathroom.'

'Cal, I—'

I closed the door and locked it behind me. Water gushed out of the taps as I twirled the faucet. I splashed a handful onto my face, staring at my red-rimmed eyes in the mirror. I looked awful, my skin dark around my bloodshot eyes. A headache pulsed at my temples. I opened the overhead cupboard and rifled through it. I picked up Em's mum's Xanax. I counted the tablets. Twenty-seven. She hadn't noticed the last time.

Before I could think it through, I'd already popped one of the tablets into my pocket, the other melting on my tongue. I dry-swallowed, thudding my chest with my clenched fist to ease its descent. I stared into the mirror, trying to recall how long before it took effect. Unbolting the door, I exited the bathroom and made my way into Em's room.

'Cal, I'm sorry.'

'It's fine.'

It wasn't fine. Em knew what I was going through and I knew Peggy was Em's nan, but she was my lifeline – the only person I'd opened up to. Without her, I felt lost.

'I should get going,' I told Em. She hugged me. I wanted so desperately to take her pain away but if I took her pain, if I absorbed it, who would take mine?

Chapter 22

INEXCUSABLE ACTIONS

My alarm jolted me out of my coma. I rolled out of bed, hitting the floor more heavily than I would have liked. I snatched one of dad's cast-off robes from my wardrobe and wrapped it tightly around my body, securing it with a wrinkled belt. Each step down the stairs cleared my head a little more and the pain started to filter in slowly, a knife slicing my heart apart.

'Morning,' mum beamed, setting down a cup of coffee and a plate of waffles drowning in a sea of maple syrup. I checked my watch. 6.30am. I'd never seen mum up this early on a school day. 'Waffles: your favourite!'

'What is this?'

'What does it look like?' I folded my arms across my chest.

'Breakfast. I've been saving up and last night, I was thinking, it's time we started to live a little.'

Yeah, waffles and coffee – living on the edge. Let's get crazy and throw some toasted almonds on there.

I pulled out a chair and eased into it. I picked up the cutlery cautiously, cutting a small bite from the waffle. I chewed once, twice, three times. The warm chewiness of the waffle mixed with the sweet syrup was a taste overload. I swallowed, instantly feeling sick as Peggy flashed into my mind. Resting the knife and fork on the waffle, I pushed the plate away.

Mum's eyebrows knitted together. 'Something wrong?'

'I'm not hungry.'

Mum tried to smile but I could see the sadness in her eyes. I should have forced myself to eat some more but I couldn't quell the queasy feeling. A few bites wouldn't have killed me. I dug my nails into the palms of my hand, a futile attempt to drive away the phantoms haunting my every waking moment.

'Cal, is everything OK?'

I met her gaze. 'Everything's peachy, mum.' I gave her a megawatt smile. Her expression softened, radiating relief.

Look at me. Really look! Can't you see me? Can't you see I'm hurting? I'm drowning and need help. I need the mum that used to tuck me in on winter nights and read me The BFG; *the mum that slipped me mint humbugs on our family trip to Cornwall when I was ten after dad said I couldn't have any; the mum that used to tell me I was her shining star and I could never do any wrong. I'm swimming in this ocean and I'm drowning. Tell me you love me. Hug me. SEE ME.*

From the sitting room, I could hear Kayleigh's giggles above Dora's 'Swiper: no swipe'. I stopped at the kitchen door, my hand resting on the handle. I took one step into the hall.

'Cal.' I glanced over my shoulder. 'There's something I need to tell you.' She fidgeted with her hand, combing loose hairs behind her ears. 'Your father's trial is next weekend.'

I sprinted up the stairs, ignoring mum's calls. I slammed my door and twisted the key in the lock. I switched on my stereo and Kelly Clarkson's *Because of You* bled out of the speakers. I screamed the lyrics, anger and fear eclipsing sadness but I couldn't arrive at school with tears in my eyes. I couldn't paint a bullseye on the back of my head like that for Niall.

I opened my drawer and photos spilled onto the floor. Mum. Dad. Matt. I searched for a pair of scissors at the bottom of the drawer and took a handful of the photos in my hand. I cut the pictures into tiny, indecipherable pieces that could never be glued back together. I cut until my hands cramped and my forehead beaded with sweat. I cut as fast as I could and then, the scissors slipped, slashing my wrist.

It was a shock, jolting me from my thoughts. It beat back the emotion that crashed over me and for a single moment, I had clarity. I watched the blood bubble from the wound. I opened the scissors and placed the blade further up my arm. I pressed down lightly and winced as the blade easily sliced through my skin. Focusing on something physical – something I could control – felt so good. I felt in control from the first time in a long time. I ran into the bathroom and washed the cuts. I grabbed plasters from the cupboard and quickly dressed the wounds, extending my sleeves down to my palms.

I couldn't control the trial or my relationship with Em. Those were elemental forces that raged outside of my domain but I could control this. I knew it was wrong. I knew it wasn't healthy but in that moment, all I cared about was the release and this was a lot easier than facing reality.

I met Em at the top of her road and we walked side by side in virtual silence. My thoughts floated around in my head like helium balloons blown around in the sky.

'Why do good things happen to evil people?' Em asked.

'Huh?' She nodded her head in the direction of the car park where Niall Marsden and Gareth Mead closed the doors to a sleek silver Toyota Yaris.

'I hope it snows.' Em stormed off.

I followed.

I plonked into my chair in Form, hard plastic biting into my back. I'd learned not to rest my thumbs on the sides of my desk. There always seemed to be fresh gum stuck to my table. I kept my hands in my lap. Mr Murphy marched into the classroom, all business with a manila folder in hand. He called the roll and when he got to my name, I could sense a shift in mood. Niall and a couple of others sniggered at the back of the classroom. Mr Murphy didn't seem to notice them or at least he didn't particularly care.

'Enough,' he ordered, cutting off the whispered conversations.

Then, the note swapping started. I heard the crinkle of paper.

'For you,' Electra mouthed, sliding the folded note across the table. My hands quivered as I opened it.

> Tick a box if you think
> Cal should just get it
> over with.

Dotted around the page were scribbled boxes, most containing ticks, and a stickman with a noose around his neck. I counted twenty-five and when I looked back at the number of people it passed by, I counted the same. I bit hard on my lip and blinked away tears. I was up and out of my chair seconds before the bell rang. I balled the note and shoved it into my pocket.

'What's that?' Em asked, waiting next to the lockers.

'A stupid joke.' I couldn't look Em in the face because if I did, I would have broken apart.

I thought that would be the worst of it, a cruel joke with a side of whispers and not-so-subtle finger pointing but I was wrong. I was so wrong. In Maths, I was solving a cubic equation, which Mr Murphy was scrawling across the blackboard in chalk.

Niall looked over at me mockingly from the other side of the room, a smirk plastered on his face. His shoulders were relaxed, his hands steepled together like a bad parody of a mob boss. He nodded his head as words continued to fall out of my mouth.

In a weird wave, I noticed everyone removing their phones from their pockets one by one. First Electra, then her friends, Jenny Carter and Mercy Graves, who sat behind her. I didn't falter but in my head, I was anxious, sweat already beading on my forehead. There were gasps followed by more whispers and a few sniggers from Niall & Co. 'The answers are 2.'

My phone vibrated in my pocket. 'And -2.'

I took it out, sliding the lock across the screen.

'Well done, Cal.'

Mr Murphy wrote my answers on the board.

> 1 Facebook notification: Three of your friends have
> liked a new page – 101 reasons why Cal should
> bite the bullet.

I didn't need to tap on it to know the kind of things they were saying about me. My grip slackened, my phone almost sliding between my fingers.

'Is everything OK, Cal?'

'Yes, sir. Could I get some air?'

'Sure. Would you like someone–'

'No! I mean, I think I'll be OK.'

'OK, but don't go too far.'

I nodded. I was beyond the point of forming words. I sped down the corridor. I barrelled through the door to the boy's toilets, kneeling down and lifting the lid on the toilet. Vomit burned my throat and splattered into the toilet bowl. I heaved again. My fingers hurt from gripping the sides of the toilet bowl too tightly but I liked that; I focused on that instead of the vomiting.

I retched some more, coughing and spitting a mouthful of

saliva. I broke off some toilet paper and dabbed at my mouth. I gave it another couple of minutes before I made it to the sinks. I ran the cold water, splashing it onto my face and washing the taste from my mouth. I smelled my clothes, glad that they still smelt faintly soapy. My phone vibrated in my pocket.

> Em: I'm going to kill him. I'm going to CRUCIFY him.
> Me: Em, don't.
> Em: No, Cal. He always does this. Someone needs to stop him.
> Me: You can't.
> Em: Then you need to go to a teacher. You need to speak to someone.
> Me: We'll talk about this later.
> Em: Cal!
> Me: Later.

"Later" arrived sooner than I would have liked. Em clenched and unclenched her fists, breathing heavily.

'You'll only make things worse.'

'Worse? Cal, are you even listening to yourself? What he's done is *sick*. You need to report him. Or if you like, I can bury him.'

'Did you hear about Mr Murphy?' I dangled this in front of her, hoping she'd take the bait.

'What?' Em replied, her interest piqued. I fed her some of the rumours I'd been hearing during P.E. The tension disappeared from her face and I knew that I'd won this round. For now.

'How was chemistry?' I asked, skirting the conversation away from Niall.

'Same old, same old. Mr Flick let us blow things up *and* it's educational.'

'Cool.' My face dropped then. Coming straight towards us were Niall, Gareth and John. I bit hard on my lip. I reflexively reached out for Em's hand, squeezing it tightly. I sensed more than saw every muscle in her body tensing. 'Keep your cool, Em.'

'I'm trying,' she said through gritted teeth.

'Don't do anything stupid.'

I honestly couldn't tell what would happen. Em stomped ahead of me, heading for a direct collision. Niall narrowed his eyes and sniggered. I felt the blood drain away from my face. An arm's length apart and Em skirted around John, knocking shoulders with him. I didn't make a sound as Niall shouldered me roughly.

'Loser,' he muttered. Gareth and John laughed.

I put a hand on Em's shoulder. Her jaw tight and squared, clenching her hands into fists so that the colour drained away – she was just about holding it together. 'They're not worth it.'

'But you *are*,' she said through gritted teeth. We rounded the corner and she pulled me into an empty classroom. I leaned back against the blackboard, indifferent to the chalky dust rubbing against my school jumper. 'I can't believe you let them treat you like that.'

'But Em—'

She held up her hand. 'I hate them. I wish Niall would get hit by a bus on the way home from school. I used to feel sorry for you, Cal.

I wanted to protect you and be there for you but now, whenever I look at you, I see disappointment. We've all got problems, Cal, and sometimes, you need to face them. You see yourself as the victim and guess what, you're a victim. Congratulations.'

'What do you want me to do? What can I do, Em?' I cried out, running a hand through my greasy hair. What good would retaliation do? If I fought back, things would get worse. I thought back to the moment Niall tased himself with Peggy's phone. The bullying had increased tenfold since then. What would he do if I fought back? What could I do when he had our whole class behind him?

'Anything.' She turned her back on me. 'Do . . . *anything*.' Her voice cracked. She left the classroom, leaving me in a pool of my own misery, treading water with cinder blocks hooked around my feet.

A year ago, I would have peed my pants with excitement if someone told me Cam Evans' arm would be touching mine but I couldn't see past the melancholic fog that clung to me, the same way tobacco smoke clings to a smoker's clothes. I rolled up my sleeves as Cam measured out our ingredients.

'Sugar?'

'Sugar,' Cam chirped, handing me a small bowl of caster sugar.

'Egg yolks?'

'Egg yolks.' He passed me a bowl of egg yolks, already beaten with tiny bubbles still appearing on the surface.

I sensed Cam watching so I chanced a side glance. 'Everything OK?'

'What happened to your arm, Cal?' His eyebrows were knitted together. His question pinned me to the wall, writhing around but unable to escape.

'Cut it. It's worse than it looks,' I replied casually, forcing a smile that I didn't feel. Instinctively, I rolled down my sleeves to cover the cuts. How could I be so careless?

'Are you sure that's an accident? It looks—'

'Why can't you just leave me alone? Saint Cameron. You didn't want to know me up until a month ago so just leave it out. I liked it better when you pretended I didn't exist.'

'I never did that, Cal. I never wanted that.' I'd hurt him. I didn't need to see him to know that. The sadness choked his voice.

'Yeah, well, people don't mean things but sometimes they just happen.'

Our conversation dissolved into silence after that. I could feel the change already – cutting off people that probed and asked questions. I isolated myself early on. I deflected questions and manipulated conversations so I wasn't the focus. I stayed quiet so I faded into the background but there was only so long I could do that before things erupted.

Chapter 23

EXPLOSIVE REACTIONS

Friday was like trekking to the end of a rainbow, the closer you thought you were getting, the further ahead it seemed to slip. A wave of dread crashed over me as I realised tomorrow would be the day I'd see dad in court, reliving all those painful memories.

Pushing it from my mind, I shouldered my rucksack, instantly wincing. I completely forgot about the fresh bruise on my shoulder. I held my rucksack by my side, closing the front door behind me. I met Em at our usual spot. She was quiet, so unlike her sassy self. This new Em unnerved me.

'Hey.'

'Hey, yourself.'

'How's everything at home?'

'Good as can be, I guess. Mum's a bit freaked out with the court case tomorrow. She hasn't been sleeping great.' She never told me this but I knew it. She woke me up three times last night, the floorboards creaking.

'Court case?'

'Dad.'

Em's mouth formed an O. The awkward silence smothered us. 'If you need me . . .' Em began.

I nodded. I'd heard that before. They felt like empty words, a Kinder Surprise minus the chocolate and the toy – just the shining foil promising something more. That's how it was now. Not unfriendly but strained.

Minutes dragged into hours but finally, we arrived at our last class of the day, double-checking my seat for fresh gum before sitting down. I stared out the window, at the shiny silver metal of Niall's Yaris. God, I wish someone would key his car.

Mr Benedict read out a passage from *To Kill a Mockingbird* and asked us to discuss Atticus in pairs and feedback to the class. Em and I spent 90% of that time talking about Lizzie's new girlfriend and her party on Saturday night, and 10% about Atticus. When it was time to speak in front of the class, Em stood up.

'Atticus is a true gentleman. He's a pillar of the community, whether other people see it or not. He fights for justice with reason and faith. He protects the innocence and rages against bigotry and prejudice.' She caught my eye as she said this. 'He's gentle and kind but he fights with fire and steel in his every word. He sees things from different perspectives and he's a firm believer that people can change.'

'Thank you, Em and Cal. Who'd like to go next?'

Niall and Gareth enlightened us about 'how much of a boss he is'. Electra and Jenny told us 'how hunky he is in the film adaptation and I'd like to put a saddle on him and ride him like a Shetland pony'. John and Steve must have been reading a different book. They mostly talked about how he was 'a brother from another mother'. It became clear that six out of the twenty-five of us had bothered to read the book.

The bell rang and I gathered my books.

'TGIF!' Em squealed and then a blast from outside made the windows shake. Students clustered around the windows but Em and I were the first to see Niall's Yaris engulfed in a fireball.

'This is an important announcement,' the tannoy in the corner blasted. 'Would all students remain indoors? Stay in your classrooms. Failure to comply will result in one month's detention. I repeat: no one is to leave their classroom until advised.' Principal Holden's order caused a stir as we watched the flames leach the colour from the car.

Niall bolted from the room. Mr Benedict called after him but it was no use. I saw him sprint down through the carpark to his car. I wasn't sure what the point was. It wasn't like he could blow out the flames. This wasn't a handful of candles on a birthday cake.

Niall stood, looking on helplessly, wringing his hands. He howled into the sky, stamping his feet onto the concrete. Something warm radiated from my chest and I realised it was satisfaction. Finally, Niall knew what it was like to be helpless; to know what it was to have zero control over the things that happened to you.

'I wonder if he has insurance,' Em remarked casually as Principal Holden glided gracefully through the car park and guided Niall back to the front entrance. He resisted but eventually folded as the flames began to flicker out and all that was left was a charred husk.

Phones vibrated and everyone, except Em and I, were messaging each other frantically. Everyone gossiped with eyes that looked like they might bulge out of their sockets if they were any wider. I heard the sirens before I saw the blue lights flashing as a police car and fire truck sped up the driveway.

The firemen got out of the car, shook hands with Principal Holden, inspected the damage and together with the police, drew up a report. I didn't see the point in them being there. I hadn't a clue what happened or what they expected to find but the fire was long extinguished before they arrived.

I wondered briefly what kind of insurance Niall had – not the kind that covered spontaneous explosions, I guessed. Nobody seemed to care how it happened but hawked the scene, thankful that it had. I couldn't speak for everyone but I was beginning to think most people hated Niall Marsden. I mean, he was Mr Popular. He was captain of the football team and the girls fancied the arse off him, but I suspected that was where mild interest began and finished.

Niall wasn't a complex character: cars, girls and football. He was the Amoeba of boys. I was glad karma had balanced things out but I was scared; scared of how erratic and irrational Niall was at the best of times and now, what that meant for me.

'What do you think happened?' I asked Em. We were a stone's throw from her house, sitting on a red brick wall that looked out across a park with a curving path and a colourful playground. She shrugged. 'I heard there's going to be an investigation. They think someone torched his car.'

'Bullshit. If someone torched the car, we'd know about it. We'd have seen someone running for the school. No one left our class. Everyone was accounted for.'

'Maybe you're right.'

'*Of course* I'm right.' She held my hand, squeezing gently.

'I heard Electra telling everyone that his father left his mother.'

'And?'

'Just what I heard.'

'I don't give a shit what's happened to him. Nothing justifies what he did to you – what he does to you.' Em sighed. 'How are you doing?'

'Good,' I lied.

'You know I'm here.'

Are you though? my mind asked. 'I know. I'm sleeping better. I'm trying to move on.' Lies. I hadn't slept more than four hours a night since Peggy died.

'Are you sure you don't want me to come with you tomorrow?'

I shook my head. 'You need to go to the funeral. Mum will be there. I just want—' My voice choked off. I couldn't believe I was going to court because of dad instead of saying goodbye to Peggy.

'It's going to be OK, Cal. Everything is going to be OK.'

Don't cry – not in front of Em.

Chapter 24

EXCRUCIATING MEMORIES

We met the usher inside the main entrance. I slipped my hands into my pocket, discreetly wiping away excess sweat. The usher was exactly how I imagined him – a balding man wearing a trousers-and-shirt combo, jazzed up with a lilac tie that didn't suit him. The surprising thing was the black waistcoat-robe combo. It seemed so out of place but it looked courtly.

'Mrs Adams,' he greeted mum with a formal handshake. 'And Cal. Right this way.'

Mum answered most of the questions as I zoned out. I was aware of the faint scribbles of pencil on paper. This was the first time I'd seen dad in six months. I tried to remember the last time I'd seen him, with mum in a cafe. I couldn't remember the details, the shock of seeing him eclipsing everything else that day with Matt.

'Cal.' I jerked my head in the usher's direction. 'Are you ready?' He gave me a reassuring smile but nothing could reassure me. I never wanted this. Sure, dad hit me but he'd spent sixteen years loving me. He'd never laid a finger on me. Was this a mistake? Did I really want to go through with this? Could I stop it, even if I wanted to? I was rolling down a hill, unable to change my trajectory. I sensed a cliff at the end of my metaphorical hill.

I nodded. The usher guided me into the witness box. The prosecuting and defending lawyers sat in front of me, absently shuffling papers. I looked across the room at the other box. It was empty. I held my breath, counting slowly. Why was this so damn hard? Why did everything have to be such a struggle?

Then, I saw him. He shuffled along, so unlike the strong man that had punched me – a shell of his former self. I got my blue eyes from dad but when I looked at him, his were tired and framed with crow's feet. His skin was pale and wrinkled. He twisted around to look at me. I stared down at my feet, focusing on my double-looped laces because having him look at me felt like a physical burn. I instinctively pressed my fingers along the healing cuts on my arm. He took his place in the box across from mine. I let out a long breath, gasping for air. I interlinked my fingers, trying desperately to stop them twitching. What would I say? What would happen? My mind was a maze even I couldn't navigate.

'All rise,' the usher boomed.

The district judge entered, not in a black robe like I'd expected but a black suit, paired with a white shirt. I gulped. Mum took me to a café not far from the court an hour ago. She coaxed me to eat some food, even a slice of toast. I recalled her grimacing at the sight of me knocking back a pot of filter coffee. The coffee had previously quenched the fire in my belly but now, it was bubbling furiously – my stomach cramping. The lights were so bright that I felt dizzy, the floor rushing up to meet my eyes.

'You may be seated,' the usher concluded after the judge took his seat.

'Good morning, ladies and gentleman. We are here to address hearing #2129 in the matter of Adams versus Adams. Is the prosecution ready?'

'Yes, your Honour.'

'Is the defence ready?'

'Yes, your Honour.'

'Prosecutor, please present your case.'

'Your Honour, the victim states that at about 7pm on the night of the 30th December at St. Andrew's, the defendant shouted and dived for him, alerting the attention of two nurses – the testimonies of which act as evidence for this case. A relative to Mr Combs, a patient undergoing a procedure in the neighbouring room, claimed she saw the defendant punch the victim in the face. Her testimony supports the victim's claim. I also have photographs of the bruising around the victim's right eye.'

Every word felt like the *bang, bang, bang* of a bullet though my chest. It was a struggle to get my thin raspy breathing under control in the tense silence between words. Not a cough. Not a sneeze. I glanced around the courtroom, inhaling the smell of freshly polished mahogany. Everyone had their ears strained.

'Distressed, the victim ran from the scene of the crime as the defendant was restrained by two security personnel. Master Adams made a statement at his home in Leytonstone a couple of days later. The defendant was granted bail and as a result, the authorities granted the victim a temporary Protection Order.'

'Thank you. Defence, please present your case.'

'My client does not deny this.'

There were a few gasps. My jaw hurt as I realised my mouth hung open. Words tumbled out of the defence solicitor's mouth, in sync with my rapid heartbeat.

'He accepts the weight of his actions and has asked that the court consider his circumstances.'

'Mr Adams, could you tell us what happened on the 30th December – *prior* to the incident?

'I was at work . . . as usual and after our lunch break, we were informed that half of us would be losing our jobs. The construction firm had over-projected and they needed to make immediate cuts.'

'How did that make you feel?'

'Angry. Nervous. Scared. I have a wife and two children. My wife told me a week before that she was pregnant. I didn't know how I was going to support them.'

'Can you tell us where you were when you got the call from the hospital, informing you about your wife?'

'I was leaving work. The line was staticky. They didn't tell me what happened, just that she was in hospital.'

'And what did you think when they told you this?'

'I thought it was the baby. I thought she was having a miscarriage.'

'So, you arrived at the hospital and located your wife's room. Then what?'

'My wife told me what happened. I worried about the baby. I—' Dad paused for a beat. 'I'm not proud of what I did. I hit my son. I was worried about the baby but that's no excuse.'

'That's all, your Honour.'

'Thank you.' Prosecutor?'

My solicitor rose from his seat. 'Yes. Cal, could you tell us what happened at St. Andrew's the day of the 30th December?'

I nodded. 'I-I-I—' I paused. I inhaled deeply. My solicitor gave me a reassuring smile. I saw mum, looking like she was about to spontaneously shatter like cracked glass, fissures spreading up her arms. 'He punched me.' The words came out, choked off with emotion. Tears pricked the backs of my eyes. 'Mum, she cut off her finger. It was an accident. I called an ambulance and it took her to the hospital and dad came and—'

Too much to handle. It was a tsunami blasting its way through a plughole and I couldn't take the pressure. I clenched my fists tighter, driving them into my eye sockets. Why did everything have to be so damn difficult for me?

'Dad came into the room and ran to mum. She said something— I couldn't hear her. Dad turned around and lunged. He punched me in the face and my head cracked against the window. Two nurses came in and wrestled him to the ground.' I didn't know the name of the nurses. Shame radiated from my chest. I didn't know the name of the people who stopped my father sending me to intensive care. 'Two security officers turned up and hauled dad from the room. I waited a minute and I ran. I couldn't—'

I rested my elbows on the podium, concealing my face behind my hands. My hands shook but I didn't care. Thirty pairs of eyes were trained on me. They'd already seen the tears.

'Would the defence like to contest this?'

'No, your Honour.'

'Does the defence wish to present?'

'No, your Honour.'

The judge reviewed the medical records and the witness testimonies. He shuffled papers and silence stretched on forever afterwards.

'It is clear to me that the defendant assaulted the victim. There is no contest here. I must take into consideration, the enforcement of the Protection Order, but also the actions of the defendant to willingly remove himself from a potentially volatile situation once the Protection Order terminated. I cannot ignore the aggression with which the witnesses have described the incident nor the medical records supporting the sustained injuries. Therefore, Mr Adams, I sentence you to two hundred hours community service, effective immediately.'

I didn't know if I was expecting relief but I certainly wasn't feeling it. I felt sick, like I was going to vomit up my liver in front of everyone. Sitting there in court, it hit me that the only thing I really felt for my father was fear. I compared the snarling animal that lashed out at me to the quiet demure man that followed the officer out of the court. Dad had always been careful and considerate. Had he always had this mean streak in him, this ability to change moods like an internal switch?

You think you know someone; you think you know what they're capable of and then they blindside you, but it's not the physical pain that gets you; it's the fear and the sadness that runs so deep you don't know how to extract it. It's in the marrow of your bones. It latches on to every cell in your body like a parasite until it fuses and there's no way to eradicate it without losing a part of yourself.

Mum looked over at me, her eyes clouded over so it was impossible to tell what she was thinking. She didn't appear outwardly sad but she wasn't blasting party poppers into the air either. I expected a reaction. Mum never reacted much these days. I wondered if I'd ever get her back, if she'd ever be able to transform back from the shell of a woman she now was.

Chapter 25

EXCISIONS

'Cal! Cal' Kayleigh's muffled voice sounded from behind Mrs Peach's double-glazed windows. Copping the McDonalds bag in mum's hand, she swiftly changed her tune. 'Chicken nuggets! Chicken nuggets!'

Mrs Peach opened the door on the latch. 'It's me, Mrs, Peach,' mum said.

Mrs Peach wore thick glasses that enveloped her face – one-part binoculars, one-part magnifying glass. 'Watch out, Melinda, there's a hoodlum behind you.'

Mum laughed, a fake laugh that sounded like the clinking of champagne flutes that changed her complexion. 'That's Cal, my son.'

Mrs Peach narrowed her eyes and grinned. It was ironic that we left Kayleigh with someone that could just about see. 'Cal, I remember when you were this big.'

I nodded, plastering a wide grin on my face. 'How are you, Mrs Peach?'

'Me? Fine, fine – never better.' Mum stage coughed. Mrs Peach unlatched the door and ushered us in. She proffered a plate of pink wafer biscuits and behind her back, Kayleigh made a face. I knew the biscuits must have gone off – Kayleigh would eat most biscuits, *especially* if they were pink – so I politely declined.

I noticed Kayleigh eyeing up the McDonalds bag wolfishly. We didn't stay long. Mum thanked Mrs Peach and we crossed the road to our flat. Inside the kitchen, I took the bag from mum and suddenly, I was Kayleigh's Number One again. Her 'chicken nugget' chant started up again. I dangled a chicken nugget as bait a few feet above Kayleigh's head. She stared at it with saucer eyes.

'Gimme, gimme, gimme!'

'What's the magic word?'

'McDonalds.'

I rolled my eyes, suppressing a smile. 'The *other* magic word?'

'*Pea*sssssssssssssssssss.'

Close enough. I broke off a tiny piece of the chicken nugget and dropped the larger piece. Kayleigh caught it in the air like Scooby Doo. I cherished that moment. It felt like the stone pressing down on my chest had lifted but that was only temporary because the letter on the kitchen table changed everything.

I rifled through the post, searching out anything for me. I wasn't sure what I was expecting to see. Bill. Another bill. A takeaway menu. A leaflet about health insurance. Another bill. I was about to throw the stack of letters back on the table when I noticed the last letter bearing my name, taped to a small package wrapped in brown paper. My name had been scrawled in barely legible letters like someone had leaned on a brick wall for support. I bit down on my lip, shoving it into my pocket as mum entered the room. I turned and smiled.

'Do you want any help cleaning up?'

'No, honey, that's OK.' She said it with so much energy; it was like having mum back again and not the hollowed-out carapace that had replaced her all those months ago.

'OK, I'm going to go upstairs and make a start on my homework.' If lying was a language, then I was fluent. I went into the sitting room and kissed Kayleigh. I might as well have been a ghost for all the attention she gave me. She eyed the TV like a god; ready to worship at its antennae morning, noon and night. I took the stairs casually, one at a time. When I got to the landing, I sprinted to my room, slamming the door harder than I'd intended. I unfolded the letter and flattened it on my desk. I traced the indented words with my finger, unable to fully focus as my mind drifted back to the time spent with Peggy. I held the paper up to my nose and sniffed. It reeked of cigar smoke. I smiled. I sat on the floor, back against the wall, facing the narrow window of perfect blue.

Cal,

I've lived seventy-five long years and if there's one thing you should know by now, it's that I'm a self-centred cow that's alienated most of my family and, because you're probably wondering, I should tell you now that I wasn't in pain. I've been in pain long enough to know the best way to face the music.

The first time you came to my house, I was deplorable. I thought you'd never come back but you did. You were persistent. I wanted you gone. I'd made my choices long before you'd arrived and I didn't need another variable, but you grew on me. You made me feel needed and wanted. I held on a little longer for you, Cal. You couldn't save me, not that far gone, but you re-injected a shot of life into this old crone.

You're a special boy, Cal, and Em will need you now more than ever. She's been hurting for a long time. My son wasn't a very nice man. I don't blame Em's mother for separating us but it broke my heart. I think it broke hers too. Thank you for being there for her. She has a lot to work through.

I couldn't think of what to leave you. I pondered it for weeks. You asked for my advice, Cal, but the truth is you have it in you. I stopped caring what people thought of me. Everyone tells you that things get better, that they'll get easier, but what if they don't? What if the bullies at school are at your university? What then? You need to do "you" because in my seventy-five years, I've never met anyone quite like you. When you embrace who you are, it'll be the best kind of armour against a world that's going to throw everything it has your way.

I've enclosed a present. I hope it helps.
Look after yourself,
Peggy

P.S. It's not a taser.

I ripped through the brown paper and opened the small box, expecting jewellery but instead, I found a small brass compass with elaborate metalwork across the front. I wrapped it in the paper and stored it in my sock drawer, next to Peggy's phone-taser. I felt the rigidity in my muscles. I didn't cry. I was all cried out. I couldn't pinpoint the emotions whirring around in my head. It was like my feelings had been thrown into a vortex, spinning around so rapidly that anger collided with sadness, the anxiety negating the shock. Left in its place was a dull hollow ache, like the piece of me that made me, "me", was missing. I couldn't feel anything – process anything. It should have scared me. Heck, it should have terrified me.

Instead, I looked at the healing cuts on my arm. I pressed down lightly, relishing the light sting. I opened the top drawer of my bedside cabinet, picking out a bottle of cheap cologne. I aimed it at the burns and sprayed twice. I pressed down harder, enjoying how it felt, loving how it took my attention off the visceral reality around me.

I took out my phone, tapping away in the search bar: "how to feel". I didn't know what I was looking for but the suggestions didn't help:

How to feel . . .Happy. I wasn't happy. I didn't see
how anything could possibly make me happy.

Better. What did that even mean?

Less tired. I wasn't tired, even though my dreams had
twisted into nightmares.

More awake. This was the problem.

Better about yourself. Fairy godmother service?
Instead, I hit search and read through a list of steps,
telling me about the "reward of healing" and "how
to feel alive in five easy steps", but I didn't want five
steps and I knew I couldn't be healed. I wanted a quick
fix. I wanted a one-step solution that would transport
me from real-life into my own little world.

I re-configured my search:

"How to make the pain stop". Suicide prevention
sites flooded my results along with ways to ease
heartache and support for turbulent relationships.
I trawled through sites for what felt like hours.
Eventually, I came across The Final Cut. I read
through the pages, ignoring the obscene drawings. I
shuddered, remembering how everyone told me

to off myself. I didn't want to die. I knew that suicide
was wrong so I closed my laptop and lay back on my
bed, letting my thoughts take me away on a cloud
of hornets.

I closed my eyes, trying to focus on clearing the painful thoughts that plagued me. Instead, images of Niall's snarling face loomed out of the darkness. The threats, the slurs, the beatings – it pressed in on all sides and I felt the air squeeze from my lungs. I remembered I had Em but that niggling voice of doubt creeped in and punctured that thought. Who else did I have? Mum was oblivious. Peggy was gone. Matt was ...

Matt. Why, after all this time, did I still crave him? Why did I still need him? He'd been so kind, so loving, but no matter how hard I tried, the memories of us together twisted and morphed so I was looking at a portrait of Matt and Alfie, Matt's smirking mother looming over them in the background.

I opened my eyes but the images poked and prodded at my mind. I pulled my bedroom door open

and listenied to the sounds of the TV downstairs. Kayleigh sang along to *Dora the Explorer*. I slipped into the bathroom, my heart doing double time as I heard the reassuring click of the key in the lock. I opened the cabinet and located my razor. I breathed in once and coughed against the overwhelming clinical air freshener that must have been sprayed in the last hour.

I took my phone out of my pocket and played the first song I found, something poppy and upbeat so the beats drowned out the noise. I grabbed mum's hairbrush and smashed it down onto the razor blades until they broke apart. I pocketed three of the four blades and rolled up my left sleeve. I held the blade with shaky hands. I just wanted to make a small cut – a distraction. I needed something to help me get past this hollow feeling eating away at my chest so I took the blade and drew it lightly across my wrist.

I watched the *drip, drip, drip* of the dark droplets splattering into the white sink basin. I held it above the plughole, watching them fall and imagining the hole as a monster – a dark vortex of sadness and anger – and as the blood dripped, I felt a sort of ecstasy. My thoughts sharpened in that one moment. I felt alive.

The blood flow eventually slackened so I grabbed some tissue with my right hand and wiped away the blood on my pale skin. I turned the faucet, watching as the water circled down the plughole, tinged pink with my blood. I did that. I created something that looked so beautiful.

I took two plasters from the cabinet and covered the cut, rolling down my jumper sleeve to hide the evidence. I entered the bathroom with an overwhelming hollow sensation taking over but I'd found a solution. There was no one to talk to. Mum was preoccupied with the pregnancy and Em. . . well, Em had made it perfectly clear that Duncan and Lizzie were her priorities. I stashed the blades in the bottom of my sock drawer next to the compass, in a pair of festive socks I no longer wore. I bounded down the stairs and into the sitting room.

'Where's the little rascal?' I shouted in a mock sinister voice. Kayleigh screamed, hiding behind the couch. She made a dash for the door but I intercepted her, throwing her playfully onto the couch. I blew kisses onto her tummy and tickled her under her arms, all the while, she protested.

'I'll get Barbie after you!'

'Not Barbie,' I replied, feigning fear. She took a Barbie from under one of the cushions and walloped me across the head. 'OK, seriously, not Barbie.'

'Tell Barbie, you're sorry.'

'What?' She hit me again. She was strong for a four year old. 'Ouch. Barbie, I'm so sorry.' I placed my arms out straight, palms facing the ground and bringing them up and down, as if worshipping a deity. Kayleigh giggled. 'I'll get us some juice.'

'Apple juice!' Kayleigh insisted.

I bounded into the kitchen breathlessly, like I'd been injected with adrenaline. I took out a sippy cup and a tall glass and filled them with apple juice. Pure. Fruit. Juice. Things were on the mend in the Adams' household. I carried them between both hands and set them down on the side table.

Kayleigh snuggled into me, drinking her juice. Out of the corner of my eye, I noticed mum peering between a crack in the double doors, smiling. I hugged Kayleigh to me tightly, like she was my lifeline.

'Cal?'

'Yes?'

'Barbie loves you.'

'Thanks.'

'Cal?'

'Yes?'

'I love you too,' she added, squeezing her tiny arms around my waist.

'You're in a good mood,' mum remarked, swirling a glass of red wine. She sniffed it once before sipping it. Her lipstick left a red smear on the rim.

'Yeah,' I fired back defensively.

'Get a glass.'

'Mum?'

'Do you like red?'

'Sure.' I hated wine but I might never have another opportunity to drink with mum again. I grabbed a glass from the cupboard and watched as she filled it halfway. I could smell the jasmine incense in the air, mixed with the fruity notes of the wine. I sipped once and tried not to pull a face. Mum laughed.

'It's OK if you don't like it. You can have whiskey if you want. A single,' she cautioned.

'Mum, should you be drinking if . . .' The baby was due in a month.

She twisted the bottle so the label faced me. 'It's non-alcoholic.' I felt uncomfortable under her gaze. She sighed, running a hand through her hair. 'I don't know how to do this.'

'To do what?'

'To say sorry. To tell you how sorry I am for everything I've put you through. I told your father about you being . . . gay and that wasn't for me to tell. Look where it's landed us. Instead of talking to you, I holed myself up in my room. I found ways to avoid talking about it until I started to tell myself that it had all worked out, but it hasn't.' I didn't know if this was a question or a comment so I kept quiet. Mum seemed to take my silence as confirmation. 'I've messed up royally. I want you to know that you can ask me anything. Is there . . . is there anything you want to know?'

'What were you like when you were my age?'

It wasn't the question mum was expecting. I surprised myself too. Mum brought the glass to her lips, smiling. She drank slowly, deeply, and placed it onto the table. 'I was . . . a wallflower. I watched the pretty girls match up with the pretty boys. I went to school. I had friends. I had parents that loved me. I had a wardrobe of pretty dresses and the last Friday of every month, mum would take me to get a cut and blow-dry after school. For thirty minutes, I felt untouchable. I felt empowered and when I went to school the next day, I'd shrink into myself.'

She got up and moved into the kitchen. Her voice snaked out to the sitting room. 'I never thought I was pretty enough, good enough, but I was. I was smart too but I got too hung up on things that were irrelevant. I almost scuppered my chances of getting into a decent university, but I did. I got into U.C.L. and I met your father in the summer. I fell fast and hard and within a year, I had you.'

'You didn't go to university because of *me*?' My voice broke at the end.

'No, Cal. I didn't go to university because of your father. I didn't go to university because he told me I had him and the baby, and I didn't need to work a day in my life. If I loved him, that would be enough.' She returned with a photo album that she placed in my lap.

'Your dad wasn't a violent man. He had it in him – I knew that – but he never hurt me. When your dad was a child, your grandfather used to beat him. If he spilled milk on the counter, left toys on the floor – little things. I'm not trying to change your mind, Cal. Whatever you do, I'll stand by you. You've been through so much but I think it's only right that you know what your dad has been through too.'

I flicked through the photo album as mum spoke. Mum, in the playground, her golden hair billowing behind her. There was one of her on graduation with her friends and she was right, she was by far the most beautiful of them all but you wouldn't notice her because the other girls take up all the space, hands cocked on hips, posing like they were on the cover of *Vogue* while mum had her hands by her sides, disappearing into the cracks.

'Mum.' I didn't know how to continue.

'It's OK, Cal. I'm not telling you this for sympathy. I'm telling you this because I see in you what I see in me. You're smart and handsome and you'll have all the girls – sorry, boys – knocking on our door. You're so good with your sister and when I look at you now,' she says, tears in her voice, 'you're everything I could have asked for and more. You're my Sun, my Moon, my North Star . . .'

'And I'll love you from near, from home and afar,' I finished, tears cascading softly down my cheeks.

'I've made a lot of bad choices in my life, Cal, but you were never one of them. Your father did something I can never forget and if it comes down to you or him, I'll fight for you. I'll never stop fighting for you.'

She motioned for me to come closer and I did. I bent down and hugged her gently, conscious of the eight-month-old bump wedged between us. I could smell the cocoa butter on her skin. I pulled away and took her in for the first time. I tried to think back to a year ago, before all this had happened, but I couldn't.

'Get some rest, Cal. I love you,' she whispered.

I walked to the door. 'Goodnight, mum. I love you too.' I was almost out of earshot when she spoke again.

'I heard about Peggy, Cal. I know how close you were to her. If you ever want to talk, you know where to find me.'

'Thank you,' I murmured.

I ran up the stairs as quickly and quietly as I could and flopped onto my bed. I left my shorts and t-shirt on, too sapped to take them off. I cried myself to sleep that night. I cried for the year I'd spent caught up on various boys and the daily drama of my life; days I could have let mum in; days I could have been reconciling our relationship. Most of all, I cried because she saw me. I couldn't believe I ever doubted her love.

Chapter 26

INHALE, EXHALE

Despite my upbeat attitude, I was already regretting the decision to go out with Em, Lizzie and Abi as we rode the Central line to Tottenham Court Road. This was my first time seeing Em outside school since Peggy. I pushed the memory into the recesses of my mind, forcing myself to focus on the present.

Abi seemed nice – calm and level-headed in a way that Lizzie was not. They were a cute couple and it was great to finally meet her in person rather than through Em's Instagram feed.

Why didn't Em invite me out on their nights out?

What did Lizzie and Abi have that I didn't?

Even now, surrounded by my friends, why did I feel so alone?

'Cal?' Lizzie interrupted my thoughts, proffering a bottle of what looked like Coke and smelt of gasoline fumes.

'No thanks.' I waved the offer away.

'We're going to a club, Cal, not a library.' She rolled her eyes.

'Give me the damn bottle.' Her green eyes glowed mischievously. There was something nymph-like about her with red waves of hair framing her freckled skin and her green playsuit that fluttered around her. She stood next to the window, leaning right back. She pounced forward with cat-like grace, handing me the bottle like it was a challenge.

I drank deep, tilting the bottle up. Abi pushed it higher with a firm hand. I swallowed three mouthfuls more than I wanted to, spluttering vodka down my t-shirt. Lizzie took the bottle. 'Jesus, good in the bedroom much.'

'Off, off, off,' Lizzie chanted.

'Off, off, off,' Em and Abi chorused.

They couldn't know how sensitive I was about my boy body, looking at the models around me with six-packs and huge biceps; waking up every morning to my pencil arms. Em knew though. Why wasn't she saying anything? Feeling the need to fill the widening silence, I asked Em, 'so where's Duncan?'

'He's visiting relatives,' she said, inspecting her black nails.

I breathed in deeply, noting how the liquid burned my throat. Why had I let Lizzie pressure me into drinking? Why did I find it so hard to say 'no' and stand up for myself?

The girls re-applied mascara and eye-liner as the train shot forwards. I was surprised by how steady their hands were. The train pulled into Tottenham Court Road where we rode the escalators to the top and swiped through the barriers with our Oyster cards.

Office blocks towered around us and shouts trailed us as we made our way to Soho. We walked past a Starbucks and swung left just as a London bus – a red, double-decker advertising *Kinky Boots* – zoomed past. Memories of Matt surfaced. I snatched the bottle from Lizzie and drank it dry. Anything to stop the hurt.

We cut through Soho, collecting wristbands at the bar before trekking on to the club. It was only a fifteen-minute walk but it took us forty-five minutes because Lizzie was wearing gladiator heels. Not to mention she was pissed. You'd swear we walked to Mordor the way she moaned.

'ID.'

We handed the bouncer our ID, praying he wouldn't watch Lizzie too closely as she teetered forward as elegantly as a rusty crane. He waved us through and I offered Lizzie my shoulder. The beats raced up the staircase to ensnare us. My foot tapped the floor as we waited to pay.

I stepped in front of Em, handing the man a twenty pound note. 'Four.'

'Cal!' Lizzie tried to give me a hug but it turned into a dangerous game of Jenga.

I held her hand, guiding her through the tightly packed club as I wondered why she would wear five-inch stilettos if she couldn't walk in them. Girls would always be a mystery to me. Lizzie shimmied her way between the boys at the bar, flashing a mischievous smile as she rested her elbow on the bar. Abi waited behind her while Em and I bopped awkwardly side by side.

I wondered what Em was thinking but stopped myself, remembering that this was a celebration; a celebration of the four of us being young and free, dancing the night away. I took her cold hands in mine and attempted a two-step that ended in me standing on Em's toes.

'Sorry.'

'It's fine,' she replied, taking a drink from Lizzie.

I took a glass from Abi. 'And the other hand,' she instructed.

I did as she asked, taking a glass in each hand. 'Two?'

'You're young, single and fit, I guess, for a boy. You're the only one who's getting laid tonight.'

'Oi!' Lizzie elbowed her in the ribs.

'What? Are you going to sneak me into your aunt's house and have crazy sex on her futon?'

'I was thinking the park but actually . . .' Abi ran a hand through Lizzie's platinum blonde hair, her other hand palming the side of her shaved head as she tongued Lizzie.

'The only thing worse than seeing you and Duncan kiss is seeing them kiss. It's like watching feeding time at the zoo.'

'Do you want in on this?' Abi motioned.

'No. No, no, no!' I stepped back but Em pushed me forward. Abi and Lizzie held down my arms, spilling my drinks as they pressed their wet lips against my cheeks. 'Ugh. Have I got lipstick on my face?' I asked Em.

'We're not wearing lipstick,' Abi said. I turned in time to see a flash of red lipstick. Lizzie struggled to hold my head in place as I wriggled. 'Now you do.' They giggled.

'What does it say?'

'Penis.'

'Very funny. Where are your drinks?' I asked Abi and Lizzie.

'We drank them at the bar. Hurry up, Tegan and Sara are playing.'

'Cheers bitches!' Lizzie screamed as I toasted Em and drained my drinks. Jagerbombs. I ran my tongue over my teeth. I inhaled deeply, waiting for everything to stop moving. I wasn't sure if it was the overbearing smell of sweat mixed with cologne, the rising heat, the music that pounded through the walls and into my bones or the drinks, but everything shifted around me.

We created a human chain, holsing Em's hand as Lizzie led the way to the stage, politely asking people to move and eventually barging her way through people who were too drunk to care or respond.

Abi and Lizzie's mouths moved in perfect sync with the words as they held hands and jumped around in circles. Em and I shouted 'closer' more than was necessary; the only word of the song we actually knew. I fist-pumped the air, embracing the beat and my ill-timed, ill-coordinated steps. At the edge of the stage, I felt like I could jump and the hands in the air would catch me or better yet, that I'd fly across the room to the balcony like an eagle.

A wave of dizziness hit me and I fell forwards. I didn't fly. I fell and there were no hands to catch me. A boy below me broke my fall. Em helped me up and I turned, ready to apologise.

Bushy eyebrows. Dark brown eyes. Glossy black hair. The room melted away and I couldn't form words. My mouth opened and closed.

Open.

Closed.

Open.

Closed.

No sound came out. I could feel heat rising to my cheeks and I was suddenly thankful for the flashing lights. Hopefully he couldn't see me blush.

'Are you OK?'

I nodded.

'Can you speak?'

I nodded.

'What's your name?'

'Cal.'

He held out his hands. 'Raj. Nice to meet you, Cal.'

'I should get back to my friends.'

'Sure. Have a good night.' He winked and my heart beat faster.

Em helped me onto the stage. 'What was that all about?'

'He wanted to see if I was OK.'

'Excuse me,' Lizzie interjected, but why are you here? You should be over there kissing that fine boy!' She jabbed a finger in his direction.

I took her hand, threading my fingers through hers, praying Raj didn't see. 'He's not interested and I'm here with you guys.'

'We're not going to hold it against you if you kiss a stranger, Cal. Go, have fun! Live dangerously.'

'I'll stay with you for a bit.'

'Fine but he won't be dancing alone for long and by then, you'll be wishing you were his man candy.'

'Man candy?'

Lizzie hm-mmed.

'Is that even a thing?'

'It's a thing now.'

'It doesn't sound like a thing.'

'It's definitely a thing. Who wants more shots?'

Lizzie marched past Raj, pinching his bum. He caught my wide-eyed look and I really wished the floor would open and swallow me whole. I offered him a watery smile before sheepishly pursuing Lizzie to the bar.

'What you need,' she said, jabbing a finger into my chest, 'is some Dutch courage.'

I watched the barman pour a line of tequila shots, placing a lime wedge above each of the four shot glasses and handing Lizzie a bottle of salt. 'Isn't tequila Mexican?'

Lizzie shrugged. 'You ask too many questions. Drink,' she said, sliding a glass towards me.

I poured a line of salt onto my wrist and brought the glass to my lips. I licked the salt, downing the tequila which burned its way down to my chest. I could feel it burn away the anxieties that had made this year an uphill trek. I sank my teeth into the lime, relishing the refreshing citrusy taste that made my tongue tingle.

Em appeared behind me, offering me something that looked orange. 'It's just orange juice,' she whispered, 'but if Lizzie asks, it's a double vodka and orange juice.'

'Thanks,' I replied, washing the jarring flavours from the roof of my mouth.

'Cal, is that—' I tried to pin my arm by my side but Em had seen. She caught my cut arm in in a pincer grip. I wriggled but it was too late. 'Cal, have you . . .?' I cast my eyes downwards, ashamed. I was too drained to cry but I heard Em sniffle. She tilted my head up so her eyes burned into mine. 'Please. Please tell me this wasn't you. Please tell me you haven't done this to yourself.' My silence damned me. 'But I was there for you. Why didn't you speak to me?'

'Because you weren't there, Em!' I burst out. 'You weren't there when I needed you.'

'I've had a lot on.' I could barely hear the words above the music. 'You don't get to tell me that *this*,' she continued, dropping my hand, 'is *my* fault.'

It didn't matter what I said. Em had that steely, determined look in her brown eyes. As she watched me, I couldn't help feeling like a butterfly with its wing pinned to the wall. Em had made her mind up. I didn't take the bait. I buried the resentment, the hurt, the shame – all of it, deep in the back of my mind because this was our night out. This was my night out and I wasn't about to let something like this ruin it.

Em leaned over Abi and Lizzie. I saw her downing the tequila shots, one by one, despite Abi's and Lizzie's protests. 'Hey!' they chorused.

'Greedy, much?' Lizzie snapped.

Lizzie and Abi raced after Em as she disappeared amid a sea of fists pumping the air, Abi's eyebrows knitted together. I was as confused as her. Em kept telling me she was there for me, that I could talk to her about anything, day or night, but when it came down to talking, she was never there to listen. Something was off but I wasn't about to bring it up with three tequila shots bubbling away in her stomach.

I spotted Abi and Lizzie next to an angsty Em, stomping unrhythmically to *Oops, I Did It Again*. Abi and Lizzie spun each other around, pretending to ignore her but glancing over every now and again.

'Do you want to get some air?'

'I can't hear you.'

'DO YOU WANT TO GET SOME AIR?' I roared, hands cupped around Em's ear. I took her shrug as a 'yes' and exposed my wrist for a stamp on the way out.

'Where are you going?' Em asked as I turned right, climbing the steps.

'Let's cross the bridge.' She followed sullenly at a distance.

I walked halfway across the Golden Jubilee Bridge, leaning against the railing as I peered across the Thames and tried to discern the shapes of different buildings of the London skyline. I spotted the Shard and the Gherkin easily when the smell of alcohol wafted into my face.

'What's up, Em? Where is all of this coming from?'

'How dare you say this is my fault. I've been there for you, protecting you at school, looking out for you. Where have you been for me? When my nan died?'

'Where were you before she died, Em?' I snapped. The words were out there. I could feel the gale blowing the water from the Thames, along with my words, back into our faces.

'Screw you, Cal.' Em turned on her heel, marching back towards the Strand. I followed.

'Em, I didn't mean it. Come on.'

I knew she'd never take my apology though, not with how much she'd drank. Why did I do this now? Why didn't I wait? I ran ahead, calling her name. I caught up with her as she tried to grasp the railing, missed and fell. I grabbed her hand, preventing the worst of it. She fell, banging her knee against the lip of the step. She cried out, fumbling for the railing as I hoisted her to her feet.

'Take it easy, Em.' Reluctantly, she took my hand and let me walk her down the stairs. Em didn't look at me, didn't speak to me as we made small steps to the bus stop. We waited among drunken men and women, snogging each other, shouting and singing, but all I could hear was Em's silence washing me away.

I stared at Em's bedroom ceiling, counting the cracks, staring at the damp leaking in from the corner. I inhaled softly, the musty smell hitting the back of my throat. My eyes watered. How did we get to this point, where we couldn't say two words to each other without an attack bubbling? This had all been brewing for a while though. I'd tried to talk to Em. At Matt's prom. After court. She wasn't available.

'Em?' I sat up.

She rolled over, the duvet pulled tight around her face. 'That was a low blow, Cal.'

'I didn't mean it.'

'But you said it. You said it and it had to come from somewhere.'

'OK, I've been thinking about it. I mean, Peggy wanted to see you and . . .'

'You don't know how hard it is,' she shot back stonily, 'to watch someone you love, deteriorate in front of your eyes.'

'You're right. I have no idea but don't pretend that my life is sunshine and roses. I get that you're suffering but I'm tortured at school. I went to court with dad and you didn't know about it until the day before. You didn't even ask how it was. You haven't answered my texts since Peggy died. I know it's hard for you but I cared about her too. I'm struggling too and you're not there when I need you.'

'Who's fault is that? I told you what you need to do, Cal. You let Niall walk all over you. Why should I have sympathy for someone that's made himself the victim?'

'I didn't ask for any of this.'

'Cal, my nan has just died, my dad isn't coming back for the funeral but yet, he wants me to move to the Caribbean with him. Become part of his second family. Leave mum behind. Do you think *I* asked for that? Life is crap but you can't hide from it. You need to face up to it.'

'Just like you've done with your mum?'

'Don't talk about my mum, Cal, not where your own mother would choose your abusive father over you,' she snarled.

I focused on deep breathing but it did no good. Everything I tried to hide, tried to push to the back of my mind, re-surfaced. Adrenaline pumped through my body and I ran.

'Wait!' Cal!' Em screamed as I closed the bathroom door, bolting it shut.

I tore open the cupboard, knocking toothpaste and cotton buds to the floor as I searched for the Xanax tablets. I needed something to distract me, something to take the pain away. I closed my mind, my heart racing. Images of mum, dad, Peggy and Matt burned into my eyelid. I cut my finger on a razor as I fumbled for an escape.

I stomped on the razor, separating the blades. I picked one up from the floor and with trembling fingers, I found the incision I'd made a week ago and pressed the shard to the scar. I sliced once and the euphoric feeling burned through my veins, commanding my attention, calling me into a bubble of ecstasy. I moved it an inch further up my arm and sliced again, sharper, more reckless.

I grinned madly, savouring the sensation, the endorphins and rush that incinerated the hurt, pain and guilt that raged around my mind like a tsunami. I pressed down on the cuts, willing more blood to blossom on my skin like a single red rose in a field of white lilies – something breath-taking and extraordinary.

I felt weaker but the feeling burned brighter.

'CAL!' Em's voice probed at my bubble, trying to burst it. 'Open the door!' The room folded in at the corners. 'CAL!' Em's voice railroaded towards me, dispersing my . . . I looked at the crimson streaks painted across my white t-shirt like a fiery sunset . . .

Chapter 27

CROSS-EXAMINATION

Beep. Beep. Beep.

'A swarm . . . a swarm of butterflies,' I blurted out.

My mouth felt like it was packed with cotton buds and my throat scraped raw. I gulped once, inhaled a deep breath. My hands reached out around me, chafing against a scratchy blanket. I groaned as the clinical disinfectant odour hit the back of my throat with every breath. Something soft connected with my hand. Fingers. Skin. I struggled to piece everything together, failing to blink away the bleariness from my vision. I reached up to rub it away but hands pressed my arm back onto the bed. Tubes rubbed against my skin.

I wanted to cry but my eyes were dry. I wanted to scream but my voice had left me. The memories hit me with G-force, leaving me winded and grasping the blankets.

Beep. Beep. Beep. Beep. Beep. Beep. Beep. Beep. Beep. Beep.
Beep. Beep. Beep. Beep. Beep. Beep. Beep. Beep. Beep. Beep. Beep.
Beep. Beep. Beep. Beep. Beep. Beep. Beep. Beep. Beep. Beep. Beep.
Beep. Beep. Beep. Beep. Beep. Beep. Beep. Beep. Beep. Beep. Beep.
Beep. Beep. Beep. Beep. Beep. Beep. Beep. Beep. Beep. Beep. Beep.
Beep. Beep. Beep. Beep. Beep. Beep. Beep. Beep. Beep. Beep. Beep.
Beep. Beep. Beep. Beep. Beep. Beep. Beep. Beep. Beep. Beep. Beep.
Beep. Beep. Beep. Beep. Beep. Beep. Beep. Beep. Beep. Beep. Beep.
Beep. Beep. Beep. Beep. Beep. Beep. Beep. Beep. Beep. Beep. Beep.
Beep. Beep. Beep. Beep. Beep. Beep. Beep. Beep. Beep. Beep. Beep.
Beep. Beep. Beep. Beep. Beep. Beep. Beep. Beep. Beep. Beep. Beep.
Beep. Beep. Beep. Beep. Beep. Beep. Beep. Beep. Beep. Beep. Beep.
Beep. Beep. Beep. Beep. Beep. Beep. Beep. Beep. Beep. Beep. Beep.
Beep. Beep. Beep. Beep. Beep. Beep. Beep. Beep. Beep. Beep. Beep.
Beep. Beep. Beep. Beep. Beep. Beep. Beep. Beep. Beep. Beep. Beep.
Beep. Beep. Beep. Beep. Beep. Beep. Beep. Beep. Beep. Beep. Beep.
Beep. Beep. Beep. Beep. Beep. Beep. Beep. Beep. Beep. Beep. Beep.
Beep. Beep. Beep. Beep. Beep. Beep. Beep. Beep. Beep. Beep. Beep.
Beep. Beep. Beep. Beep. Beep. Beep. Beep. Beep. Beep. Beep. Beep.
Beep. Beep. Beep. Beep. Beep. Beep. Beep. Beep. Beep. Beep. Beep.
Beep. Beep. Beep. Beep. Beep. Beep. Beep. Beep. Beep. Beep. Beep.
Beep. Beep. Beep. Beep. Beep. Beep. Beep. Beep. Beep. Beep. Beep.
Beep. Beep. Beep. Beep. Beep. Beep. Beep. Beep. Beep. Beep. Beep.
Beep. Beep. Beep. Beep. Beep. Beep. Beep. Beep. Beep. Beep. Beep.
Beep. Beep. Beep. Beep. Beep. Beep. Beep. Beep. Beep. Beep. Beep.
Beep. Beep. Beep. Beep. Beep. Beep. Beep. Beep. Beep. Beep. Beep.
Beep. Beep. Beep. Beep. Beep. Beep. Beep. Beep. Beep. Beep. Beep.
Beep. Beep. Beep. Beep. Beep. Beep. Beep. Beep. Beep. Beep. Beep.
Beep. Beep. Beep. Beep. Beep. Beep. Beep. Beep. Beep. Beep.

'Nurse!' Em.

'Calm him down.' A panicked chorus of voices shouted over each other. Someone tugged at one of the tubes and I felt something cold injected through the tube and into my bloodstream. I immediately felt calmer, the clouds in my mind dispersing.

Em was by my side, knelt down and staring into my eyes with a mixture of fear, sadness and relief. I gazed around the room, focusing on the white bed covers and blue blanket. I clocked the nurse staring at me and my heart thudded in my chest as I realised where I was.

'It's OK, love. We've given something to relax you. Press the bell if you need us,' she spoke to Em as she exited the room. Shame flooded my body and I looked away, at an empty vase on a bare table at the end of my bed.

'I'm so . . .' Em choked. I knew she was crying. 'I'm so sorry, Cal. I didn't mean it. I didn't mean any of it.' She reached for my hand again but I pulled away, like she was a disease that would infect me with a touch. 'This is all my fault.'

It wasn't Em's fault. It was mine. I'd let things build, ignored them, brushed them under the carpet. I was so focused on finding a boyfriend, so desperate to pave over the cracks in my own family and at school.

'Em, it's not your fault.'

'I didn't know about any of this.' I noticed my arm was encased in thick bandages. I couldn't see the cuts but I could feel them pulse under the bandages. 'I love you so much.' Her fingers reached for my hand. I jolted at how cold they were.

'I love you too.'

'I didn't mean for this to happen.'

'I know. What happened, Em? What did they ask you?'

She wouldn't meet my eyes.

'What happened?' My mind reeled. I wasn't sure that I could handle it but I needed to know what happened after I cut myself.

'I found you with the . . . and . . . then you were . . .' She took a deep breath and started again. 'I caught you as you collapsed. You'd blacked out. I rested you on the floor and staunched the bleeding as best I could.' I could hear the tears in her voice, the quaver in her tone. 'I called an ambulance. They cut you out of your t-shirt and they asked me . . . questions.'

Questions. I didn't like where this was going. 'Em, what did they ask you?'

'Lots of things. They asked me about your family and your history. I told them I didn't know anything about your . . . They know, Cal. They saw the cuts.'

Cutting had been a release. Me and the razor blade. Water washed the few drops of blood down the drain, a whirlpool of pink that sucked my pain down the plughole.

I tried to turn my head, but my neck was stiff and a pain radiated out from my chest that could have been guilt or the weight of the last month making itself known. Em wrapped her arms around me, anchoring me to this bed, to this room, to the moment, in the here and now. Tears *drip, drip, dripped* onto my neck.

'I don't know where to start. I don't know how it got so bad. The cuts – they distracted me from everything.'

'I wish you'd spoken to me.'

'I did, Em. I tried to talk to you at Matt's prom. At the park. You never answered, never asked. I get it, Duncan is a big part of your life.'

'You're still a big part of my life, Cal.' I looked away. I wanted it to be true. I wanted to feel loved and wanted, but I didn't. Words disappeared as soon as they were said. They lived in memory. Whether we acted on them or not was anyone's guess.

I ploughed on, desperate to unload the burden I'd been carrying with me for months. 'I cut myself a couple of weeks later and the escape – the control.' Em's eyes radiated disapproval. 'It took away the pain, Em. That's all I ever wanted.

'A distraction. But then Peggy died and she was the only one that would listen, the only one that I could talk to. The court case. Dad. I couldn't cope and when you . . . I couldn't cope.' I sniffled, hiding my face behind my hands. I didn't want Em to see me when I was crying, when I was ugly.

I resisted Em's efforts to remove my hands from my face but she overpowered me easily, pinning my palms to the blue blankets. 'I am so sorry for what I said, Cal. I've been a shitty friend. You're right. I haven't been there for you and that stops now. I had no idea. There's not much I can say about your family. No matter what happens, I'll be there, but this,' she continues, holding my arms out so I could see my bandaged wrists, 'is *not* the answer. This needs to stop. I've lost Nan. I can't lose you too.'

'I wanted to save this for your birthday but I think you could do with it now.' She handed me something heavy in a brown paper bag. It felt like a book. I unfolded the paper and carefully removed the present. I stared at the cover. In glittery, loop font, Em had spelt out "EXTRAORDINARY". I turned the pages, lingering on each image as I took in the photos. Em and I were in every picture.

Em tying my once-long-hair into pigtails on a reluctant, four-year-old Cal.

Em and I drinking wine from a juice box last summer in Abbots Park.

Last Halloween, Em, dressed up as Harley Quinn and I, in Batman's cape and cowl.

'You're steel like Superman, you have the smarts of Batman and the heart of the sweetest boy I know. You'll get through this.'

I fingered the Batman cowl masking my photo-identity and it made me wonder. Who am I? Who are we? Do we define ourselves by the people we meet? The things we do? The words that leave our lips? Maybe the thoughts that ricochet off the walls of our fragile minds? What we leave behind? What had I left behind?

A fractured family.

Holes in hearts.

Words that would never leave my lips; the same words that would let me spread my wings wide like an eagle taking flight for the very first time.

Pain.

Sadness.

Cowardice.

I was Cal Adams but what did that mean?

Sixteen-years-old.

Black hair.

Blue eyes.

Short.

GAY.

Was that me? The essence of me? If I filled a bottle of memories, what would I include? What had I done? Everyone told me to "be me", that I would be a shining bloody star when I embraced myself but I couldn't figure out who I was, let alone who I was going to be.

Em clicked her fingers in front of my face. 'Earth to Cal.'

'Thank you,' I whispered. She hadn't forgotten about me

'Knock, knock,' a feeble voice announced from the door.

Mum. I immediately averted my gaze. How could I look her in the eye? How could I sit there in the same room without feeling like the walls were pressing in and out? I fidgeted with a loose thread in the blanket.

'I'll leave you two to talk. See you in a bit,' Em told me, squeezing my hand once.

'Cal.' Mum choked on the word. Tears pricked the backs of my eyes. 'I'm – I'm so sorry.' Did I hear that right? I heard her shoes squeak against the linoleum as she strode towards me, grabbing me around the waist and embracing me in a bear hug. I folded into her like origami.

'I was so busy sorting things out, with Kayleigh and the baby that I completely lost sight of you.' She pulled back and pinched my cheek. 'Sometimes, I forget that you're only sixteen. I put so much pressure on you, looking after your sister. And your father, I should have spoken about it sooner but I-I—'

'It's OK, mum. It's OK.' It was because finally, I got it. I understood that mum was struggling with finances, making pennies stretch to pounds. I got it. I mean, things weren't great for me but I'd seen her at midnight, sleeping on a sea of bills and mortgage notices when I'd gone downstairs to pour a glass of water.

I looked at her then, ten years older than the mum I was used to seeing. Greying hair. Bags under her eyes. Cracks in her pale skin. Snot dribbled from her nose and I was acutely aware of the baby bump squished between us. When had she gotten so big?

'Can we go home, mum?' I widened my watery eyes.

She looked at me, really looked at me and I could see that emotion was tearing her apart. 'Oh, baby. We need to see the doctor.'

'It was an accident. It was one time and-and-and—'

I bawled in front of her. The pain of emotions bubbled to the surface. I felt the embarrassment and helplessness at school, the physical and mental abuse I suffered every day. I recalled Matt's betrayal. I remembered dad and how he hadn't wanted me. I thought about Peggy, how I'd lost the only person that had ever really seen me, noticed me, listened to me.

'Breathe, Cal.' A pressure on my shoulders. Mum caressed my hand as blind panic possessed me. A groan. A moan. A scream. Mum. The grip on my shoulders slackened. Mum. I could hear her. I focused on her, on how she was doubled over, clutching her stomach, clutching her baby bump.

I tried to push back my thoughts but it was like opening the vault for Fort Knox with plastic cutlery. I wheezed, watching helplessly as Em bounded into the room and back into the corridor, screaming, waving her hands. I thought about everything that happened, about how the memories were branded in my mind. I could never erase them. They would stay with me forever.

So why was I trying to press the DELETE button?

Why had I been trying to ignore them?

Why was I trying to pretend they didn't exist?

I opened my mind, letting them reach the deepest recesses, opening myself up to the pain and fear and the intimidation that already dwelled in the darkest corners. My arms shook and I could feel sweat beading on the palms of my hands. I inhaled a deep, shaky breath and exhaled a sudden burst of air. I tried again, focusing on me and the moment. Mum needed me. My heart hammered away. I focused on the *thump thwump, thump thwump, thump, thwump*, counting the seconds and feeling my heart beat a little slower, slow enough for me to fully open my lungs and inhale enough oxygen to stop the shakes, to see things a little more clearly.

I unhooked the IV bag and slid it onto the bed so I could kneel closer to mum. I reached out my hand and she squeezed tight.

'It's going to be OK. I'm here.'

A nurse rushed into the room, quickly assessing the situation. Two aides followed close behind, one pushing a bed. The bulkier of the two depressed the bed and dropped down the sidebar while Em and I watched.

The scene lasted seconds. I tried to follow but the nurse ordered me to stop.

'But she needs me. I'm family!' I shouted as she clamped down on my fingers, preventing me from unhooking the IV bag from the stand.

'You're a patient and you're not to leave the ward until the doctor sees you.' The D-word left a sour taste in my mouth.

'It's OK, Cal. I'll go with her. I'll be back once she's settled down. Everything will be OK. You'll see,' Em said, offering me a fragile smile. I didn't believe her. She couldn't make that kind of promise. I nodded as she grabbed her bag and scurried after the nurse.

The room felt big and empty without mum and Em, the walls expanding and contracting. I noticed things about the room that had eluded me at first. The *tick, tick, tick* of the black-and-white clock on the wall to my left told me it was 1.40pm. It reminded me of Peggy's bizarre, cat clock. The walls were a mint colour, reminding me of that time Em made mojitos and I vomited puce green into her toilet bowl all night.

I picked at a hangnail, tearing the skin with my teeth. A woman ambled into the room, her face serene beneath a beehive of jet black hair. A pen poked out the side. She wore black heels that *click, click, clicked* on the grey linoleum. She stopped at the end of my bed, flicking through my chart as she spoke.

'Hello, Callum.' Red flag Number One. 'How are you feeling?'

'Fine.' I kept my voice neutral, devoid of any emotion she might have tried to use against me.

'I'm Dr Dempsey. Would you mind?' she asked, gesturing to the chair to my left. I shook my head from side to side. 'I'm one of the resident doctors here at Whipps Cross. 'You're sixteen?'

No, I'm thirty-one. She had my bloody file open in her hands. I nodded. 'Tell me about last night. What happened?'

'I cut myself.'

'Why did you cut yourself, Callum?' Red Flag Number Two.

'Seemed like fun at the time.' I shrugged. I didn't want to open up to her. I didn't want her picking with acidic fingers at wounds that were still fresh.

Dr Dempsey slid her glasses off her face and folded them on the windowsill. She sighed. 'While I'm concerned for your wellbeing, Callum, there are dozens of other patients on this ward that need my attention and a whole other ward of people lying on trolleys in A&E that are waiting for me. So, while you lie there, avoiding my gaze, consider that. And,' she continued in a caustic voice, 'if you won't consider that, maybe you'll think about your family and your friends. Do you think they want to spend every Sunday afternoon wondering if and when their son and friend will wake up?' I would have cried but my tear ducts were empty. 'Stop!' she ordered, grabbing my wrist.

I looked down at my hand. I'd torn the skin with my nails. Blood trickled onto my skin and dripped onto the bed. I watched as Dr Dempsey went to the sink and grabbed some paper towels. She handed them to me and I pressed them against my finger. The scratch of pen against paper arrested my attention.

'What are you writing?' I murmured.

'You have no control, do you? Once you have the urge, you do it. You don't think about it. Is that accurate?' When I didn't answer, she pressed further. 'What goes through your mind when you have the urge to cut?'

Cut. I hated that word. I thought about Christmas time, at school, before the bullying started, when we used to cut out paper snowflakes and hang them on the tree at the back of the class. I remembered haircuts as a child when dad had to hold me down in the seat so the barber wouldn't scalp me. I recalled how mum trimmed the hydrangeas in our garden with shears during hot summer days. All that was marred now by the scars on my arms. I hated that nasty little word.

'This isn't easy and you're not the first person that I've seen that's self-harmed. For what it's worth, you're not the worst case I've seen, and there is hope, Callum. Things can get better. You can get stronger.' I bit down on the inside of my cheek. 'If you're not going to do it for you, please, think of your family. Think about what they're going through.'

'I just want it to stop.'

'Want what to stop?'

'The pain. I have so much pain inside me and I don't know what to do with it. It hurts.'

Dr Dempsey nodded like she understood. 'Have you spoken to anyone about this? Does anyone know how you've been feeling?' I shook my head from side to side. 'That can't be easy dealing with all of that emotion. I think it would help if you spoke to someone. I'm not saying it's as easy as a chat and a cup of tea, but we can help you.'

'You want me to see a therapist, you mean?'

'It's—'

'I'm not crazy.'

'Nobody thinks you're crazy, Callum.'

'Stop calling me that. My name's not Callum. It's Cal. CAL!'

'I'm sorry, Cal. This must be tough. We can help you.'

Why was it so hard for me to admit what I already knew – what mum and Em knew? I tried to think of the point where it all went downhill, where things started to slip out of reach. I thought I could control my feelings, box them up and feel only what I wanted to feel. God, I really was an idiot.

I thought of mum and the baby in her belly, and Em, and I started to realise that this had been something I thought I could control. I couldn't speak about the pain because it choked me. I wanted everything back the way it was, before dad lost his job, before I came out and my world turned upside down, but I knew that could never happen. I knew it wouldn't be easy but it had to be done. I balled my hands in the white sheets.

'I need help.' The voice, smothered by emotion, didn't sound like mine.

Dr Dempsey scribbled on her notepad. 'This is a huge step, Cal. You're really brave.' I couldn't tell if she meant it or not. It didn't seem brave. I was a modern day Humpty Dumpty and even I had no clue how to Pritt Stick the pieces back together again. It did feel right though, and the tension flushed out of my muscles.

A nurse opened the door and stormed into the room. Her eyes widened when she saw me. She stood on her tiptoes to whisper into Dr Dempsey's ear. Irritation flashed across her face and then something more indecipherable.

'What? What is it?' I asked.

'Your mother would like to see you, Cal. The nurse will take you to theatre.'

'Theatre?' I exclaimed, almost choking on the word.

'There have been complications with your mother's pregnancy.'

Chapter 28

EXUDING CALM

I put on my trainers and followed the nurse through the corridors and into a lift. All the time I wanted to shout at her to move faster. We descended to the lower ground floor and stopped outside a theatre marked LG-2. The nurse opened the door, ordering me to sanitise my hands. I slipped into the scrubs she held out and put the covers over my shoes, and a blue paper hat on my head. A scream pierced my ears. I made a move for the next door. The nurse grabbed my shoulder and squeezed.

'Your mother is having a Caesarean to save the babies.'

'Babies?'

'She's having twins. The umbilical cord is wrapped around one of the baby's neck. Speak to her. Keep her calm. If we anaesthetise her, it could harm the babies.'

I nodded.

We entered the room. Immediately, the overlapping *beep, beep, beep* of mum's and the babies' heartbeats sharpened my thoughts, reminding me what was at stake. I heard mum moaning from behind a half dozen nurses and doctors. The nurse guided me past them to mum's side. I glimpsed blood and fought down the urge to vomit.

Mum noticed me immediately and her eyes sparkled, distracting me from her ashen, sweat-soaked skin and the vein pulsating at the side of her face. She knotted her fingers in the covers and twisted. Two nurses held her in place. Mum reeled. What could I do to distract her? My train wreck of a life was enough to distract anyone but I needed to keep her calm.

'I love you.' I choked on the words. I reached for her hands and let her grasp mine. 'I love you so much. I'm . . . I'm sorry – for everything. It doesn't sound like enough. It's never going to be enough but when we get out of here, when we take the babies home, I'm going to look after you and Kayleigh. I'm going to make things right. I'm going to get help.'

I bit back the tears. I was failing her. I was letting my emotions get the best of me. *I don't know if there's a God out there. I don't know if I believe, but I believe in mum. I believe in her spirit and compassion. I believe in her respect and her love. I believe in her charisma, magnanimity and fighting spirit. Please let her be OK. Please let the babies be OK. Don't take them away from her. Don't take her away from me. Don't punish her. She doesn't deserve it. I'll get help. I'll look after the babies. Please, let me make things right. I've lost so much of me already. I can't lose her too. I can't lose all I have left.*

Whispers sliced through the room and mum groaned. *Oh God. What do I do?*

'I remember when I was four and you took me to Brighton and let me play on the stone beach. We got ice cream and the sun shone and I can remember the heat and the waves lapping against my ankles. I remember you tucking me in at night, reading to me, and letting me get into your bed when I had nightmares. Holding my hand when I got my first jab and you took me to McDonalds and told me how brave I was – how much you loved me.

'You're so brave and I'm here. I'm not going anywhere. I'm standing here and I'm done running.' I squeezed her hand tight.

'My beautiful boy.' Her voice was breathy, hissing through tight lips as she cut off the blood circulation to my fingers. 'Cal.' She released one of my hands and with shaky fingers, brushing a strand of hair behind my ears. 'I love you too, my amazing, incredible b-bo—' She screamed.

Beep, beep, beep.

The clinical smell pierced every pore in my body.

Mum roared.

My head spun. The nurses scurried around. I watched mum, eyes clenched shut. I had no idea what she was going through. The contractions. The Caesarean. The potential pain of losing something that you'd carried for over eight months. Seeing her son in a hospital bed, cuts branding his arms. Torn between husband

and son. I had no idea, but it was like a veil had been lifted and I could see everything clearly for the first time.

'The first baby is out, mum. It's—' I strained to overhear the doctors. 'It's a girl. Kayleigh has a little sister!'

Mum released a strange sound, somewhere between a laugh and a groan. 'Just ... what we all ... need.'

I laughed. Seconds later, the other baby was out. They rushed the tiny thing into a basket and wheeled him out through the double doors. Fear spiked in my chest. 'The second baby's out. He? I think it's a 'he' and he's beautiful – a beautiful baby boy.' I fought the acrid taste building at the back of my throat.

Mum's body seemed to shrink in on itself. She released my hand. I linked my hands tightly, fearing my worry would show. The nurses hurried about, cleaning up while the doctor approached mum.

Please don't say it.

PLEASE don't say it.

Please DON'T say it.

'Congratulations, Mrs Adams. You've had a boy and girl.'

'Can I hold them?' mum's voice was frail, like cracked china.

'Let's get you cleaned up and back to your room,' he responded dismissively.

Pre-birth, mum would have followed up and pressured him. Now, her hair was matted to her scalp and her skin was shiny with sweat. Her eyes creased heavily around the edges when she closed her eyes and sighed deeply. I wasn't religious. I didn't believe in God, but I still sent out a silent pleading prayer to the universe that my baby brother would be OK.

A whoosh cut through the air as the doctor pulled back the curtain, jolting mum from her sleep. Mum's doctor stood at the foot of her bed, framed by two junior doctors that held notepads. A nurse accompanied them, meticulously drawing blood samples and checking her vitals throughout the exchange.

'Mrs Adams.' Mum blinked against the phosphorescent lighting. The doctor hesitated. I knew what he was going to say. My heart thumped wildly in my chest. I dug my chewed fingernails into my palms. 'How are you feeling?'

'I'm fine. How are my babies?'

'May I?' he asked, gesturing to her belly.

'Of course.'

The doctor squeezed his hands into a pair of blue gloves. Mum loosened her gown. He asked her, 'does this hurt?' and, 'what about this?' Mum shook her head each time. I wasn't sure if she was lying. She kept peppering him with questions about the babies; how they were doing; when she'd get to see them.

His gloves made a slapping sound as he removed them. I anticipated the next words out of his mouth, instinctively inching closer to mum.

'Mrs Adams, the nurse will wheel your baby girl up to you in the next hour. Your boy – one of his lungs hasn't developed. We're doing everything we can. Right now, it's too soon to say . . .'

If he's going to die.

Mum wailed, kicking off the covers. The junior doctors wrestled her as she attempted to rip out the IV drip. She pushed them away and when her screams became silent sobs, they took a step back. I watched mum curl up into a ball and bite her nails, unsure how to help.

I didn't realise I was crying until hot tears tickled my cheeks. I ran the sleeve of my gown across my face and sniffled. I pulled up a chair beside her and massaged gentle circles into her back until she was still.

Please. Please let him be OK.

The sun blinded me as mum and I exited the hospital. I felt bad about leaving mum by herself but someone had to collect Kayleigh. A welcome gust of wind tousled my hair as I stared up at the cloudless blue sky.

I hopped up the stairs, two at a time, and wrapped my knuckles twice on

Ms Peach's door.

'It's me, Ms Peach. Cal,' I prompted, when there was no sign of her loosening the three chains bolting her door.

'Cal! You can't be too careful. Would you like to come in for a cuppa?'

'Sorry, Ms Peach: I need to get Kayleigh home and cook the dinner. Maybe tomorrow?'

'You're a sweet boy, Cal,' she told me, unhooking the last of the chains.

'Cal! Cal! Cal! Cal!' Kayleigh bounded through the hall, jacket zipped and rucksack on both shoulders.

'Bye bye, sweetheart.'

Kayleigh ignored Ms Peach, dashing two doors down to our flat. 'Look after yourself, Ms Peach.' I waved, running to catch up with her. Kayleigh had chocolate ice cream smeared across her face when I entered the kitchen. 'Cold.' Her teeth chattered as she showed me her chocolate-stained fingers.

'Come here. Let's get you cleaned up and I'll cook dinner.' I took a wet wipe from the table and wiped her face and hand.

'Cal?' I turned, a pot in hand. 'How's mummy?'

'What do you mean?' I tried to make my voice as chirpy as I could, to mask the pain and the grief that we'd endured at the hospital.

'Mummy isn't here.'

I swept my hands under Kayleigh's arms and hoisted her into the air. 'Mummy is at hospital and guess what!' 'Wha'?' I zoomed her around the kitchen like Supergirl. She pulled at my greasy hair. 'Cal! Wha'?'

'You have a baby sister AND a baby brother. Mummy is going to bring them home really soon.'

Kayleigh flashed a toothy grin and frowned. 'Are they sick?' 'No, silly!' I lied. 'They're OK but . . . well, because mummy has two babies, she needs a little help. She needs some rest and the nurses can help her.'

'Oh.' Kayleigh looked pensive for a moment, disappearing into the sitting room. She emerged seconds later, haphazardly bounding around the room on a pogo stick. I emptied a bag of pasta into the pot and half-filled it with water.

'Careful,' I told her, as I put the pot on the hob to simmer.

Chapter 29

EXTRA SUPPORT

'Hey, Kayleigh, should you really be drawing pictures on the walls? What will your mum say?' Em's voice emanated from the hall. I rubbed sleep from my eyes, sitting up on the couch as Em's voice reached me. 'Is Peppa Pig.'

'Where's Cal?' I couldn't hear Kayleigh answer. 'Cal?'

'In here,' I tried to say but it came out as more of a whimper. Em perched herself in the only armchair while I relaxed back into the sofa.

'I don't think I can do this, Em.' I let the words fill the air. If Em was surprised, she didn't let it show. I pressed my palms into my eyes.

'Hey.' She took my palms from my watering eyes. 'You will *not* cry on my watch.' Rubbing circles onto my left hand, she continued, 'you called me. You reached out, Cal.'

'I'm weak, Em. I can't do this by myself.'

'None of us can do this by ourselves. That's what friends are for.'

'But if I can't mind my sisters, be around my family, go to school, what use am I?'

'Your first therapy session is tomorrow, right?' I nodded. 'Write down how you're feeling. Bring it with you. When dad broke our family apart, mum took me to a therapist. I kept a diary of my feelings. It helped. It *helps*.'

'What – wait: you've been to therapy?' Em nodded. 'You never told me.'

'It's not really a conversational touchstone, Cal, and besides, this is about you. I know it's tough and if the sessions don't work out, we'll cross that bridge when we come to it. Just give it a chance. Cal,' she continued when I didn't speak. 'Promise me you'll give it a chance?'

I exhaled, my shoulders slumping. 'I promise.'

'Good. Have you heard from your dad?'

That caught me off-guard. Em asked about mum, about my siblings, about me. She asked about school sometimes, when she was sick but she never asked about my dad. She never picked away at that scab. The saliva in my mouth turned to glue, sticking words to the back of my throat with each swallow. 'No,' I told her, trying to force the words from my lips. 'He doesn't want to know.'

'Do you want him to?'

No one had ever asked me that. I pondered it for a minute. 'I'm not sure. I'm so ... angry.'

'You've never spoken to him, so you don't know what he thinks or how he feels.'

I wasn't sure I wanted to hear his side. 'Maybe you're right,' I lied. All the ways that it could blow up in my face raced through my mind.

'You don't have to do this on your own.' I'd heard that before. It was Em's mantra this year but every time I needed her, she wasn't around. A crash – followed by a howl – sounded from the kitchen, jolting me out of my reverie 'I'll get Kayleigh. You get some rest.'

'Are you sure?'

'Positive.'

'Thanks.'

Em left the room and I cuddled deeper into the couch. Em had let me down but that was in the past. My head hit the pillow and I wondered if it was something I could let go, something I could really forgive. She stood by me at school when everyone else skirted me in the corridors like I was toxic. She defended me against Niall. She made me laugh. I thought about how much Em has anchored me that year, how many times I would have drowned without her steering the ship.

I rolled over, facing away from the couch. I planted my feet on the scuffed carpet, expecting it to tilt suddenly and send me hurtling through the air. Em was slumped in the armchair, watching trash TV. Kayleigh was probably upstairs playing with her Barbies.

'How's your mum?' Since the hospital, Em seemed go probe more. I know she meant well but resentment bubbled beneath the surface. Whenever I asked her about her family, Em shut down. I wondered if she told Lizzie or Duncan. Probably.

'I'm not sure. She spends most of her time in the hospital.'

'That's understandable.' It was but something inside me didn't want to accept that. Something inside me wanted to smash a glass or kick the kitchen door in. The emotion smothered me every night and as much as I wanted to get better, as much as I wanted to heal, I wasn't sure that could happen. 'Your brother will be alright,' Em told me.

'I know,' I replied but I didn't know and it made me borderline feral. I wanted to shout and scream. I wanted to bleed the emotion from my heart and dissolve the thoughts in my head as they chewed away at my mind at night.

I didn't tell Em how buttering Kayleigh's toast in the morning was an Olympic challenge not to cut. I didn't tell her how I burned myself making the baby's bottle last night and it felt so good and at the same time, so bad. I'd spent hours asking myself if it was deliberate, unconscious. I should have been getting better but I felt myself unravelling.

'I have to meet Duncan. If you need anything – *anything* – you let me know.'

'Are you and Duncan doing OK?'

'We're good. He was asking for you.' Em confirmed.

I nodded. 'Tell him I say "hi".'

'Will do.'

'Are you mad?'

She stops at the door, her hand propped on the handle. 'No.' I believed her. 'We've all made mistakes. I've made mistakes. You're still here, Cal, that's the important thing. Look after yourself.'

I walked into the sitting room and sat down on the couch. I flicked through the channels before deciding I wanted food. I opened the cupboard next to the sink.

'Shush, I'm hiding,' Kayleigh whispered, hunched on two big bags of fusilli pasta, wedged between a box of porridge and an industrial-size bottle of ketchup.

'From who?'

'Em. I've been hiding for an hour now and she still hasn't found me.' She giggled.

'Em had to leave, Kayleigh. Come on.' I offered her my hand. 'Let's get you some ice cream.'

'Ice cream, ice cream, ice cream! Chocolate, chocolate, chocolate!' she shouted.

I spooned the last scoop of chocolate ice cream into a bowl and handed it to Kayleigh. Her face told me that she was not impressed so I took a chocolate flake out of the cupboard and sprinkled half of it into her bowl. She trotted off into the sitting room. My phone pinged.

> Em: Shit, forgot to tell you that Kayleigh has been hiding in the kitchen cupboards for the last hour.

I sauntered into the sitting room and plopped onto the couch next to Kayleigh. She scooted down a seat, shielding her ice cream from me. I laughed so hard that she threw me a funny look. In the moments of absolute darkness, I needed to snatch the moments of light with both hands before everything swallowed me whole.

Chapter 30

MEETING THE EXPERTS

'Hello, Callum. I'm Dr Daly.' She extended her manicured hand, a delicate gesture followed by a gentle shake, like a sudden jerk might cause my scars to open and bleed me dry. I glanced once at her face, at her dark inquisitive eyes and her small nose; the contrast of black and white facial features, defined eyebrows, dark eyes and raven black hair on a canvas of pale stretched-too-tight skin. I didn't meet her eyes after that. 'Would you like to take a seat?'

I sat but not because she told me to. I wanted to. Both of my wrists were scarred but my right one was marred worse than the left so I covered it with my left hand, trying to make it look like a natural habit. Her white dress was covered in embroidered

red, purple and pink blossoms in a dozen different shades, tied together by a deep, purple silk sash. I liked that.

'This is a safe place, Callum. Anything you tell me here doesn't leave this room. Do you understand?' I nodded slightly. 'Would you like to tell me a bit about yourself?'

I searched the room for something to fixate on while I decided how to answer that. The walls were a rich colour somewhere between gold and maize. She had a desk with a recliner chair and a small coffee table to the side with two, faded red velvet chairs. The floor was carpeted and when I ran my stockinged feet over it, it made me smile – though I never let Dr Daly see. She'd asked that I leave my shoes by the door with hers. I complied. She didn't wear stockings and her toenails were painted crimson red, revealing very little.

A vase of orange tulips rested on the coffee table between two, small china cups and a ceramic teapot.

'What would you like to know?'

'Anything you'd like to tell me.' She beamed at me with a smile that I was sure she'd spent the last decade perfecting.

I asked myself what I wanted to tell this woman. Not about Matt. I was still having a tough time dealing with that. Not about my dad. I hated him. And certainly not about school. 'I'm sixteen.' Two weeks ago, that would have been the easiest sentence in the world to announce but somehow, it felt like learning how to breathe again after a lung transplant. Why was it so hard? 'I have two sisters.' I didn't want to talk about my brother so I didn't mention him. 'And mum. Kayleigh is four. She likes Peppa Pig.

Arya was born a week ago.' Mum picked the names Arya and Aydin. I loved them. They feel bespoke. Special.'

She took a long sip from her teacup, motioning for me to do the same. I did and when I scrunched my face in distaste, she remarked, 'camomile tea. It's good for centring the mind.' She sipped her tea again, puckering her lips once, twice. 'What is your relationship with Kayleigh?'

'Well, she's my sister.'

'But what is she to you? How does she make you feel? How do you feel about her?'

'I love her.' It was the first thing that came to mind. It was as natural as breathing or putting your hands out when you start to fall.

'There's a bit of an age gap between you and Kayleigh.'

She let the words hang in the air and I thought, *duh! Someone give this woman a medal.* Mum had me with dad when she was sixteen. I knew I was an accident when I was eight and I heard dad complaining about going to Butlins again and that 'it would have been Antigua if it hadn't been for that bloody accident'. Twelve years later and I loved him now about as much as I loved him then. I knew what I was and what I was not.

I suspected Dr Daly's tactic was to lull me into a false sense of security and probe ever so slightly. 'There is but I don't love her any less.'

'How about your mother? What is your relationship like with her?'

I hesitated for a moment. 'Mum tries her hardest. She always has.' My voice squeaked before I finished the first sentence.

'This is a safe place, Callum. Anything you say here will stay between us.'

'I know.' Did I?

'I'm here to help. I want to help but you need to let me in.'

My shoulders deflated. How did I explain my relationship with mum to this woman? I loved mum. I really did but there was this huge, emotional black hole in my chest that I was struggling to understand. Every time I confronted it – every time I demanded answers – I found myself with even more questions.

The more and more I thought about it, I felt a pulsing headache at the sides of my head. I alternated between tapping my temples and massaging them with my middle and index fingers.

'I can't. I can't do this now. I can't talk about her.'

Dr Daly passed me a box of tissues with a kitten design pencilled on the outside. I took one and dabbed at my eyes. 'It made me difficult to talk about your family but here, in these four walls, we will need to discuss your relationships. We need to look at your support system and the people in our life so they can better support your recovery. If there is any tension, this needs to be ironed out. In this room, you are my priority.'

Dr Daly's eyes burned into me, eager to scribble notes into her notepad as soon as I left the room. 'I see many different patients, Callum, with many different concerns. It's my job to determine the best course of action for each patient. I'm going to make some suggestions, some you may not like but I'd like you to hear me out. The first, is group therapy. You'd sit in a two-hour support group session every Sunday and continue a one-hour session every

Wednesday as an opportunity to discuss any feelings one-to-one. The second, is family therapy.'

'No!' I protested.

'It's clear there is some . . . tension between you and your mother. I think it would be beneficial for the both of you. I fail to see how you can move forward without healing that relationship. The last option is to continue as we are though I must advise you that this would be the least beneficial to your recovery.'

'One-on-one. For now,' I added, addressing the unmistakable look of disappointment that she tried to hide from me.

'I'm also going to prescribe a course of antidepressants that we'll review each week. Citalopram. Take one tablet a day. Now, Callum, I must warn you, these tablets will take up to two weeks to take effect. It's important that you're aware of your emotional triggers; those things that upset and stress you. Navigate these situations carefully. The tablets will help but you need to put your wellbeing first.'

I nodded.

'Now, I want you to close your eyes and think of somebody who makes you feel safe. Conjure up an image of him or her into your mind as you last saw them. Think of what that person means to you and why you chose them. I would like you to bring this person to our session on Monday so we may discuss your relationship with them.'

'Monday?' I blurted out.

Dr Daly crossed her legs and placed one hand atop the other, pressing down on the silk sash that rippled across her lap. 'Your mother was concerned. She asked that we have some additional one-to-one sessions for the first week.

Mum. I didn't know whether to hug or slap her. She was one of the main causes of my messed-up psyche and now, I was enduring a weekly programme of therapy sessions like some nutjob. I thanked Dr Daly for the session even though it felt like one step forward and three steps back. Maybe that's how therapy worked. A little regression to pave the path for progression. Or maybe I was deluding myself.

I thought about the person that I felt most safe around, the person that came to mean so much to me this year. Peggy was dead. There was no way I could bring her to the session but I could bring Em. Peggy would want me to bring Em and maybe, therapy would help her too.

'Hello, Callum.' Dr Daly welcomed me into her office as Em and I sat side by side.

Same tulips. Same therapist. Different dress. Today, she wore a plum dress that cut off just below the knees.

'Hi,' I replied sheepishly. 'Actually, my name is Cal,' I pointed out, hoping I didn't sound rude.

'My apologies.' She waited a beat. 'Would you like to tell me who you've brought to our session and why?'

Em took my hand and squeezed gently. 'Em. My best friend. I brought her because . . .' Why did I bring her? There were so many points that she'd let me down but I let her down too. Maybe this could be a fresh start for the both of us. 'Because, she's my everything. She stands by me when no one else does. She helps me, supports me. I'm comfortable around her.'

'Nice to meet you, Emily,' Dr Daly extended her arm and shook Em's hand, correctly guessing her full name. Em just smiled sweetly. 'I think it would be useful to give me some context. Talk me through your friendship. How long have you known each other? Where did you meet? That sort of thing.'

'I met Em on our first day of school. Em was clinging to her mum's leg, afraid she'd leave her. Her dad had left a few weeks before,' I explained, 'and Em was afraid that she was being left behind.'

'My father—' Em froze, her shoulders tensing. 'My father left my mother. Up and moved halfway across the world. I was afraid of letting go and Cal saw me from the other side of the classroom. He walked up to my mum. He held out his hand and asked me to paint. I took his hand and he brought me to his table. He squirted blue paint onto a paper plate and we smeared it across our hands and stamped it down on coloured paper. I forgot about my dad and my mum. Cal helped me cope . . . when things got tough. I know what it's like, problems at home, feeling alone; feeling like you can't talk to anyone.'

'Thank you for sharing that, Emily. That must have been a tough few years. Can you tell me what Cal is like as a friend?' The scribble of pen on paper irritated me as much as the overwhelming scent of rosewater that forced its way up my nostrils.

'Cal is amazing. When I got older, learned what my dad did, he brought over cakes and listened to me rant late at night. We'd walk in the park. Sometimes . . .' She hesitated.

'Go on, Emily. Anything you say can only help Cal's progress.'

'At school, he's different.'

'Different, how?' Dr Daly prodded.

'He's not himself. I mean, he is, but he's not the Cal I know, and I get it. School hasn't been easy.'

'What happened at school?' Alertness hardened Dr Daly's eyes. I resisted the urge to elbow Em in the ribs. Dr Daly looked from me to Em. Em opened her mouth to speak. I cleared my throat and they watched me.

'She's talking about the bullying,' I informed her. 'She's talking about . . . this.' I remove my t-shirt and stand up so she can see the mostly yellow bruises.

'How long has this been going on for?'

'Since I started secondary school, but it's gotten worse in the last year.'

'Why didn't you tell anyone?'

'No one was listening. The teachers didn't notice, didn't see what was going on. Mum was preoccupied with the pregnancy and the bills. Dad couldn't come within one hundred metres of the house. And Em . . .'

Em looked beyond Dr Daly and out the flower-framed window. 'I've tried to help but he won't tell anyone. He won't ask for help.'

Dr Daly rounded on me. 'Have you told someone? Does your mother know?'

I shook my head. 'She doesn't know but I'm going to tell her. Tonight.'

'Well, that's a step in the right direction. Tell me, Cal, what can your friends and your family do to help you? How can they make things easier for you at home?'

271

I pondered that for a minute. 'Nothing. Nothing that they're not already doing. Em is incredible. I know she's there when I need to talk. She makes me smile when I don't feel like smiling. She makes me laugh when I don't feel like laughing. She's everything to me. I need her to just . . . keeping doing her.'

'Is there anything you'd like to say to that, Emily?'

'You need to open up to other people, Cal. You need to talk to your mum. If I'm not there, you need to be able to talk to her. I don't want to see you like that again'

'I will. I want to get better. I want to be stronger.'

'It's a learning curve', Dr Daly added. 'This, all of this, is going to help. I'm going to ask you to try something. Try sitting down with your mother in the evenings. Put aside five minutes where you ask her about her day. Tell her about your day. Let her know what's important to you. Let her know how you feel. It's important to have the support of your family through this process. You need to heal your home and you'll heal your mind. Thank you for coming to today's session, Emily.' Em nodded. 'I'll see you on Wednesday, Cal.'

'Thank you.'

I breathed a sigh of relief as we closed the door to her office. If the first session was like picking at a scab, then the second one was picking the scab clean and soaking the wound in malt vinegar. I hoped it would get better. I prayed it would get easier.

Chapter 31

ALMOST EXACTLY AS PLANNED

I heard the jingle of keys, the scratch of metal on metal as mum found the lock. She entered the sitting room, carrying Arya and Aydin in a twin baby carrier 'Come say hello to your baby brother and sister, Kayleigh,' mum announced.

Kayleigh bounded across the room, ogling them with saucer eyes. 'Can I hold them?'

'Not just yet, sweetheart. We need to be really careful.'

'Could you do mummy a favour and get their dummies from her locker?' Kayleigh bunny-hopped out of the room and up the stairs, if the sounds were anything to go by.

'How was your session?' I shrugged. 'That good?'

I thought about what Dr Daly and Em said and sighed. 'She

said I need to start talking and not just to Em. I need to start talking to you about . . . things.'

'Is that why you look like you're being marched to the gallows?'

'I just don't . . . I don't know how to talk to you. That sounded mean, I'm–'

'After everything that's happened, you're finding it hard to connect with me. I understand, Cal. A lot has happened. Twins.' She gestured to the chair and the Moses basket. 'Peggy. Your father,' the words curdled as they rolled off her tongue. 'I-I'm as much to blame for all of this as your father. How could I not see what was happening?' Her eyes watered but her gaze was fierce and fiery, like an avenging angel.

'You don't have to tell me anything you don't want to, but can I ask one favour?' I nodded. 'If,' she said, gritting her teeth, 'you feel yourself going back to that place, promise me you'll talk to someone? It doesn't have to be me,' she quickly added.

'I promise.'

'Thank you. I have to take Aydin to the hospital on Saturday. I know it's a lot to ask, but would you mind watching your sisters for a couple of hours?'

'Of course,' I told her instinctively.

'Thank you. I'm not going to pry. When you want to talk, you know where I am.'

'Thanks, mum.'

'Now, could you have a look for your sister? It shouldn't take that long to find the dummies.'

I glimpsed Aydin as I stood up, his fingers fragile like

matchsticks. 'Kayleigh?' I called up the stairs, my knees cracking as I arrived at the top. 'Kayleigh, where are—'

'I'm a baby too!' Kayleigh gurgled.

She lay in mum's bed, the duvet tucked around her neck. An assortment of teddies kept guard as she sucked on the dummy.

'What on Earth are you doing?'

'I'm a baby too, Cal. I need a blankie and dummy.'

I sat down beside her, clawing her hair out of her eyes. 'Is this because of the twins? Kayleigh, I love you so much and mum loves you to the Moon and back, but you have Arya and Aydin now too. Mum has to love us all equally but it doesn't mean she loves you any less. She'll be still there to cook you dinners and do your homework with you. I'll still be there to read you bedtime stories. Your brother – Aydin – well, he was in the hospital for a long time. He was sick and he's not as strong as normal babies.'

'Is he going to die?' she asked, hugging her pink unicorn teddy tight to her chest.

'Of course not. He's just a bit sick and he needs mum's attention for a little while. Aydin needs his big sister to be strong and right now, he needs his dummy. So, how about you bring it down to him?' Kayleigh kicked off the blankets, one hand cradling her pink unicorn teddy as she stomped out of the room. 'Kayleigh?' She stopped. I took the dummy from her and rinsed it under boiling hot water. I handed it to her and she ran down the stairs. I entered the room just as she placed it in mum's hand.

'Thank you, sweetheart.' She kissed Kayleigh on the forehead. Kayleigh beamed. Mum leaned into the Moses basket and worked the dummy into Aydin's mouth. 'Can you keep an eye on him for a minute?'

'Sure,' I responded, taking the seat she vacated. I listened to his raspy breaths, amazed at how something so tiny had the potential to knit us all back together again. I felt a bit like Humpty Dumpty; pieces of me scattered all over the place but slowly, this family was putting me back together again in ways that they'd never know.

I relaxed back into the sofa, something niggling at the back of my mind; something I couldn't quite put my finger on. Kayleigh plonked down on the couch next to me, leaning on my shoulder. Mum appeared at the doorway, holding a Kodak camera. The flash went off and Kayleigh looked at mum. I blinked. Mum. That flash was all it took to clear the fog in my head. I knew what I wanted to do; what I *needed* to do.

I sat, looking into the lens of mum's battered iPhone camera. I stood and brushed the creases from my t-shirt, stopping to pick at a loose thread. A pang of satisfaction pulsed in my chest as it started to unwind, reminding me of everything that led up to that single moment. I flicked my tongue over my dry lips and ran a hand through my greasy unkempt hair, seeing it flop back into place like clockwork on the camera screen.

I asked myself again if I really wanted to do this, if this was something I needed to do. Em never had to come out as straight so why should I have to come out as gay? Why should I tell the world that I was gay? Anonymous trolls would forever be armed with this information, using it to fuel their cannonball comments.

Fudger.

Batty boy.

Gayboy.

Bad enough at school. Could I endure people across the world seeing me admit what I am – *who* I am.

This isn't for them. This is for you. This is all about you. Peggy's voice echoed in my mind. That mentality would bow under the weight of a hundred users telling me to kill myself. Putting something so personal and intimate out there for thousands of people to view and critique, and it wouldn't be a book or a film or a TV program they'd be criticising. It'd be me. It was a huge part of who I was but it wasn't all of me. It didn't define me but I wanted to wear it with pride and for people to know and understand.

I tilted my head back, staring up at the ceiling, spotting new cobwebs above my closet. I inhaled deeply, breathing in the smell of the eucalyptus and pine diffusers that mum got me. She said they'd help me sleep at night. My sleep was still riddled with six hours of nightmares but I grew used to the smell, basking in the freshness and the lavender oil that mum dotted onto my pillowcases.

'I'm Cal and I'm sixteen years old,' I practiced but even though it was my voice and they were words that I had spoken before, they seemed hollow and empty. I tried again. 'Hi, I'm Cal. I live in East London and yeah, I want to . . .' I trailed off, my voice growing smaller and smaller, dissolving into complete obscurity.

I scratched at my arms and immediately stopped. I realised that I was biting a hangnail and that was worse so I took the bottle of Stop 'n' Grow from my chipped bedside locker. I twisted the cap and applied a thick layer onto my nails. The methodical process calmed me and the clinical scent sharpened my mind.

'Jesus, how did I get here?' The words were mine and they felt more natural, my voice strong like titanium instead of bending like iron heated over a Bunsen burner.

My nails dried and I started picking at the plasters covering my wrists before I realised it. I slapped my hand and bit down on my lip. I opened the first drawer of my locker and removed a small red, stress ball in the shape of a heart that Dr Daly gave me. I squeezed it hard and relaxed, squeezed again and repeated the process, inhaling and exhaling deep breaths until my heart stopped hammering away in my chest like a drum solo.

The funny thing that they don't tell you is that the urge to cut, to make the pain stop, doesn't just go away. It's something that sticks with you and it's how you process and plan for it that shapes it. It's asking for help and talking about it that keeps those demons locked away. If I had to go through it again, I wasn't sure I'd walk away from it.

There wasn't a quick fix for depression and anxiety. I knew this. I knew it'd be a struggle and a journey and there were numbers I could call, people I could speak to, pamphlets I could read but when I felt that way, I liked to process it alone. Not because I felt I had to but because I wanted to. I liked to think things through and find my inner strength. I knew I could speak to mum but I found it difficult when she decided to lock away every sharp object in the house, including Kayleigh's Crayola scissors which, let's face it, couldn't cut through Christmas card. I suppose she meant well but it made me feel worse. Given everything she'd gone through, I had no right to contest it either.

I knew she worried and I wished I could reassure her but I was too busy trying to figure things out for myself, making sense of where it all went wrong and the moment I lost my identity and threw myself into relationship after relationship with a bunch of shitty guys that made me feel worse; relationships that stole my self-confidence and self-esteem. I don't blame the guys I dated through. I chose to repress what happened with dad. I chose not to talk to mum. There were moments where she wanted to speak and I shut her out, moments where she'd invited me to share a glass of wine and I told her I was tired and lay in my bed for three hours, staring at the ceiling, wallowing in misery.

Maybe this video would help things and if it didn't, it would help me. It would let me help others and tell everyone who I was and that I wasn't ashamed. I wasn't ashamed to be gay. I wasn't ashamed to tell people that I liked boys but I refused to be defined as the "gay boy" because I was so much more than that. I had so much more to offer. To the guys at school that called me names and made up new nonsensical ones, I wanted them to know that they chipped me but I would never be broken. I might fracture like we all do but I wouldn't shatter like a cheap vase.

I was so much stronger than they would ever know. To the girls that laughed along with the boys, I wanted them to know that I felt sorry for them, that they would push someone to the edge to attract a guy's attention. None of them were worthy of my pity.

None of them deserved it. So, when I leaned over my chest of drawers and hit the red dot to start recording, I knew that while I had no script, the words would flow out of me like the Thames through London.

I sucked in one last breath of air, focusing on the smells around me and the subtle *thud, thud, thud* of Kayleigh downstairs, either upset that she couldn't have chocolate ice cream or pretending to be a dinosaur again. It was hard to tell with her.

'You don't know me. If you've seen me at school or in the streets, you might think you know me. You might think you know all there is to know about me but I've been keeping a secret for some time now and finally, I'm ready. I'm ready to talk about it.

'For the last year, I've been bullied for being who I was. I didn't even know what it was, who I was because let's face it, who at sixteen knows who they are? What they want? I barely knew what it was to be gay and the boys at my school spat it out with so much poison that I decided to hide it, that I would be anything other than gay because being gay was accepting I was different, and if I was different, if I stuck out in any way, I was punched, kicked, spat on, pissed on and threatened.

'Taunted for something I couldn't possibly comprehend.

'Tortured for who I was and not knowing what that even meant.

'Scarred, marked, bruised for my silence.

'But I'm done being silent because I've found my voice and I'm upset with myself for not finding it sooner; angry that I let this go on for so long. My friends tell me I'm brave but the truth is, I was a coward. I'll date outside the nightmarish prison my school has become. I ran away from my problems when I came out. I'll tell my friends and my family who I am and though I shouldn't have to tell anyone else who I am, I'm choosing to tell you. I'm choosing to own my truth. I'm gay. I'm coming out because it's my choice – my decision – and the bullies and the trolls in this school can't keep me quiet any longer.

'You can beat me, you can break my bones but as long as I own my truth and stand tall, you'll never break my spirit. I might cry but when those tears dry, when the stains on my cheeks disappear, it'll only make me stronger.

'This summer, I went to a really dark place and I let everyone push me there, but these scars,' I say fiercely, ripping the bandages from my wrists, shoving them in the camera line, 'are a reminder that I'm stronger than you might think and what doesn't kill me will always make me stronger.

'To anyone that's watching this, questioning, unsure of themselves, feeling like they've only got one choice left, remember that there are always choices and while this has been a tough road for me, I wouldn't change it for the world. The people that love you will accept and support you,' I mused, thinking about Em, mum and Peggy. 'And the people that don't accept it – well, that says more about them than it does about you.' I stared pointedly into the camera, channelling my father and Niall.

'There are thousands of people out there that will love you. Surround yourself with the people that love you and love yourself.'

I put down the camera, exhaling the pent-up emotion from the last nine months, expelling it from my body.

Things get better.
Things will get better.
Mum. Kayleigh. The twins. Em. People that love you. Reasons to live.
Live for you. Love you.

Chapter 32

EXHIBITION

'Are you sure you're ready for this?' Em asked but I could still feel the tickle of her felt tip pen along my ribs. I'd have laughed if it weren't for the words she inked across my skin.

'No,' I answered honestly, 'but I'm tired of pretending.'

This was the scariest thing I'd ever done. Exposing myself to the school. Letting them see every inch of who I was. I balled my hands into fists, released them and waggled my fingers, exhaling the tension from my body. I'm not sure if it was something I needed to do but I knew that I wanted to and that was enough for me.

I used the bar on the wall of the disabled toilet to lower myself onto the cold, grubby tiles. I tore the packet open and took out the spare fine-tipped marker. I started scrawling across my bare legs while Em worked the tip of her marker down my back, curlicues and gentle flicks so beautiful on words that were pure poison. It almost felt therapeutic.

Almost.

I remembered what would happen when we finished, and my skin was concealed by my rough scrawl and Em's loopy script. *What am I doing?* Em shook me, jolting my head back and forth.

'Sorry, you looked like you were doubting yourself,' she announced, caressing my head, 'don't.'

I could feel the ink pressing down on my skin like tiny weights, accumulating into hundreds of kilograms of secrets that I'd been holding onto for years and now, the whole school was about to find out who I really was. I bit down on my lip hard, relishing the pain.

Em pressed her palms down onto my shoulders, forcing me to face her. I noticed that she wore a new fragrance, spicier than I was used to but not unpleasant. 'Look, there's some things I can help with and others I can't. This is one of those things I can help you prepare for but you need to do this alone. I know you're frightened but think of it this way, they already think you're gay. They already taunt you. What's the worst they can do?' I looked down at the ground because there was a lot Niall could do and had done. 'Look at me,' she ordered, forcing my chin up with a vice-like grip. 'I love you. I'll stick by you no matter what happens. You're so brave doing this and the people that love you will stick by you.'

'Great, one person will stick by me.'

'Do I need to slap you again? You're not a leper, Cal. There are people that like you, love you even. You've been through so much and I refuse to throw you to have a pity parade. Jesus,' she added, 'you could at least try to look like you're headed somewhere a little better than the electric chair.' Em unlatched the cubicle door. 'Ready?' I nodded. Em took my uniform and stuffed it into her rucksack.

I pushed out of the bathroom. My feet were cold against the chequered marble floor. The bell rang and students filed out of their classes, slapping each other on the back. The girls whispered and gossiped while the boys guffawed and shoved each other out the doors. I waited for them to see me. Even though it was freezing in the hall, I was burning up with the heat as one by one, their gazes locked onto my boy body.

Every part of me that I loathed, my big hips, my pale skin, my skinny legs were on display for the whole school. Some looked confused. Others laughed. A couple of boys aimed their iPhones at me. I fixed a smile on my face and cocked my hip. I wouldn't let them see my fear. I wouldn't feed them my tears.

I marched determinedly down the hall, to the west wing of our school. I wanted Niall to see me. I wanted him to see my bravery and how strong I was.

I reached the Physics lab and Niall marched towards me with Gareth and John flanking him. He smirked. Gareth looked to Niall for direction and John was clearly baffled. I didn't have their bodies. I didn't have their footballer thighs and six packs but I was slowly beginning to love what I did have, what I've always had. They didn't have my smarts or my charisma.

They walked towards me, a head-on collision. 'Careful,' I

whispered, smiling at how I kept the tremor out of my voice, 'you wouldn't want to catch *gay*.' I deliberately knocked Niall's shoulder and moved forward. The bathroom was about twenty steps away. I was almost there. My hand touched the cold metal. I pushed, Em close behind me, her phone aimed at my back. I walked to the nearest stall while Em threw her weight against the door. She slid her rucksack across the tiles and I picked it up.

'Cal.' My hand was on the doorframe. I looked at the bank of mirrors. Shit. Cam. 'What are you—?'

I turned so he could take in the full spectacle. 'Ta-da.' I waved my hands dramatically.

He came closer, his fingers pressing lightly on the words I'd branded into my skin. My skin tingled where he touched me. I took a pair of jeans from Em's bag and slipped them over my hips, turning my back to him. I felt so vulnerable under his gaze.

'Why?'

'Because I'm tired, Cam. I'm tired of everyone in this school hating me for something I haven't even figured out. I want to just go to school one day without being beaten up but that doesn't happen so, I might as well give the school a show. I want them to see that I'm stronger than a handful of words.'

'But I've always thought you were strong.'

'But you never told me.'

'I tried to show you. I tried to talk to you and show you I cared. I left a message on your locker.'

'Wait – what?'

'I'm here . . .'

'That was you?'

'Signs of a serial killer,' Em interjected.

'I didn't – I mean—'

'It's OK. I understand.' It made me smile, seeing Cal blush.

I understood now.. I shut him out. I remembered when Niall locked me in the storage cage. He tried to ask me if I was OK and I shut him out. 'I'm sorry.' I looked at the tiles on the floor, distracting myself by the patterns because I couldn't look at the hurt twisting his infectious smile into sadness. I was such an idiot. I'd spent the last year ignoring my friends and my family because I wanted someone to care about me and all along, I had someone who was listening all that time.

'It's OK . . . as long as you're OK?' It sounded like a question but I didn't say anything. 'I wish . . . I wish you didn't have to go through this – all of this to discover that.' He hugged me. I relaxed. 'Have you still got your marker?' Em cleared her throat and handed it to him. The felt tip grazed the bare skin under my nipple and I smiled as his loopy letters tickled me. He finished, popping the lid on the marker with a *click*. He opened my fist and curled my finger around the marker. 'Look after yourself, Cal.' Em moved aside and let him exit the bathroom.

I rushed to the line of sinks, leaning over the basin to peer into the mirror. I was dazed, unable to clearly make out the reverse message.

'What does it say?'

'It says "Brave."'

Tears leaked down my cheeks.

I cried for everything I'd lost up until then and everything I'd gained.

I cried for all the pain I had to go through to get to this point and the pain I had unintentionally inflicted.

I cried for each of the boys I willingly and stupidly gave my heart to.

I cried because I wasn't smart enough when I needed to be, stronger when I ought to have been.

I cried because it took a hospital trip to realise what an amazing support network I had.

I cried for the old Cal, the Cal that was naïve and should have known better, but the new me – the new Cal – he knew better and he'd love as loud and as proud as he possibly could. I wouldn't cry another moment for the people that had hurt me. I'd cried my tear ducts dry and the only tears I'd offer up from this point on would be for the people I loved and loved me. The only tears I'd shed would be out of love because that's what I wanted all along.

L.

O.

V.

E.

Dr Daly's glasses rested on the bridge of her nose. The vase held new flowers, orchids maybe, I couldn't be sure.

'How did that make you feel, Cal?' she asked, after I'd finished telling her about my stunt at school.

'Nervous. Queasy . . .' There were so many words to describe how I'd felt but there was one bobbing above the others. 'Free.'

'That's great. "Coming out" is a big deal but you did it in front of the whole school. That's incredibly admirable.'

'Thank you.'

'How are you feeling now?'

'Lighter. Positive Hopeful. Everything feels easier. I guess I didn't know how much the secret was weighing me down.'

'That's excellent. Sometimes we're not aware of subconscious thoughts and feelings. We push things to the back of our mind, repress experiences, but they manifest in other ways. What about the urges? How are you coping?'

'It's still there. When I get stressed or upset, my mind wanders. I've been using the stress ball though and the tablets have helped.'

'For most people, self-harm isn't something that ever goes away. It's a very visceral struggle but you seem to be coping well. It's important that you don't put yourself in any situations that might cause you additional stress as you recover. I'm glad to hear you're making strides. How is your relationship with your mother?'

A loaded question if ever there was one. I felt more comfortable around her now than I did a month ago. I felt like I could ask her anything but guilt also radiated from my chest when I thought about how I'd shouted at her; how I shut her out when all she was trying to do was help.

'That good?' I tried not to smile. Who knew Dr Daly was capable of humour?

'We're getting there.'

'OK. So, why can't you look me in the eye and say that?'

'Because it's still ... I'm still ...'

'Breathe, Cal.' She waited a beat. 'Therapy is supposed to help you. It's not always going to be fun but when we work through your issues, you'll be in a much better place.'

'I guess I'm feeling guilty. Mum tried to help me and I shut her out. I should have supported her better during her pregnancy. So yes, I feel pretty shit thinking about me shouting at my pregnant mother, going out with boys and having my heart broken, when she still stands by me after all the mistakes I've made and that I'm still making.'

'What makes you think that you're still making mistakes?'

I pulled up my sleeves, showing her the cuts. 'This – all of it – it's not going away and I'm still having thoughts. When I'm in Biology, I'm thinking it would be so easy to pocket the scalpel and make a slight cut in the toilets; to release a bit of the pain because *this* is so hard.' The words flowed out of my cracked lips. 'Everyone keeps telling me it gets better and "you're doing great,"' I mimicked, 'but you know what? They have no clue how hard this is for me. They have no idea how I'm feeling and all they can do is offer me up empty words. They don't know how addictive it is, or the guilt that I'm feeling for all the things I've done to all the people I care about. They have no idea what it feels like to feel like every part of your life is this . . . *square*; I'm a circle and school, my home life, being with my friends – it's all square – and the only time I actually felt like a square was when I was with Matt or the other guys that wore me down.'

She offered me a box of tissues. I took two sheets and she placed the box on the table next to her. She spoke as I dabbed at my eyes. 'You're right. The people surrounding you, they have no idea what you're going through.' She flicked through the pages of her diary and scribbled something down. 'Maybe speaking to someone your own age, someone that's been where you've been might benefit you.' I remained silent. What did I say to that? 'And as for the guilt you're harbouring, you need to let it go. Guilt is such an ugly thing. If you let it, it'll smother you. You need to let it go, find a way to work through and process it.'

'I've been trying but—'

'What if you wrote letters? What if you wrote down your feelings? It might help you make sense of your emotions and thoughts. You don't have to send them but as an exercise, it might prove therapeutic.'

It took me a moment to take it all in. I could write what I couldn't say. I thought about her offer, to put me in touch with someone that had been where I'd been; someone I could relate to. Would that help? Was I ready for that step? Would it really make things easier? I didn't see how it could make it any worse.

'If I did want to meet this person, how would it happen?'

'It would happen here in my office. I'd introduce you, maybe stay for a few minutes and leave you to chat or, if you felt more comfortable, I could stay for the full session.'

I nodded, wondering if talking to someone who'd been through it would help me. 'This person, they've recovered. I mean, they're doing well?'

The muscles in her face relaxed. 'Yes. Very well indeed. I wouldn't put you in contact that with someone I believe would cause you any pain or distress. You still have a way to go. I can prescribe different medications and treatments but it all comes down to you, Cal. It comes down to you and those thoughts and you need to exert control over them. You need to be strong. I honestly believe talking to someone that's been where you've been might help you.'

At some point, I had to listen. I had to open myself up to healing. 'Yes,' I told her, 'I'll do it.'

'Excellent. I'll speak to him today and see when he's free.'

Chapter 33

EXTENDING APOLOGIES

I paused at Leytonstone tube station, recalling all the times I passed by this spot. Nights out in Central London with the girls. Trips to Abbotts Park with Em. Prom with Matt. I faced the tree, running my fingers over the message carved there:

The world is watching, Cal,
so give them something
to watch.

I'd never noticed it before. It wasn't Em's style and mum was busy with the twins. Peggy couldn't leave the house alone. Who did that leave?

'Looks like you took my advice then.' The voice sounded behind me, making the hairs on the back of my neck rise.

'Matt. You did this?' He nodded. Matt's voice still made butterflies flutter in my stomach. I remembered our kisses; how we melted into one another, lying beside him in his bed; slow dancing alongside him, hands on hips as we glided across the dancefloor. He looked as beautiful as ever, as groomed and clean-cut. I immediately picked up on the sadness in his blue eyes though, missing the sparkle that I was so used to seeing.

He picked at a loose thread on his jumper, so unlike the boy I fell for. I couldn't help looking at Matt's Instagram pics. No signs of Alfie but there was a boy in his photos. I can't say that didn't hurt. 'Cal. I—'

'Let's talk over coffee.' We walked across the road. I held the café door open. 'A latte and a gingerbread latte,' I told the barista. Matt tried to hand him a ten pound note but I put one hand on his and tapped the card reader with my debit card. 'I got this.'

'Thanks.' The hiss of steam and the gurgle of espresso shots mingled with excited chatter. My heart wouldn't stop beating. I tried to tell myself it was because the noise set me off but I knew better. 'Cal.' Matt took my hands. I recoiled. He breathed deeply. His musky cologne made me reminisce about all the good times; movie nights, coffee dates and our trip to the theatre. 'I probably deserve that. I know you might not believe me but Alfie planned that photo. He planned to split us up. I didn't know anyone was watching, let alone taking a photograph.'

'Thanks,' I told the barista, taking my coffee. I walked to the door and held it open, keeping my distance from Matt. 'Would it have changed things if you'd known?' I asked.

'He's my ex, Cal. We have history. I can't ignore him but I also can't pretend that the one-second flash showed exactly what happened.'

'You really hurt me.'

'I know. I tried to make things right. You blocked me, ejected me from your life, stopped going to Armin's classes.'

I pondered that briefly. 'It wasn't easy for me.'

'Is there a chance – *any* chance we could get back together?'

If Matt had asked at the wrong time, I might have said 'yes' but so much had changed. I was confronting my demons. I'd announced who I was to the whole school – the whole world. Everyone knew who I was. I had a baby brother and two sisters that needed me. Everything had changed. *I* had changed and I knew then that things could never go back to the way they were.

'I'm sorry, Matt.' I moved in for a hug, holding Matt the way he held me when I'd seen mum with dad.

'Can we be friends?'

Could we be friends? 'I'm not sure.' I paused a beat. 'I have a lot to work through. Maybe . . . maybe when I work through my own issues, we could go for coffee?'

'Gingerbread lattes?' Matt piped chirpily.

'Regular lattes,' I deadpanned.

'I miss you, Cal.'

'I miss you too, Matt.' It was true. I missed him but I wasn't sure there was another chapter in our book, if there was anything left to read. If there was, I was in no state to take that chance.

'That video was something else.'

'You saw it?'

'Saw it? I bet everyone in East London has seen it!'

That made me instantly queasy. I pressed 'publish', pushed the video out into the world, but I'd ignored the buzzing notifications in my pocket throughout the day. I didn't want to know what people thought. I didn't think I was ready to face it.

'I can't believe you ever compared yourself to Alfie.'

'What do you mean?' A knee-jerk reaction.

'You're brave and kind and compassionate. Alfie is none of those things.'

'But Alfie is rich and beautiful.'

'You're beautiful.' I hoped I wasn't blushing. I stopped at the foot of the pedestrian bridge. 'Sorry, but you are.'

'I have to meet Em,' I said, diverting the conversation.

'Where are you headed?'

'Abbotts Park.'

'Cool, I can walk you there.'

I wanted to tell Matt 'no', that I was OK, but I couldn't help falling back into that comfortable companionable space I found myself in six months ago. It was one of the only times I can remember us walking in silence, but I liked it.

I spotted Em pacing back and forth at the park gates. 'This is me,' I announced, hoping he wouldn't want to walk me right up to the gate. 'Take care, Matt.'

'Take care, Cal.' He hugged me tight. I could feel his lingering touch on my shoulder, around my back. I sensed him watching me as I made my way over to Em.

Em's eyes narrowed. I looked over my shoulder at Matt, sheepishly waving. 'What's he doing here?' she snarled.

'Em, it's OK. I invited him. I needed to speak to him. I needed . . . closure.'

Em stopped tensing. 'OK, but if he breaks your heart again then I'm going to break his face.'

I didn't tell Em that you couldn't break a heart again when it was already broken. 'It's not like that. We're just . . .'

'Just?' Em pressed.

'Just friends, I guess.'

'OK, but if he hurts you again, I'm going to hurt him.'

I rolled my eyes. 'What's in the bag?' I asked, eyeing the massive carrier bag by her feet.

'I'm glad you asked.' My stomach cramped with dread. 'We're going rollerblading.'

'OK,' I agreed reluctantly, 'but only if I can have the blue blades.'

She handed me the pink rollerblades. We walked to a nearby bench and slipped off our trainers. I tried to do the clasps on the rollerblades and failed. Em flicked them into place with ease. 'You're freakishly strong.' Em shrugged, handing me a helmet and kneepads. 'Aren't you going to wear anything?'

'Pros don't need helmets.'

'Are you saying I'm not a pro?'

'I'm saying that you've the coordination of a newborn pup at the best of times.'

'Thanks.'

I fastened the Velcro straps and clicked the helmet in place. It immediately started to itch but I tried to ignore it, determined to prove Em wrong. I stood up, slipped and immediately fell on my bum.

'Smooth,' Em chimed.

'Aren't you going to help me up?'

'Help yourself.'

'Rude.'

I crawled onto my knees, hands clamped around the bench as I tried to balance one skate, then the other. The skates diverged and I was a centimetre away from ripping the seams in my jeans. I exhaled, bringing my legs together.

'It's like riding a bike.'

It was, only, I'd never learned to ride a bike. The spokes on the wheel terrified me as a toddler, almost as much as the wheels on these skates gave me palpitations. I released one hand from the bench. Finger by finger, I let go and stood tall, knees slightly bent.

'I'm doing it!' I exclaimed, rolling gently forwards.

'You absolute daredevil. Now come on,' Em grabbed my hand and skated beside me, hoisting me alongside her.

'This is a bit too fast, Em,' I cried out.

A toddler waddled past me alongside his mother, easily outpacing me. 'I've seen atoms moving quicker. You're doing fine. Trust me.'

'Thanks, Em.'

'I'm just holding your hand.'

'No, I'm talking about everything. For standing by me. The skating. The chats.' I stumbled forward, Em holding me up so I didn't fall. 'You're a lifesaver.'

'I'm glad you're still here. I wish I'd been there for you. I wish I'd done things differently.'

'Don't. Wishing gets you nowhere.'

'But I could have stopped it.'

'I don't know that you could.' Sure, Em not being there was a catalyst to what happened, but I needed to take responsibility for my actions. It might still have happened even if Em was there, if Em was free to talk.

'It scared me so much, seeing you in my bathroom. Seeing you in hospital.'

'It scared me,' I replied honestly.

'How is therapy?'

'Good. I'm meeting someone this week – a past patient. I think it might help, to talk to someone that's been where I've been.'

'I'm glad,' Em said. 'Dad wants me to move to Tobago.'

'Oh. What do you want to do?' I quickly recovered, masking my anxiety.

'I'm not sure. He's my father but . . . he has this whole other life. Another family. He broke our family apart but . . . part of me wants to meet my sister. Half-sister. I'd like to get to know her. What do you think?'

'I think that I'm probably not the best person to give advice.'

Silence cloaked us but it wasn't unpleasant. It was nice to

feel the cool breeze on our faces, to hear the leaves rustling and children shouting, pounding the tarmac with tiny feet.

'I want to see Peggy,' I blurted out. I hadn't been to the cemetery. I didn't know where she was buried. I was at court with mum and dad when I should have been holding Em, saying my goodbyes to Peggy at her funeral. 'Will you come?'

'Sure,' Em shot back casually but I knew her thoughts were anything but casual. 'Pothole,' she shrieked, letting me go as she skirted around it. I bent my rigid knees, willing myself to the right, leaning ever so slightly towards the dandelions sprouting out of the grass beds. My skate was inches away from impact but I avoided it. Em reached out for my hand and we wobbled-skated through the park.

Every obstacle that came my way felt like a pothole but I had mum, Kayleigh, the twins and Em. I had everyone I needed to make it through the darker moments.

I touched the heart-shaped, white marble stone decorating Hugh's grave. Peggy was put to rest next to her second husband. I closed my eyes, trying my best to channel my thoughts her way, wherever she was.

I'm not very good at goodbyes. I never got the chance to say a proper goodbye, not when you were alive and not at your funeral. I wanted to say thank you for listening to me when it felt like I couldn't turn to anyone else. Thank you for seeing something in me that I couldn't see. I think I'm finally starting to understand.

I came out at school this week. I was terrified but you were right: it's out there and I can't take it back. I don't want to. I'm finally ready to accept it. Now that everyone knows about it, I feel lighter.

Wherever you are, I hope you're at peace. I hope you're reunited with your husband and catching up on all the good times, puffing a cigar and knocking back a glass of Scotch.

I opened my rucksack, removing three tumblers that I set in the dirt. I unscrewed the bottle of Scotch and poured three generous measures. I placed one on the grave and handed the other to Em. Raising my tumbler to my lips, I clinked Em's and Peggy's glasses.

'To Peggy,' I toasted, downing the contents.

'To Peggy,' Em echoed solemnly.

A strong gust knocked over the glass, Scotch spilling into the dirt. I thought then that she must be out there, somewhere, and maybe she'd heard me.

'Typical nan. She never could say 'no' to a drink.'

Chapter 34

FAMILIAL EXPECTATIONS

'What's this?' mum asked, examining the pots and pans billowing steam into the kitchen. Kayleigh watched *Dora the Explorer* in the living room and the twins gurgled away in their high chairs at the table.

'It's dinner,' I informed her, draining the pasta and spilling it out onto three plates. I unplugged the blender and poured the marinara sauce over the pasta before spooning the meatballs out of the pan.

'Have you hit your head?'

'Can I not make dinner for my family?'

'I don't think you've ever made me dinner before.'

'A first for everything,' I replied, gesturing for her to take a seat.

I sprinkled some parmesan onto the plates before serving one to mum.

'Kayleigh!' I called, lifting her by her arms and airplaning her into her seat.

'At least you're not going to fail Food Tech,' Mum noted. I glared. 'Speaking of school, you're mid-term results came in this morning. A "B" in English Lit. Not bad.' She winked.

We ate our meal in silence. When I finished, I looked up, catching mum staring at me.

'What? Have I got something on my face?'

'I'm just thinking . . . how lucky I am to have such a beautiful boy.'

'Cake, cake, CAKE,' Kayleigh demanded, banging her cutlery against the table.

'We don't have any cake, Kayleigh,' Mum remarked.

'Actually,' I said, removing the empty dishes from the table. I placed the Cherry Bakewell in front of mum. 'I made your favourite.' While chocolate was our family's favourite everything, Cherry Bakewell was mum's favourite cake.

'Cal.' She reached over and hugged me. Pre-empting a tantrum, I handed Kayleigh a bottle of chocolate sauce. 'It's delicious,' mum told me as we watched Kayleigh cover her dessert in a sea of chocolate.

'I really think we should do something about that,' I whispered.

'You try taking the chocolate sauce from her,' mum fired back.

Kayleigh scooted off her chair and tottered into the living room. 'I'm sorry, mum. For everything.'

'I love you, Cal. Nothing and no one is going to change that.'

She kissed my cheek. I took Arya and mum lifted Aydin out of the high chair. Mum asked if she could take a family picture. I manoeuvred Arya into the crook of my left arm on the sofa and Aydin into the right. Kayleigh sat down beside me.

'On the count of three: one, two three. Cheese!' mum shouted.

'CHOCOLATE!' Kayleigh chirped as the camera flashed.

Some things never changed.

I stared at the next name on my list,

Dad

I didn't know what to say. Dad had never been the best father. He wasn't going to win any awards for parenting any time soon. He kept us fed and clothed though he'd never loved me the way a father should. He'd rejected me when he hit me in the hospital but he was still Kayleigh's father and mum's husband. I needed to write something but I couldn't articulate my thoughts on the page. I fell back onto my bed, staring up at the ceiling.

'Knock, knock.' mum opened the door, my baby brother in her arms. I could hear his wheezy breaths from across the room. I closed my window.

'How is he?'

'He's doing good. He's been drinking just fine. The nurse says it will boost his immunity.' *Give him a better shot of survival*, I imagined her saying.

'I want to visit dad,' I announced. Mum gawked. The words hung in the air between us, a force field that neither of us wanted to penetrate.

Mum sat down on the bed next to me, opened her mouth once

and closed it. She bent down to kiss my brother's forehead, a distraction. 'Are you sure that's a good idea?'

Are you sure you're strong enough?

If it goes wrong, will you start cutting again?

I sighed. 'I need to speak to him.'

Mum nodded. 'Maybe we can invite him around for dinner tomorrow evening?'

'Sounds good,' I lied, swallowing against the lump in my throat.

'Do you want to talk about it? About anything?'

Yes. No. I wanted to talk to Em, but she was out for dinner with Duncan and his parents. I could speak to Mam but what if she disapproved? *You'll never know if you don't try*, Dr Daly's voice sounded in my head. So, I told her. How I'd felt at the hospital. When Matt cheated on me. When Peggy died. How worried I was to face dad. How hard it was testifying in court. She hugged me so tight that I thought she might hug away my problems but the feelings lingered when she released me.

'No matter what happens between you and your father, I will always love you, Cal. If it comes down to you and him, I will choose you. I'm not excusing your father but he was never a sentimental man. He was never one to wear his emotions on his sleeve. He grew up with five brothers and his mother – your grandmother – died shortly after we started dating. He has issues too, issues that he has to work through and if he doesn't,' she continued, kissing the crown of my head, 'then that's his loss.'

'Thanks, mum.'

'There's something I've been meaning to discuss with you.

Principal Holden has summoned me to your school for a meeting Monday morning. Something about you stripping down to your boxers and parading around the school, though I suspect there's more to the story than she's telling me.' She rocked Aydin gently in her arms. 'Would you like to tell me?'

It should have been easy for me to open her mouth and tell her what happened – exactly how and why it happened. I'd already told her about Peggy, Matt and dad, but the 'why' was far more complicated than I knew. I opened my mouth but words wouldn't come out. Mum watched me, concern flashing in her eyes. I needed to tell her. I didn't want her to worry but, of course, she would. Any mother would worry when they knew what I'd been putting up with. She needed to know. I took a deep breath and did the only thing I could think of. I removed my t-shirt, exposing the dark purple and fading yellow bruises peppering my arms and shoulders.

Mum snatched my arm in her free hand, turning it over, pressing a finger to the bruises and wincing. 'Who did this to you?' She set Aydin down on the bed and took my hands in both of hers. 'Who did this to you?' she repeated, her voice like steel.

I'd always wanted one moment with my mum for us to chat freely and openly, to reconnect, and that night, I got what I wanted. Whether I liked it or not, mum knew. I told her everything. She now knew about Niall and the full extent of the bullying. The slurs. The physical abuse. I showed her the death threats and she made me take snapshots. I told her how they cut holes in my boxers. I relayed the physical threats for my lunch money which didn't seem so laughable then, looking back on it all. I didn't cry. I was proud of that. Those bastards didn't deserve my tears.

Mum knew and what she did with that information was up to her now.

Chapter 35

EXPOUNDING THE FACTS

I sat in English, scribbling notes to Em, trying to find out about her weekend as we read *The Love Song of J. Alfred Prufrock*, when a fist rapped on the door.

'Excuse me, Mr Benedict, but Cal Adams is to go immediately to Principal Holden's office,' the tall, gangly boy relayed.

Mr Benedict nodded and I followed the boy to the office. I knocked on the door and waited.

'Come in,' Principal Holden announced.

I pushed open the door, clocking the empty chair next to mum. 'Mum?'

She didn't look sideways. She watched Principal Holden, a latent fury darkening her eyes. 'Hello, honey.'

'Cal, I've called you here to discuss your actions at school on Friday afternoon. I am aware that you walked the halls of this school in your underwear. I want to remind you of the serious nature of these actions. This is grounds for suspension. We are a mixed school and as such, we ask our students to show respect for one another.' Mum scoffed. 'Is there something you'd like to say, Mrs Adams?' Principal Holden's voice was prickly. I wasn't sure I liked where this was going.

'If wearing underwear around a school is punishable by suspension,' mum acknowledged, her voice deceptively thick and sweet like honey, 'then what's the punishment for corralling your students to kill themselves?' I felt the air whoosh out of the room when she dropped the k-word.

'I'm not sure I follow.'

'No, I can't imagine you do, holed up in your office when your students are abused on an almost daily basis.' She removed her phone, swiping across the screen and placing it onto Holden's desk.

'This is—'

'Deplorable? Repugnant? Disgusting?' My heart beat frantically in my chest. I fought the urge not to cry, not to hug mum, and tell her how much I loved her.

'All of the above but I don't see how this has any bearing on Cal's actions or this school. We can investigate but the likelihood that these actions are school-related is—'

'100%. I've contacted Facebook in relation to this and they were kind enough to release the email address of the fake account that created the group. Niallmarsdenisboss69@gmail.com. Does that sound like anybody you know, Principal Holden?'

'I see. We shall definitely be investigating this but—'

'I'm not finished,' mum interjected, fishing for a hairband in her pocket and tying back her glossy hair into a high ponytail. 'Cal has had his belongings destroyed, has been called every gay slur in the book, has been burned with metal rulers and had pencil parings dropped in his hair. He's been assaulted and threatened more than once by idiots with butter knives. He was locked in the storage cage at the side of the school and urinated on, had his locker filled with death threats and bananas. Need I continue, Principal Holden?

'If you'd sat down and spoken to my son about why he wrote on his body and walked the halls in his boxers, you might have discovered some of these answers rather than wasting my time here on a Monday morning when I have three young children to care for, one of whom who has just come off life support. If your teachers weren't blind to the happenings in your school, perhaps you might have been able to prevent some of what my son has gone through.

'No doubt, I relayed what has happened to Cal prior to this term. These hate crimes, these threats that he's has been subjected to are frankly, beyond belief. I'm incredulous how you can run your school from this blind spot of an office. I wonder what the other parents will think when they hear about this.'

'I don't think that's necessary.'

'And not just the parents. If you're prepared to victimise a victim, then perhaps the media will be interested in hearing about this. I'm not sure if you are aware but my son has filmed a rather moving video that's fetched 250,000 views online. People are listening and there are people out there that are against the kinds of homophobia that this school has become a breeding ground for. My son will not be a victim here anymore.'

'No. You're right. I—' I'd never seen Principal Holden look so flustered in her life. Beads of sweat dotted across her made-up forehead. 'There will be an investigation into these matters. I-I assure you. This won't be ignored.'

'You see to that. In the meantime, Cal will be coming home with me. Heaven forbid, he has to sit in the same class as some of the rabid boys that have been driving him to suicide for the last year.' She threw Holden a pointed look. 'Cal, grab your bag.' I shouldered my rucksack. 'Good day, Principal Holden.' Mum smiled tightly.

We exited the office, a cool breeze playing with my fringe. It wasn't until we were in the car that I started to breathe evenly, my heartbeat slowing. Mum had her hands braced on the wheel with stiff frozen arms.

'Mum, thank you.' I didn't know what to say and suddenly, it didn't feel like enough. She nestled her face in her arms and rested them on the steering wheel. She started to sob. 'Mum? Mum, are you OK?'

'I'm sorry, Cal. I'm so, so sorry.'

I didn't ask her what she was sorry for. I coaxed her into my arms. She lifted her head from her arms and rested it on my lap, mascara streaking her face. I held mum close to me. I wondered if she thought of me as her anchor.

STOP picking at your hangnail.

Stop PICKING at your hangnail.

Stop picking at your HANGNAIL.

'Are you OK?' mum asked. I wondered what gave me away; my asthmatic breaths or the red foam heart that I'd been squeezing tightly in my hand. It had googly eyes that bulged whenever I clenched it. At first, I found it funny but there was nothing funny about seeing my father at dinner. I hunkered down on the ground, palms flat on my knees, heaving deep breaths in and out of my lungs.

'Fine,' I wheezed.

'If you want, I can tell him—'

'No, I need to do this.' Mum took my hand as the doorbell rang. I jumped off the sofa and dashed into the hallway, nervous energy buzzing through my veins as I pressed down on the doorjamb and looked out at dad.

'Cal.'

I just stood there. It was like I was underwater, unable to breathe. Dad watched me with pleading eyes. I opened the door and ran into the kitchen, stirring the Bolognese sauce that clearly didn't need stirring.

'Hello, Richard.' Out of the corner of my eye, I saw dad peck mum on each cheek.

'Daddy, daddy, daddy!' Kayleigh bounded out of the living room in her pink onesie and right into dad's arm. He helicoptered her around the room. She giggled loudly, tears streaming from her cheeks, reminding me that I needed to think of the bigger picture.

I hadn't noticed before but Dad held a square box and a small package, wrapped in coloured paper. Presents for the twins. He set them down on the countertop next to sauce stains and stray fusilli pasta shapes.

'How's school?'

'Fine,' I mumbled.

'Fine? As and Bs across the board, Richard. My little brainbox.' Mum kissed the top of my head before handing him my end-of-term results.

'Wow. Better than your old man could have done.'

'OK, everyone sit. Sit, sit, sit. I'll dish up the dinner.' Aydin and Arya were both asleep in the sitting room despite Kayleigh's bunny hops to her seat next to dad. I carried the salt and pepper shakers, and parmesan cheese to the table. Mum lifted the lid on the simmering sauce, steam rising into the air. It wasn't long before the rich tomato smell reached my nose.

Mum set a plate down in front of Kayleigh and I. I waited for mum to sit while Kayleigh dug her kiddie cutlery into the meatballs, carving up her food. Mum placed the final two plates down and took her seat. 'This is lovely.' Nobody said anything. I felt awkward as it was. Dad looked nervous, something I'd never witnessed before.

'The sauce is phenomenal, Mel.'

'I know. Those Food Tech classes are finally playing off. Right, Cal?' She smiled.

'You made this?'

I nodded.

'Don't look so surprised.'

'I'm just . . . I just . . .' Dad looked down at the food solemnly. 'Excuse me.' His chair screeched across the wooden floor. He stood, racing from the room, slamming a door behind him.

All that I could hear over the sound of my own rapid heartbeat was Kayleigh gnashing down on her dinner. 'What was that about?'

Mum frowned. 'I-I don't know.' I could tell this wasn't going the way she thought it would. 'I'll go see what's happened.'

'No,' I told her when she reached the door, 'I'll go.' Mum watched me warily, a look that asked if I was sure. 'Yes.' I closed the door gently behind me out of habit. Each step towards the end of the hall felt heavy and the rich sweet smell of tomatoes had disappeared, replaced by stale sweat. I blew my fringe out of my face as I knocked gently on the bathroom door. Once. Twice. Three times. I toed the door open.

A cold breeze blew through the open window, raising the hairs on my arms. The bathroom was empty. I checked behind the door, pulling back the shower curtain. No dad.

Did he run from the house?

Could he not stand the sight of me?

Could he not bear being in the same room as me?

That's when I heard it: the unmistakable sound of muffled sobs.

I knocked on my bedroom door. 'Dad.' I pushed the door open. Dad sat on my bed, facing away from me.

'Cal,' he said, taking his face from his hands. He vigorously wiped the tears from his red-rimmed eyes.

It was such a strange sight to see dad crying. The same man that hit me at the hospital was this sad little man, crying on his son's bed. It didn't add up. Torn in two ways, I watched from the door, unable to move. I felt like my legs were roots, burrowing under the floorboards and into the earth.

'Sorry.'

'I don't understand,' I blurted out.

'Sit?' I wasn't sure if it was a command or a question. Dad's voice was undeniably broken. I sat beside him, awkward and rigid. 'I've missed so much.' Silence. I didn't know what to say to that. 'Even when I was here, I missed a lot.' Dad blew a breath through his lips. 'I've wanted to come to the house, to explain.'

'Then why didn't you?' I snapped.

'Your mother advised against it. Said you were going through a lot and I didn't want to make things worse. It's been so difficult being away from you and Kayleigh, from your mum and the twins.'

'You should have thought about that before you punched me.'

Dad winced. I almost felt bad. Almost. 'I should have. I lost myself at the hospital. I was worried about the baby – babies. When I saw your mum at the hospital, I didn't know it was her finger, I thought she'd lost the baby.'

'So, it wasn't because I'm ... gay?'

'I can't pretend it won't take some getting used to, but no. I was worried about your mother. I shouldn't have hit you. I shouldn't have done that, not when you were looking after her, not when you were there, and I wasn't.'

'Oh' was all I could manage. All this time, I thought dad hated me – hated who I was – but he didn't. With the rug pulled from under my feet, I didn't know where to look or what to think.

'That never should have happened and I'm not going to sit here and tell you an apology is going to make it all better. We both know that it won't, but if you'll let me, I'd like to try to make things right.' Dad held out his hand. I wasn't sure if I was ready for this. Any of this. My mind was a maelstrom of conflicting thoughts. I ignored my head and listened to my heart. Listened to my gut. I took dad's hand and he squeezed it tight. He was sorry. I didn't need him to say it. It radiated off him in waves. I could never forget what happened but over time, maybe I could forgive him. Dad pulled back, hands clasped on either side of my face. 'So, what's this I hear about a boyfriend?'

I told dad about Matt, about our relationship and the kind of person he was. He listened. He asked questions. It didn't feel like he was prying. I didn't tell him everything. I trusted him with tidbits, to see if he could handle it, to see if he'd really changed. I waited until the end of the story, waited for dad's reaction.

'He's a fool,' dad commented. 'Anyone that makes a Bolognese sauce that good won't stay single for long. Now come on, let's get back to dinner.'

Dad, Kayleigh and I sprawled out on the couches, watching a kid's show I didn't know the name of. Mum went inside to make herself a cup of tea. I couldn't relax. Something about dad still unnerved me. I guessed that would be the way things would be for a while.

Scissor Sister's *Take Your Mama* blasted from the kitchen. I stood up, confused. Mum appeared in the doorway with a cake bearing a dozen lit candles.

'What's this?'

'Your "coming out" cake.'

'What?'

'It's chocolate,' dad chipped in.

'Chocolate,' Kayleigh cheered and when she saw mum and dad nervously watching Aydin, she apologised.

'But why?'

'It's a celebration of who you are, what you mean to us – what you mean to this family. We love you, Cal, and we're sorry it took us this long to get back on track.' I stood up. In white icing, a message was spelt out: *Chocolate is my favourite everything*. 'Chocolate is this family's favourite everything,' mum continued, gesturing to Kayleigh, whose eyes looked ready to fall out of their sockets.

'Make a wish,' dad told me.

'I already have everything I could possibly want,' I said, my voice cracking.

I blew out the candles anyway and thought about everything good in my life. Mum. Em. Kayleigh. Arya. Aydin. Maybe dad. I had at least five reasons to be thankful; five reasons to love and to live and to channel all my energy into getting better. Going to my therapy sessions. Talking to mum. Opening up to dad.

Some people didn't get a single chance at life but I'd been given a second chance and I was going to grab it with both hands and live my life to the fullest.

Mum served me a big slice of cake while dad handed me the colourfully wrapped present I noticed earlier. I stared at it, confused. I thought it was for the twins.

'It's for you. I hope you like it. Your mum picked it out.'

I tore back the wrapping paper, excited to see what they'd got me. Through the clear plastic packaging, I could see a pair of furry, red sex dice.

'Em ...'

'They're Decision Dice!' mum chirped, a smile plastered on her face.

'Thanks,' I told them, still trying to figure out what decisions they'd help me with. I could see three faces on either dice: 'kiss', 'bite' and 'lick', and 'elbow', 'lips' and 'hips'. I had no idea what mum was thinking but I sat on the couch, mum on one side, dad and Kayleigh on the other. We ate chocolate cake and surrounded by family, there was nothing else I could have wished for.

When life gives you lemons, you can make lemon juice and moan how it isn't something more, picking faults in everything or you can infuse it into your drink to dull the pains and aches of everyday life.

But sometimes, you turn it into something amazing like the lemon meringue pie Cam and I made last week and suddenly, it's nothing to do with lemons. It's about love and life, family and friendship. It's all the things you can't put into words and all the things that you can. It's everything we are and everything we share and sure, our meringue had cracks and the pastry could have been more golden on the outside but you can't pave over the faults;

you can't wash away the past but sometimes, when you make mistakes, you get a second chance.

And this, well, this was my second chance. This was my new beginning.

Chapter 36

AN EXTRAORDINARY END

I rubbed my palms on the new jeans mum got me today. They must have been paying mum well because I've never owned a pair of Levi's in my life. I hooked my thumbs through the loops of my jeans to stop my hands from fidgeting. Lana Del Rey's *Ride* pumped loudly through my headphones. It popped up on shuffle last week and I'd been listening to it ever since. It soothed me. It helped stop my heart racing so fast when I went for my first proper job interview at Ben's Breads in Stratford.

My skin still smelt like eucalyptus from the bath oils. I held my arm to my nose and inhaled deeply. I didn't know why I was so stressed and sweaty. It wasn't like I'd never been to see Dr Daly before. We'd had six sessions together over the course of the month. This wasn't just any session though. I was meeting someone today; someone that self-harmed. I knew it was a 'he'. I didn't know what he looked like and I didn't know why that would even be important. I was panicking. I slipped a hand into my pocket and squeezed the stress ball. The wind rustled the crisp autumnal leaves across the path, the sun beating down on my face as I closed my eyes and tilted it towards the blue sky. I focused on the sharp browns, reds, oranges and yellows.

Breathe, Cal. Deep breaths. You can do this.

This should have been nothing. I stripped down to my boxers and marched through the halls, bearing homophobic slurs inked across my skin; the same slurs that Niall and everyone else had called me.

I'd put a video out to the world that now had half a million views and it had only been live for four days. Buzzfeed called mum, asking if I'd do a live interview in London. I'd braved school last year, after my dad had hit me and I'd been bullied in new and inventive ways every day. Matt betrayed me, building me up to incredible heights and plunging me into unfathomable depths. I'd had Everest highs and Atlantis lows but I'd dealt with all. I was stronger and happier than ever, but it was thoughts of the unknown that unnerved me.

I counted my steps up to the front door. I had an uneasy feeling in the pit of my stomach. I couldn't tell if it was from that dodgy burrito me and mum had earlier or something else entirely. I belched, the taste of spicy beef at the back of my throat making me nauseous all over again. I placed my hands on my knees and sucked in a deep breath. I opened the door and the receptionist flashed me a smile.

'Cal Adams,' I informed her.

'Thank you, Mr Adams. Please take a seat and Dr Daly will be with you shortly.' I picked up a magazine. Housekeeping. It figured they wouldn't have any gossip magazines here. I couldn't imagine captions telling you to be your skinniest self would go down well in a place like this. I flicked through the magazine, mostly looking at the colourful, glossy pictures.

I was alone in the waiting room. Acoustic music filled the room from an old radio. I closed my eyes and tried to focus on the chords. I thought of Matt, playing me a song in front of a crowd of Japanese tourists at Southbank. Memories flooded my vision, some good, others bad, but what was important to me was that I played them out and embraced them, otherwise I'd never learn from my mistakes.

'Cal,' Dr Daly called. I started. How did she creep up on me like that? 'Tired?' she asked.

I shook my head. 'Just . . . thinking.'

'Only good things, I hope.'

I nodded. I smelt the rosewater before I stepped over the threshold to her office. 'So, when does he arrive?'

'He's already here.' Dr Daly smiled, pushing the door open and letting me step into her office. I took two steps into the room, gripping the back of the chair for support, my knees weak. Dark hair. My height. Dimples. White teeth. He was beautiful but it wasn't his beauty that threw me; it was the familiarity. Then, he spoke.

'Hi Cal.'

'Cam,' I said and a million emotions tugged at my heart, memories racing through my head. Nervousness. Nostalgia. Happiness. Anxiety. Shame. Guilt. And something else fluttering away under my skin. I couldn't describe how it felt because it was completely alien. Completely unexpected. The door closed and Dr Daly took her chair which she'd positioned at the side of the room.

'Well,' she announced, 'let's begin.'

RESOURCES

If you or someone you know is facing some of the issues that Cal has faced, you might find you need someone to talk to. Below are a list of charities and organisations in Ireland and the UK where you can find out more. Please note that contact information is correct at time of publication.

IRELAND

Belong To (National Organisation Supporting LGBTI+ Young People in Ireland)
www.belongto.org / 01 670 6223
(Monday – Friday from 9am – 1pm & 2pm – 5pm)

Transgender Equality Network of Ireland (TENI) (non-profit organisation supporting the trans community in Ireland)
www.teni.ie / (01) 873 3575

LGBT Ireland (national organisation, providing support, training, and advocacy to improve the lives of LGBT+ people)
lgbt.ie / 1890 929 539

Jigsaw (provide vital supports to young people with their mental health)
www.jigsaw.ie

There are a number of regional phone numbers on their website where you contact the one most relevant for you.

UNITED KINGDOM

Mermaids (family and individual support for gender diverse and transgender children and young people) – www.mermaidsuk.org.uk / 0808 801 0400
(Open Monday to Friday; 9am – 9pm)

Stonewall
www.stonewall.org.uk / 0800 050 2020
(Lines are open Monday to Friday; 9:30am – 4:30pm)

Switchboard LGBT helpline (the LGBT+ helpline)
switchboard.lgbt / 0300 330 0630
(Open every day; 10am – 10pm)

Mind (offer support and advice on mental health and wellbeing)
www.mind.org.uk/information-support/for-young-people/
www.mind.org.uk/about-us/our-policy-work/equality-human-rights/mental-health-and-being-lgbtiqplus / 0300 304 7000
(Open every day; 4.30pm – 10.30pm)

NORTHERN IRELAND

Cara Friend (provide regional LGBTQ+ youth groups across Northern Ireland)
cara-friend.org.uk / 0808 800 0390

Belfast Trans Resource Centre (community hub for trans, non-binary and questioning people and their families and friends)
belfasttrans.org.uk / 0300 302 3202

The Rainbow Project (promote the health and wellbeing of LGB people and their families in Northern Ireland)
www.rainbow-project.org / (028) 9031 9030

ACKNOWLEDGEMENTS

The first word – the first page – is an exciting journey filled with infinite possibilities. That new-project energy bubbles in your veins, fingers itching to create immersive worlds and colourful characters but as the story goes on, you feel the walls narrow. You fall. You stumble. You backpedal. You make mistakes. The story becomes something more than you thought it would be and stronger still, because the energy and passion of those around you, keeps you afloat and helps drive you to the finish line of something momentous. For me, this person is – and always will be – the incomparable Jake Hope. Mentor, friend, agony aunt and more, Jake's support buoyed me in the more turbulent times of my life when this book was written and helped shape it into something beyond my initial vision. For this – and for everything you do, Jake – I am eternally grateful.

I am grateful to have parents that paid for my English and Creative Writing courses and supported me – even when they did not understand.

Lisa, Ann-Marie, Kelly and all my friends who gave me valuable feedback – a big thank you!

Thank you to Tanja and her keen reading students that championed my story long before it was published and gave feedback that helped this story to be the strongest it could be.

A huge thanks to Mrs Fitzsimons who taught me that the power of words can change a world. You are wondrous and magical. Thank you for helping and believing in me when no one else would.

Thank you to Nicky Matthews who helped shape my writing style and gave constructive feedback that I still use to this day and Laura Dodd – you're a superstar!

A massive thanks to the UCLan Publishing team (Hazel, Toni and Charlotte) who have worked tirelessly to publish my work and let my story be told. Hazel – you are as compassionate and kind as you are determined and diligent – all admirable qualities that leave me in awe.

A special thanks to the authors that gave writing advice and kind authorly chats at different points of my life – Lu Hersey, Sue Wallman, Katherine and Elizabeth Corr, Juno Dawson, Siobhan Curham, Non Pratt, Patrice Lawrence, Anne Fine, Alex Bell, Sarah Crossan, Jess Vallance, Alexia Casale and Lisa Williamson. I cannot the lovely UKYA bloggers who championed and supported me before I was ever published – Sally (@thedarkdictator), Michelle (@chelleytoy), Georgina (@georginahowlettwrites) and Virginie (@chouettblog).

A special thanks to readers. I hope you enjoyed this story and you love Cal just as much as I do.

ABOUT THE AUTHOR

C. G. Moore has travelled to the furthest reaches of space and time, has fought all manner of monsters and done battle against forces of evil.

A keen champion of reading, C. G. has enjoyed stories in all their shapes and sizes since early childhood and has made a career of working with them.

C. G. is a freelance editor and marketer who has written for Bookmachine, Writing.ie and many more. He runs the #YAtakeover, an online festival dedicated to bringing readers and writers together. He has hosted physical and online events as part of Litfest, and the CILIP Carnegie and Kate Greenaway medals.

When C. G. is not reading or writing, he can be found wrapped up in aerial silks, baking or getting lost in nature with his sassy Jack Russell, Ruby. He currently lecturers on the MA in Publishing program at the University of Central Lancashire where he shares his love of the written word.

HAVE YOU EVER WONDERED HOW BOOKS ARE MADE?

UCLan Publishing are based in the North of England and involve BA Publishing and MA Publishing students from the University of Central Lancashire at every stage of the publishing process.

BA Publishing and MA Publishing students are based within our company and work on producing books as part of their course – some of which are selected to be published and printed by UCLan Publishing. Students also gain first-hand experience of negotiating with buyers, conceiving and running innovative high-level events to leverage sales, as well as running content creation business enterprises.

Our approach to business and teaching has been recognised academically and within the publishing industry. We have been awarded Best Newcomer at the Independent Publishing Guild Awards (2019) and a *Times* Higher Education Award for Excellence and Innovation in the Arts(2018).

As our business continues to grow, so too does the experience our students have upon entering UCLan Publishing.

To find out more, please visit
www.uclanpublishing.com/courses/